"You have something to tell me, don't you?"

"Yes."

Serena swallowed. "Is my mother dead or alive?" She'd been afraid to ask that, but now she couldn't avoid it.

"She's dead," Ethan answered. "Jasmine died from the injuries she received in that car crash the night before your birth—just like your grandmother told you."

She bit her lip. "Somehow...I guess...I hoped she was alive."

Ethan had grown very still beside her and she knew there was more. "What is it?"

"Your grandmother didn't tell you the whole truth. I searched a little deeper and found..."

"W*hat*?"

"Jasmine Farrell gave birth to twin girls."

It took a moment for the words to sink in, and then she leaped to her feet. *Twin girls.* Around and around the words went in her head until she had to accept them. "That means the stripper's my sister. My twin. My double!"

Dear Reader,

Has anyone ever claimed to have seen someone who looks like you? How did you—or would you—react? Would you shrug it off? Laugh? Or would you think about it constantly?

That's what happens to Serena Farrell in *The Wrong Woman*. She hears about a woman who's a dead ringer for her. She can't stop thinking about the other woman and is finally driven to hire a private investigator to find her.

Ethan Ramsey, the P.I., appeared in two of my other books, *Straight from the Heart* and *Emily's Daughter*. Now he faces a case that intrigues him—as does the blue-eyed, red-haired Serena. If there are two women like this, he has to see them!

Serena's and Ethan's lives become entangled in ways they don't expect. I hope you enjoy their quest to find the woman who looks like Serena. (And if someone sees a person who looks like you—laugh about it. That's the best reaction.) Thanks for reading my books.

Linda Warren

P.S. You can reach me at LW1508@aol.com, www.superauthors.com, www.lindawarren.net or you can write me at P.O. Box 5182, Bryan, TX 77805. Your letters will always be answered.

Books by Linda Warren

HARLEQUIN SUPERROMANCE

893—THE TRUTH ABOUT JANE DOE
935—DEEP IN THE HEART OF TEXAS
991—STRAIGHT FROM THE HEART
1016—EMILY'S DAUGHTER
1049—ON THE TEXAS BORDER
1075—COWBOY AT THE CROSSROADS

The Wrong Woman

Linda Warren

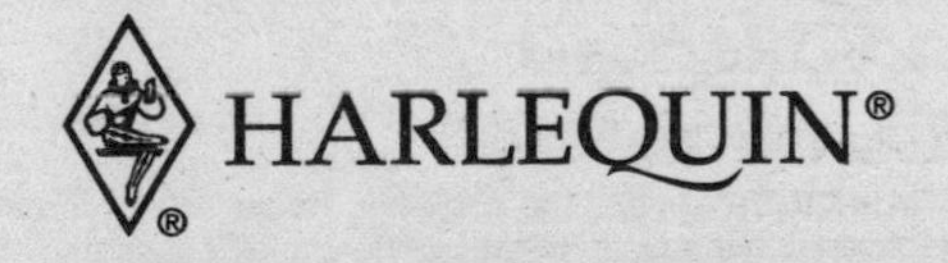

TORONTO • NEW YORK • LONDON
AMSTERDAM • PARIS • SYDNEY • HAMBURG
STOCKHOLM • ATHENS • TOKYO • MILAN • MADRID
PRAGUE • WARSAW • BUDAPEST • AUCKLAND

ISBN 0-373-71125-5

THE WRONG WOMAN

This edition published by arrangement with Harlequin Books S.A.

Visit us at www.eHarlequin.com

Printed in U.S.A.

DEDICATION

To Diannia Dudake Landry, my cousin, my sister, my best friend all rolled into one. I pray that in the years ahead, we'll be as close as in years past. Thanks for just being you and always being there for me. And hopefully, one of us will always remember the way home.

AKNOWLEDGMENTS

A special thanks to
Joe and Joanna Johnston and Jim Gatewood for sharing their expert knowledge and for being so nice. And to Laurie Fay for continuing to answer my many questions with such patience. Any errors are strictly mine.

CHAPTER ONE

"WOW, ETHAN, take a look at her."

Ethan Ramsey didn't raise his head. He twisted the beer in his hand, felt the coolness of the glass against his fingers and wondered what would happen if he took a swallow. Would he want another? Then another?

Travis glanced at his brother and noticed his preoccupation with the beer. "Why'd you order the damn thing? You know you're not gonna drink it."

"A test, I suppose," he answered solemnly.

"Damn, Ethan, you beat anything I've ever seen. You have the strongest willpower of anyone I know. You went through a bad spell with liquor, but you had good reason. Under the circumstances, any man would've lost it."

Ethan didn't answer. He kept twisting the glass, trying to decide if any man had a good enough reason to obliterate the world from his mind.

"Check out the stripper, Ethan. You won't regret it."

Ethan wasn't interested in the stripper. He was more interested in getting Travis out of the strip club. He didn't want to be here in the first place and would never have come on his own. Unfortunately he'd allowed his younger brother to make their evening plans and—

"Ethan!" Travis called above all the jeers and yells.

Ethan turned toward the girl. She was beautiful, stunning, actually, with long legs, a tiny waist, full breasts, creamy skin and hair the color of rich copper. It hung down her back and she tossed it around her in seductive movements. She was taking off the few clothes she had on and the men were going wild. Ethan focused on her face and the blue of her eyes. They were blank, desolate, a look he'd seen many times in the course of his career. He'd been an FBI agent until he was injured in the line of duty. Victims, especially the abused, had that look. The girl hated being on stage in front of all these men. She was being forced to strip. He knew that without a doubt, and anger surged through him.

He told himself it was none of his business. But that didn't work. He kept staring at the girl's face and realized he had to get out of there or he'd do something stupid.

He stood abruptly. ''Let's go.''

Travis's head jerked toward him. ''What? We've only been here thirty minutes.''

''Let's go,'' Ethan repeated in a voice Travis clearly recognized. Moodily he followed Ethan outside to the truck.

Ethan got behind the wheel and Travis crawled into the passenger side. ''You have a way of ruining my whole day,'' Travis complained. ''I forgot that annoying little habit of yours.''

''It's two in the morning,'' Ethan reminded him as he backed out and pulled into traffic.

''So what?''

''So you're thirty-eight years old and still going to strip joints. When the hell are you gonna grow up?''

''Whenever I damn well please,'' Travis returned, leaning his head back. ''I'm not like you and Pop. I don't want a life that's so structured you're old before your time. I have to be myself.''

Ethan rolled his eyes at the tiresome cliché. ''Fine,'' he muttered, ''but that also comes with a price.''

"Oh, God," Travis groaned. "Don't preach to me."

Ethan didn't say anything else because he knew they'd get into a full-blown argument. That was the last thing he wanted, especially when Travis had had too much to drink. Not only that, Ethan couldn't shake his feeling about the stripper. It still bothered him, and he was taking it out on Travis. His brother could make his own decisions—even if *he* didn't like them—and Ethan had to respect that.

As they drove up to Travis's apartment, Ethan couldn't resist asking, "Did you notice the redhead's eyes?"

Travis sat up straight. "The stripper?"

"Yeah."

Travis laughed. "Her eyes? No, I wasn't looking at her eyes and if you were, you're getting as stodgy as Pop."

Ethan turned off the engine, letting that last remark slide. "Someone's forcing her to strip."

"What?"

"Didn't you see how scared she was and how she hated the men yelling and leering at her?"

"No, I didn't see any of that. Shut off your FBI radar. You're imagining things."

Was he? He didn't think so, but he had to forget it. He wasn't an agent anymore. He was a rancher; he did P.I. work on the side, but only when people asked for his help, and the only people who needed his help right now were his family. He'd spent years working all over the country; that time away had come with personal casualties—a divorce, not being home when his mom died, a bullet to his hip and…the loss of a son. Even now, he had to stop before he'd let himself think those words. That pain would never leave him. Sometimes… He stopped his thoughts and glanced at Travis, who was lounging in the seat, head nodding. These days, family was his top priority. He had to find a way to talk to Travis without arguing.

He'd come to Dallas for that reason—to try to get Travis home for a visit. Their father and Travis had been at odds for years. It was time for family unity. Their sister, Molly, had just gone through a bitter divorce and she needed family around her, but getting Travis home was proving to be a more difficult task than he'd figured.

When Ethan had arrived in Dallas early that evening, Travis was preparing for a gig. He played in a local nightclub three nights a week. Travis grew up strumming his guitar and singing anywhere he could. He didn't like ranch work, which was a constant source of contention between him and Pop. After high school, Pop had wanted him to go to college, but Travis headed for Nashville to become a country music star. When it didn't happen, his pride wouldn't let him come home. They didn't hear much from him after that, but Ethan had ways of keeping tabs on him. Travis now worked as a foreman for a construction company. He was staying in one spot finally, and Ethan knew it was time to talk.

After the gig, Travis had insisted on the strip club, which certainly wasn't to Ethan's taste. He'd gone along, trying to be patient, but his patience was wearing thin.

They reached the apartment building and Travis unlocked his door. "You can have my bed," Travis said as they went inside. "I'll use the sofa bed."

Ethan removed his hat and placed it on the coffee table next to an empty pizza box and some beer cans. Travis wasn't much of a housekeeper. "Sleep in your own bed," he replied. "I'm not an invalid." He hated when people treated him differently because of his hip injury. "Besides, I'll be up early," he added in a softer tone.

Travis rubbed his chin. ''I don't have to work tomorrow, so I ain't getting up early.''

''I'll probably be gone before you wake up.''

''Damn, Ethan, what's the rush?''

''It's hard for Pop to handle the ranching chores by himself.''

''He does it when you're off on one of your cases,'' Travis reminded him.

''I always get Roy Dawson to help him,'' he told him. ''Pop's sixty-five, Travis, and he's slowing down.''

Travis shoved both hands through his hair. ''You want me to come home. That's why you're here.''

Ethan pushed a mound of clothes aside and sat on the sofa. ''Yes, for a visit. Is that so bad? Molly's having a rough time and she could use your support.''

''Bruce is a bastard, leaving her for a twenty-year-old girl. The man must be going through a midlife crisis.''

''Yeah.'' Ethan stood and stretched. ''That's Bruce's problem. I'm not sure what yours is. Your whole life has been a midlife crisis.'' The words came out before Ethan could stop them. He had a habit of speaking his mind, and sometimes that wasn't good.

Travis bristled. ''Don't think that because of your injury I won't punch you, Ethan.''

''And don't think that because of my injury I won't punch you back.''

There was a tense moment, then Travis burst out laughing. ''Do you remember when we were kids and we used to fight over really stupid things? You were five years older, but I just knew I could take you.''

Ethan smiled. ''Yeah, but you never did.''

Travis sobered. ''No,'' he admitted. ''I have an advantage now, though. The years are on my side.'' He playfully poked Ethan in the stomach. ''Want to fight, old man?''

Ethan shook his head. ''No.''

''Me, neither.'' Travis sighed regretfully, then suddenly hugged Ethan. ''God, it's good to see you.''

Ethan hugged him back. ''You'd better go to bed before you pass out.'' The beer had taken its toll and Travis was slowly going down.

Travis moved away. ''I'll see you in the morning.'' In the doorway he paused. ''Sure you don't want my bed?''

''Sure.''

''Night Ethan.''

''Good night, Travis.''

Ethan stared at the sofa with all the clothes and the coffee table with the leftover remnants of a meal. How did Travis live like this? If Molly could see it, she'd have a fit. Or maybe not. Molly wasn't herself these days; her husband's betrayal had hit her hard. But Travis could always make her laugh and Ethan hoped that having him home for a weekend would cheer her up.

He shoved the table to one side and dropped the clothes on the floor beside it. He unfolded the bed and saw that it already had sheets. That was good, he supposed. He didn't even want to think who might've slept on them last. He was too tired. He flipped off the light, threw off his jeans and shirt and crawled in. It had been a long day—too long. His hip would probably ache tomorrow, but that was a casualty he'd learned to live with.

As he drifted off to sleep, it wasn't his hip or his family that was on his mind, it was the redheaded stripper. What was her story? Why was she stripping against her will? She needed help. No. He resolutely turned over. She didn't need *his* help. It was none of his business—absolutely none.

THE NEXT MORNING Ethan picked up all the clothes and put them in the washing machine. He cleared away the trash and washed the dishes in the sink. By the time Travis stumbled out of the bedroom, Ethan had the clothes folded and the room as clean as he could get it.

Travis scratched his head and glanced around the apartment with bloodshot eyes. "Damn, Ethan, when did you turn into my mother?"

"There's no coffee or food here, so I had to do something until you dragged yourself out of bed. Get your clothes on. I'm hungry and I desperately need coffee."

"Yeah, I can tell," Travis said with a grin. "I'll take a quick shower and we'll be out of here in ten minutes."

"Hurry."

In no more than seven minutes, Travis emerged from the bathroom with his wet hair slicked back and dressed for the day. Ethan was surprised at the transformation. He'd have sworn that Travis would have a hangover for the rest of the day. Years ago a hangover was a daily occurrence for Ethan; he quickly shook off the thought.

"Tell you what," Travis said as he fastened his watch. "I have to check out a job in Fort Worth—make sure the materials I ordered were delivered. We can eat at a café not far from the site."

"How long will it take to get there?"

Travis slapped him on the back. "Don't worry, brother, I'll have you there in no time."

Ethan followed in his truck. He was heading back to Junction Flat as soon as he'd talked to Travis. That was the reason he'd hung around this morning; he had to try once more.

The café was a typical down-home kind of place with red gingham curtains and country music playing on a radio. They sat in a booth and Ethan ordered coffee immediately.

"Thanks for straightening the apartment," Travis said. "I usually do that on the weekends."

"Just be glad your sister didn't see it."

The waitress brought the coffee and took their order.

"Speaking of Molly...how is she?" Travis asked.

"Not good and neither is Pop," he said truthfully. "Molly's depressed and Pop's worried about her, and it's getting to him."

"My being there's not gonna help."

"You might be surprised." Ethan met his eyes.

"Ethan," Travis groaned, and changed the subject. "How's Cole handling all this?"

"He's angry as hell at his father, which is understandable. I'm just glad he and Molly are at the ranch with us. Listen, they'd both like it a lot if you could come for a visit...maybe just a weekend. That's all I'm asking. A weekend out of your life."

Their breakfast arrived and Travis didn't answer. They ate in silence. Finally Travis wiped his mouth. "Okay, I'll come home next weekend."

Ethan smiled—he couldn't help it. "Thanks," he said. "Why don't you call Molly and tell her?"

"So she won't think you pressured me?" Travis grinned.

"Something like..." His voice trailed off as he noticed a woman sitting in a corner by herself. There were papers scattered on the table and she was reading them as she drank coffee. Ethan blinked. It couldn't be, he told himself. But there she was, the redheaded stripper. Looking a bit different, but it was her, he was sure of it. Her hair was pulled back and clipped in a knot, and she wore a brown business suit. The face was the same, though. He had studied it thoroughly last night and he'd know her anywhere.

"Ethan, what are you staring at?" Travis asked.

"I can't believe it."

"What?" Travis turned and followed Ethan's gaze. "Well, I'll be damned! It's her, isn't it?"

"Turn around and quit staring."

Travis glanced at Ethan. "I'm going over to say hi."

"No," Ethan said. "Her life is her business."

"You said she was scared and being forced to strip. Well, she doesn't look too scared now. I'm gonna prove to you how wrong you were."

Before Ethan could stop him, Travis was out of the booth and marching toward the woman. Ethan slowly followed.

"Howdy," Travis said, and she raised her head. Ethan recognized the sparkling blue of her eyes, but he saw no fear in them today, just annoyance.

"Do I know you?" she asked.

"No, but I know you," Travis said glibly.

She arched a fine eyebrow. "You do?"

"Yeah, and you look as good with your clothes on as you do with them off."

"I beg your pardon?" she said in a haughty tone. "If this is a come-on, it's not working and I wish you'd leave."

Ethan put his arm around Travis's shoulder. "You'll have to excuse my brother. He's forgotten his manners. We're sorry if we bothered you."

Travis shook off Ethan's arm. "Yeah, and to make up for it, when you get off work tonight, I'll take you out for an early breakfast. How's that?"

She frowned. "Get off work? What are you talking about?"

Travis placed his hands on the table and leaned toward her. "The strip joint, honey. If you want to keep it a secret, that's fine with me."

"A strip joint? You think I work in a *strip joint?*"

"I know it for a fact," Travis told her. "And you don't just work there, you're the star attraction."

Her eyes narrowed to mere slits. "If you don't leave me alone, I'm calling the police."

Ethan knew when enough was enough. If the woman had a secret, it was hers to keep. He caught Travis by the collar and pulled him away. "Sorry, ma'am," he said. "I apologize for the intrusion." He pushed his brother toward the door.

Outside Travis straightened his shirt. "What the hell did you do that for?" he growled. "She may be able to fool you, but she can't fool me."

"She has a right to her privacy."

"You didn't think so last night. You wanted to rescue her."

"Something's different today. I can't explain it."

"She's all prim and proper and..." Travis let out a long breath, his irritation evaporating. "God, she's a beautiful woman, isn't she?"

"Yeah," Ethan agreed, glancing through the café window. In that instant he made a decision. "Stay here. I'll be right back."

"What are you—"

Travis's words faded as Ethan entered the restaurant. He took out his wallet and removed a business card, then walked over to her table and placed it in front of her. She drew back as if to brace herself.

"My name's Ethan Ramsey. I'm a private investigator. If you need any help, just give me a call."

Her eyes caught his. "Contrary to what your brother

might think, I am *not* a stripper. He's mistaken me for someone else.''

''If you say so.'' Ethan knew he should walk away, but he couldn't tear his eyes from her face. She was so sincere—and so different from the woman last night. What was it that pulled him to her? He didn't know, but he had to do what he'd told Travis—respect her privacy. He tipped his hat. ''Good day, ma'am.''

''Mr. Ramsey?'' she called, and he turned back.

''Does she really look like me?''

He was taken aback by the question, but he answered truthfully. ''A dead ringer.''

''I see,'' she murmured, and rose to her feet. ''I assure you it wasn't me.''

''You've said that.''

''And you don't believe me?''

Ethan took a step toward her. ''I'm not sure what to believe, but the woman last night hated stripping. I thought she might need some assistance. That's why I left my card. If you're not her, just throw it away.'' He inclined his head and walked to the door.

SERENA FARRELL stared after the tall man and she noticed that he limped slightly, but it didn't diminish his aura of strength and capability. Not that she needed either one. A stripper? It was too ludicrous to think about.

As she stuffed papers into her briefcase, she could see him through the window talking to the other man. They were definitely brothers—same brown hair and eyes. Ethan Ramsey was the leaner and taller of the two. His brother also had an attitude, while Ethan seemed compassionate. He had warm eyes, and for some reason he seemed worried about her. There was no need to be. She wasn't a stripper who required his assistance. She was a teacher and taught art at a local high school. She'd met the father of one of her students here this morning; he worked during the week so she'd arranged to meet him on a Saturday. His son had remarkable artistic skills, but he saw that as being sissy and not macho enough. She'd tried to convince him otherwise, but the father was macho to the core and didn't like his son sitting around drawing pictures. She didn't understand why he couldn't accept his son's talent and encourage him, but then, dealing with parents was the hardest part of her job.

"Hey, Serena, who was the good-looking guy you were talking to?" Daisy, the waitress, asked.

"Which one?" she countered with a smile. The school where she taught wasn't far away, and Serena often came in here for coffee. She became acquainted with Daisy and she liked her.

"The Clint Eastwood type with the boots and the hat."

Serena picked up the card. "Said his name's Ethan Ramsey. He's a private investigator."

"Do you need a private investigator?"

"No. He thought I was someone else."

"He used a line like that? I didn't figure he was the type."

Serena started to tell her about the stripper part, but decided not to. She didn't want any more rumors to circulate. There were enough already. More than enough.

"You just can't tell, can you?" she replied as she collected her briefcase and slid the card into her pocket. She'd throw it away later.

Daisy quickly wiped the table. "No, you sure can't, but he could use that line on me any day of the week. I served him coffee and breakfast, and all he said was thank-you. All the guys go for you."

"Maybe he noticed the wedding ring on your finger."

Daisy twisted her hand. "Oh, yeah, forgot about that."

Serena smiled. "I've got to go. See you later."

"Oh, Serena," Daisy called before she could leave. "I'm sorry about your grandfather and all."

The smile left Serena's face. "Thank you," she said, and walked out.

As she got into her car, she reflected that everyone was sorry about her grandfather...*and all.* But it didn't change a thing.

AS SHE ENTERED THE driveway, Serena saw that all the other cars were gone. Her grandmother's monthly bridge meeting took place this morning, and Serena was glad it was over. She had to talk to Gran and she couldn't put it off any longer. Her grandmother had to stop spending money. They were broke; it was that simple. Her grandfather had died three months ago and left them heavily in debt. Her grandmother wasn't helping by ignoring the problem.

She went in through the kitchen and found the house completely quiet, except for the ticking of the old grandfather clock in the hallway, which only emphasized the silence. The lady Gran had hired to serve refreshments must have gone. She and Gran had argued about it this morning. They couldn't afford to pay someone for maid services, but as usual Gran had turned a deaf ear to her pleadings.

As Serena started for the hall, the kitchen phone rang. Startled, she merely stared at it. She hated answering it these days. It always seemed to be a bill collector.

She took a deep breath and picked up the receiver. "Hello."

"Ms. Farrell, please."

"This is Ms. Farrell."

"This is Mr. Wylie from the bank." Serena knew exactly who it was. She'd heard his voice more than she wanted to during the past three months. "I'm sorry to bother you on a Saturday, Ms. Farrell, but this is getting serious. We *have* to have an installment on your grandfather's note. We can't continue to let this go on. If we don't receive at least a partial payment by the end of the next week, we'll have to start foreclosure proceedings on the house. Your grandfather put it on the note as collateral. There'll be a notice in the mail."

Serena swallowed the painful knot in her throat. "I'm doing the best I can, Mr. Wylie."

"I know, Ms. Farrell, and I hate to do this. I'm aware of your situation, but my superiors are demanding restitution for this loan."

Serena glanced outside to the beautiful May day. The sun was shining, the trees were flourishing and the grass was greener than it had been even a week ago. A perfect day in an imperfect world. She recognized that now she'd have to do something that would break her heart.

"I'll be in next week, Mr. Wylie," she said.

"Oh, Ms. Farrell," Mr. Wylie replied, surprise in his voice, "I'm so glad. I'm aware that this house has been in your family for years and I hated to take it away from you."

Serena couldn't respond, couldn't say that without this house, her grandmother would lose all hope, all sense of pleasure in life. What she said was, "I'll see you at the end of the week," and hung up the phone.

Serena continued down the hall into the den. Her grandmother, Aurora, was reclining in a chair with a blanket over her feet. At seventy-one, Aurora was regal with a polished Southern charm. She had grown up in Georgia and moved to Texas when she was fifteen. Later, she'd married Henry Farrell. They'd had one daughter, Jasmine, who died shortly after a car accident more than thirty years ago. Jasmine was almost nine months pregnant with Serena at the time, and while both parents had died from their injuries, Serena had been safely delivered. After Jasmine's death, Henry and Aurora had raised Serena.

They gave her a storybook life. They lived in a lovely home in an affluent neighborhood. Serena attended the best schools. Her life was full and happy, and she'd never wanted for anything. After college she'd returned to Fort Worth and gotten a job teaching. She met Brad and they were making plans to get married when her grandfather passed away.

Her life changed that day. While she was still trying to deal with the grief of losing her grandfather, she discovered he was deeply in debt. That storybook life had been a fiction all along, paid for by loans. She'd never discussed finances with her grandfather, so she was unaware of their money problems. His family had owned a pharmaceutical company, which he'd inherited. The company had evidently been in a financial bind, and her grandfather had taken on private investors. The investors soon bought him out, but her grandfather had maintained a position in the firm with a salary—a salary that did not accommodate their lifestyle. His savings were gone and he'd taken out a second mortgage on the house, as well as a series of loans. His life insurance had paid off some of them, but Serena was still struggling to save their home. She'd never had to worry about money before; now it was all she ever thought about.

Her grandfather had tried to shield Gran and her from everything, letting them live in a fictitious world—a world without dark clouds or storms. He used to say, "I want my girls to have nothing but rainbows." That wasn't real, though. Now the real world had surfaced with a vengeance, and Serena wasn't sure how to cope. But she was trying.

Serena kissed her grandmother's forehead. Aurora opened her eyes, their blue a little faded. ''Oh, darling, you're home.''

She sat on the stool at Aurora's feet. ''We have to talk.''

''It's about money, isn't it,'' Aurora said tiredly. ''You know I don't like talking about money.''

''We have to,'' Serena insisted. ''You have to stop spending so much. We don't have any money,'' she said bluntly. ''We barely get by with your social security and my paycheck.''

''I don't understand how we could be broke. Henry always took care of everything. I never had to worry.''

That was the problem, Serena thought. Henry had borrowed and spent more and more to make sure Aurora and Serena had the life he wanted them to have. Serena had explained this repeatedly to Aurora, but she never fully grasped the situation. And to be truthful, Serena *wanted* her to have the life she was accustomed to, just like her grandfather had. She found herself weakening. She decided against telling Gran about her conversation with Mr. Wylie, even though she knew she should. Aurora would be so distressed, and Serena was determined to avoid that. Besides, she'd figured out a way to stop the foreclosure.

Serena kissed her forehead again. ''We'll talk later,'' she said, and headed for the stairs. She'd do anything for her grandmother. That was why she didn't understand Brad's attitude. When they found out about her grandfather's debt, Brad urged her to file for bankruptcy and put her grandmother in a seniors' home. Serena was appalled at such a suggestion. She'd been raised to be honest, loyal and dedicated to family. Brad was asking her to do something that went against every belief, every instinct she had. They argued back and forth, and finally Serena broke the engagement. She couldn't live with a man who was so heartless; it made her wonder how long Brad would have stuck by her if she'd taken ill. Not long, she supposed. She didn't regret her decision.

All her waking hours and many fretful nights were spent thinking of ways to make money. She used her talent as an artist to get a contract with a local greeting-card company, but it took a long time to receive her payments. She also painted portraits. Children were her specialty and she had a number of commissions lined up, but it still wasn't enough to meet the bills. They *would* make it, though, she vowed.

She entered her grandparents' room and stopped for a moment. There were pictures of her all over. The decor was done in different shades of blue, from deep cobalt to baby blue. The bedspread and drapes were a floral chintz, as were the cushions in various chairs. As a child, she'd called this the blue room, and it was her favorite place. Each morning when she woke up, she'd run across the hall to her grandparents' room and jump into their bed, snuggling between them. So much love, so much happiness… She choked back a sob. She'd wondered many times how her grandfather could do this to them, how he could hide their financial reality, but she knew he'd done it out of love. And now she'd have to do the same thing.

She crossed to the divan in the small sitting room and picked up her grandmother's purse. She removed a key and walked to the dresser, where she opened her jewelry box. Among the jewels was a small wooden box. Serena popped the lid and stared at the diamond earrings lying on a bed of velvet. Her grandfather had given them to

Aurora on their wedding day. They'd belonged to his mother and someday they'd belong to Serena. Jasmine was supposed to have worn them on her own wedding day, but at eighteen she'd eloped, to the heartbreak of Aurora and Henry, especially since they disapproved of her choice of husband. Jasmine became estranged from her parents soon after that. Then she and her husband were killed, and Aurora and Henry gladly took Serena.

Serena didn't know much about that time, and she knew nothing about her father. Her grandparents refused to even mention his name. They held him responsible for Jasmine's death. Serena shook her head. She was getting sidetracked.

She glanced down at the diamonds in her hand, remembering how Grandfather had told her she'd wear them at her wedding and her eyes would sparkle as bright as the diamonds. Well, the wedding was off and the only thing that made her eyes sparkle these days was tears.

She took the diamonds across to her room and slipped them into her purse. She'd hock them and buy a fake set, replacing them so her grandmother wouldn't know. Her eyesight was getting so bad she wouldn't see the difference. As long as there were earrings in the box, she'd be satisfied. Gran didn't wear them, anyway. She always wore the diamonds and pearls Grandfather had given her for their twenty-fifth wedding anniversary. Serena turned and caught sight of herself in the mirror.

Liar, thief, an unfamiliar red-haired woman seemed to say.

She stepped closer to the mirror. Was that her? She had a desperate look about her that she didn't recognize.

Oh, God, she was stealing from her grandmother, but what else could she do? Losing the diamonds was better than losing their home, she tried telling the woman in the mirror. Then why did she feel like the lowest creature on earth?

She sank onto the bed and refused to let sentiment drag her down. She had to do this for Gran and herself. She'd do anything to keep Aurora happy and comfortable—even lie and steal. No one was making them leave this house, not as long as she had breath in her body. And if she had a hard time looking at herself, she'd sell all the mirrors, too.

She got up and went to fix lunch. In the doorway she paused and rested her forehead against the doorjamb. The weight of all her problems paralyzed her for a moment. Her grandfather had told her that behind every cloud was a rainbow…not that he acknowledged many clouds in his world. *Oh, Grandfather, where's my rainbow?* She needed one—desperately. Just one tiny rainbow. And a handsome stranger with a heart of gold wouldn't hurt, either. Suddenly Ethan Ramsey flashed into her mind and she thought of the stripper who looked like her. He didn't seem to be a man who would lie. So *was* there a woman out there who looked like her? She let herself think about it for a moment. Since she didn't know anything about her father, there could be a cousin who resembled her, someone she'd never heard of.

She pulled Ethan Ramsey's card from her pocket. He'd said he wanted to help her. It was probably a line, just as she'd told Daisy. What did it matter? She was wasting her time thinking about it; she had enough problems. On her way out the door, she threw the card in the trash.

CHAPTER TWO

DRIVING HOME, Ethan couldn't get the redhead out of his mind. Was she an expert liar or was something else going on? The woman of the night before was afraid and had a hard edge that suggested she'd been living a rough lifestyle. He recognized that immediately. The woman today was a complete contradiction. She was softer and had a veneer and polish that came with wealth and privilege. If she was stripping against her will, that would account for the fear he'd seen yesterday, but it didn't explain the hardness. What was the woman's secret?

As he drove across the cattle guard, dust spiraled behind him. He was home in Junction Flat, Texas, a small ranching community of less than a thousand near San Antonio. There was a saying in Junction Flat: "Don't let the mesquite, the cactus and the rattlesnakes get to you. Junction Flat is a good place to live." And it was—this was where Ethan had always gone when things got too hard, and he planned on staying here for the rest of his life.

A few years ago Pop had given the ranch to his three children, with the stipulation that he be able to live on the property until his death. Molly and Travis didn't have any interest in ranching and sold their shares to Ethan. So the entire ranch now belonged to Ethan, and he was content living out his retirement in his quiet, rustic hometown.

Before he drove around back to the garage, he noticed Bruce's Mercedes parked in front of the white sandstone house. He frowned, wondering why his ex-brother-in-law was here. Since the divorce, which was finalized two months ago, Bruce and Molly hadn't spoken, as far as he knew. There was only one reason Bruce would come out here and face everyone—Cole, his seventeen-year-old son.

When he climbed out of his truck and walked toward the house, he heard raised voices. As soon as he entered the kitchen, everyone grew quiet. Pop was holding Molly, who was sobbing into his chest. Cole was screaming at his father, "Get out and leave us alone!" When he saw Ethan, he said, "Make him leave, Uncle Ethan!"

"Son, I just want to talk to you," Bruce begged.

"I never want to speak to you again." With that, Cole turned and stormed out the back door.

Ethan took a long breath. Bruce had a right to see his son, but Cole had refused to see or talk to Bruce since he'd found out about his father's betrayal. His mother's pain had only increased the boy's feelings. The situation was volatile and emotions still ran high. It was time for everyone to cool off.

Ethan looked at Bruce. "I think you'd better go," he said firmly. He walked to the front door and held it open.

Bruce's features tightened and Ethan could see he was undecided, but at last made a sound of exasperation and headed for the front door. Ethan followed him out onto the long veranda

"Ethan, I want to talk to my son." Bruce shoved a hand through his blond hair. His eyes were green like Cole's.

As much as Ethan hated what Bruce had done to Molly, he understood his desire to see Cole. Cole was the innocent victim in Bruce and Molly's divorce, and neither seemed willing to make it easier for him.

"He just needs some time," was the only thing Ethan could think of to say.

"Molly's turned him against me."

"Don't lay that at Molly's feet," Ethan told him, although he knew it was partly true. "*You're* the reason Cole's upset. He's old enough to know what's going on."

"You're a man, Ethan. I thought you'd understand."

Ethan grunted in disgust. "I understand that a twenty-year-old is more attractive than the thirty-five-year-old mother of your child."

"It wasn't like that," Bruce denied.

"Who are you trying to kid?"

"Molly and I were having problems. You knew that. Hell, everyone knew, but Molly chose to ignore them. She wouldn't listen to me and I got tired of banging my head against that rock-solid pride of hers."

Ethan had been away during the early years of Bruce and Molly's marriage, but since he'd settled in Junction Flat five years ago, he'd become aware of the tension between Molly and Bruce. Last year things had intensified, and Molly had stayed at the ranch some nights because she and Bruce had argued. Bruce worked all the time, she complained, while he said Molly was too involved with Cole's school. Cole was on various sports teams and Molly never missed a game. Bruce attended as many as he could, but he was often out of town. Another issue between them was that Molly volunteered for anything and everything, even though Bruce had asked her not to. Then, when Bruce was home, he liked to go to the club and play golf. Another problem. Molly hated golf. Their spats never lasted long and by the next morning they always made up. Ethan was careful to stay out of their affairs. He did support his sister, though.

''I don't want to hear this about Molly,'' he said in a warning tone.

''Your sister's not an easy person to live with.''

''Oh, but she was an easy person to support you while you went to law school. Easy for her to do your cooking and laundry and raise your son.''

''I don't want to get into it with you, Ethan.''

''Then don't talk as if Molly's to blame for all this. *You* made the choice here.''

''Ethan.'' Bruce sighed bleakly. ''I can't lose my son. I can't.''

The pain in Bruce's voice touched Ethan, even though he didn't want it to. He understood a man's love for his son.

''Cole is seventeen. He's a kid, yet he's almost a man. Give him some time and space. Don't pressure him, Bruce. That's the only advice I can give you.''

''Ethan—''

Ethan held up a hand when he sensed that Bruce was about to tell him things he didn't want to hear. ''Molly is my sister and I'm on her side. What you did was unconscionable and I can't condone it. You hurt the two people who loved you the most. Now you have to deal with the consequences.''

Bruce's eyes darkened, then he glanced toward the corral, where Cole was saddling a horse. As Cole swung into the saddle and set off at a gallop for the woods, Bruce nodded and walked to his car.

ETHAN WENT BACK into the house. Pop was sitting on the sofa with his face in his hands.

''Pop, are you okay?'' he asked.

Walt Ramsey raised his head. ''Is he gone?''

''Yeah. Where's Molly?''

"In her room. Every time she sees him, she screams and cries and comes apart at the seams. I don't know who she is when she acts like that, and I don't know how to help her."

At the distress in his father's voice, Ethan sat beside him. "It'll get better."

"I don't know, son. She's loved him since she was ten years old. She can't forget all those years of loving."

Molly and Bruce had met in fifth grade. When Molly graduated from high school, she was pregnant, and she and Bruce had married soon after. Bruce went to college, then law school, and Molly had worked to support them. She had shouldered the financial responsibility for a lot of years, and now that Bruce was a lawyer and making good money, he'd traded her in for a newer model. At least that was the way Molly put it. She'd never suspected he was sleeping with his new receptionist. The whole sordid mess had devastated Molly...and Cole, too.

"We just have to be here for her."

"I could kill that bastard with my bare hands."

That was the sentiment of everyone in the Ramsey family, and Ethan found it difficult at times to control his temper with Bruce, but his ethics prevented him from doing anything stupid. Besides, he knew there was always another side, even if he preferred to ignore it. Family was family, after all, and had to come first. Most importantly, Bruce was Cole's father, and that one fact kept Ethan grounded enough to have a normal conversation with the man.

"Did you see Travis?"

Ethan looked at his father. "How did you guess I went to see Travis?"

"I know you, son, and you're doing everything you can for Molly."

"Yeah, but nothing's working."

"So is he still playing in bars and honky-tonks?"

Ethan rubbed his hands together. "He's still playing in a band, if that's what you're asking. He has a steady job with a construction company, but he's never going to give up his music."

Pop climbed to his feet. "Got that from your mom's side of the family. They were always playing and singing somewhere, then the worthless lot wanted me to feed 'em." He shook his head. "A man should make an honest living for his family. Work hard and forget about havin' a good time."

Ethan stood up, too, knowing he had to say something that wasn't easy. "That's your way, Pop, but Travis has his own way. That doesn't mean you're right and he's wrong. It just means you're different, and we have to accept that."

Pop opened his mouth to object and Ethan stopped him. "Travis is coming home next weekend. For Molly's sake, I want peace in this house. And a little laughing, playing and singing wouldn't hurt."

Pop clamped his lips together, then said, "I'd better check on Cole," and walked out.

"He's ridden off into the woods," Ethan called.

"I'll find him," Pop muttered. The back door slammed behind him.

Ethan sighed. Did old wounds ever heal? He could only hope so. Well, next weekend would have to be a start. He headed toward Molly's room, then spotted her in the kitchen.

There were groceries on the table, and she was putting milk and juice in the refrigerator. He was trying to think of the right words to ease her pain, but when it came to his sister, he was never very successful. These days,

Molly was like a keg of dynamite just waiting for someone to light the fuse, so unlike the smiling, easygoing woman she'd once been. He had to be very careful.

With her petite frame, short brown hair and brown eyes, Molly looked much younger than her thirty-five years, and it angered him to think of what Bruce had done to her confidence and self-control.

"How are you, sis?" he murmured as he poured a cup of coffee.

Instead of answering, she asked, "Do you know why he came here?"

"To see Cole." He sat at the table and wrapped his hands around the mug.

"Yeah, that's the excuse he used, but he really came to tell Cole he and that teenybopper have set a wedding date. They're having a big wedding and he wants Cole to be in it. Can you imagine? Now I know he's lost his mind."

Ethan didn't comment or he'd explode with the absurdity of it all. He was worried about Molly. Bruce was all she ever talked about, and Ethan realized she was never going to get over his betrayal without a lot of help.

"Sit down," he said. "I need to talk to you for a sec."

"Sure." She grabbed a diet drink out of the refrigerator and opened it. Sitting down, she asked, "Have you heard something about the wedding?"

"No," he answered, cradling his cup.

"Good," Molly replied, tapping her fingers on the table. "He's got some nerve coming out here. It's one thing hurting me, but it's another when he hurts Cole like this. Rumors will be flying all over Junction Flat and San Antonio. We'll never be able to live this down."

He reached for her hand. "Molly, you have to stop

thinking about Bruce and this girl. He's made his decision. Now you have to get on with your life.''

She stared down at their hands. ''I can't.''

He knew that. She couldn't let go of seventeen years of marriage and she couldn't let go of Bruce. But she had to, and she had to understand what all this was doing to her son.

He cleared his throat. ''I want to talk about Cole.''

She glanced up. ''What about Cole?''

''Can't you see how miserable he is?''

''Yes.'' She smoothed the Coke can with her thumb. ''I don't know how Bruce can do this to him.''

There was silence for a moment, then Ethan said, ''You're hurting him, too.''

Molly's head jerked up. ''What!''

''Right now Cole's resentment at his father's betrayal is feeding off your anger and pain. He can't move beyond that.''

''That's Bruce's fault, not mine,'' Molly put in quickly.

''So instead of helping Cole deal with this, you'd rather see him torn apart?''

Molly jumped to her feet. ''I don't want to talk about this,'' she said angrily.

Ethan caught her arm before she could walk away. ''Molly, Bruce is Cole's father. You can't change that, and you have to realize that Cole's gonna have a part in his life.''

''No!'' Molly shook her head wildly. ''I don't want Cole near that…that woman.''

''Oh, Molly.'' Ethan got up and took her in his arms.

''What did I do wrong, Ethan?'' she cried. ''I tried to be the perfect wife and mother. I was so happy when I could quit work and be at home full-time. I loved the cooking, running the household, entertaining. I had parties for Bruce's associates, and I made sure our home was a place Bruce and Cole could be proud of, but—''

''Sis, you have to stop looking at the past and start looking toward the future.''

''I wish I could, but I can't get Bruce and *her* out of my head. She's only three years older than Cole and—''

''You're dwelling on this too much,'' Ethan said. The age thing was a big problem for Molly. Bruce falling for a younger woman had somehow reduced her worth as a woman. Her confidence was gone and her personality had changed completely in a few months.

''You've always been the rock in our family, and I know you have the strength to survive this,'' he said into her hair. ''When you found out you were pregnant with Cole, you held up your head and faced everyone. When Mom died, you were the one who kept us all together, even though you were hurting, too. And when I was shot, you helped us all stay sane—including me, and I wasn't an easy person to deal with at that time.''

She straightened and wiped away tears with the back of her hand. ''I can't seem to stop crying and I don't even like myself these days.''

''Why don't you go back to work?'' he suggested. She'd been drifting in and out of depression for months, and now was the time to do something about it.

Her face crumpled. ''You don't like having me here?''

''I love it and so does Pop, but you need another interest—something to get your mind off Bruce. And to show Cole that you're gonna be okay.''

She shrugged. ''What would I do? It's been so long since I've worked.''

''You have a friend who's got a gift shop and another who owns a boutique. Maybe you could help out until you decide what you want to do.''

Molly walked to the sink with a thoughtful expression. She came back with a dishcloth and washed down the table, which it didn't need. "I'll think about it," she finally said.

"Good." He gave her another hug.

Her arms gripped him so tight he could barely breathe. "What if he marries her, Ethan?"

His heart ached for the sadness in her voice, but she had to face the truth. "Oh, Molly. You have to accept it. It's going to happen."

"I know, but—"

"Travis is coming home next Saturday," he slipped in. He'd wanted Travis to tell her himself, but now he had to use whatever was at his disposal.

She drew back and brushed away a tear. "He is?"

"Yep, so you'd better dry those tears and get a room ready."

"Oh." She clapped her hands together. "When's he coming? I want to fix a big dinner and have the house spic and span. I hope he brings his guitar, because I want to hear his songs. Oh, Ethan, this will be fun! Thank you."

"What did I do?"

"You made him come home. I know you did, but I don't care. It'll be so good to see him. I'll fix his favorite—chicken and dressing. It won't be like Mom's, but I'll box his ears if he says anything."

The transformation in Molly was amazing, and that was because she was thinking about something besides Bruce and his new love. He should've done this sooner. Molly had to learn that there was life after Bruce.

SERENA AWOKE with a start. She sat up, shook back her hair and turned on the lamp. She'd been dreaming and it was so real. There was a stage and she was standing on it, taking off her clothes. Men were yelling at her, but she continued to undress under their leers and whistles. Her skin still crawled with revulsion and she quickly checked—yes, she had her nightgown on. She wasn't naked.

"I am not a stripper," she said out loud. "It's isn't me." Then why did it *feel* like her? Damn Ethan Ramsey for putting the idea into her head! "I am not a stripper," she said again, and settled back in bed, trying to calm down. But it wasn't easy. The feeling of disgust wouldn't go away.

Her usual worry was about money. Now she was also troubled by the thought that there might be a woman who looked like her. A woman who apparently lived nearby—and worked as a stripper. She couldn't get it out of her head. She studied the picture on her nightstand—a picture of Jasmine. She had red hair and blue eyes, as did Gran. It was a trait in their family, although Gran's hair had gone completely white. The woman in the picture did look like Serena. Her hair was brighter and her face slimmer, but they definitely resembled each other.

If the stripper was a "dead ringer" for Serena, there had to be some kind of family connection. But what? Deciding to talk to her grandmother, she got up and went into Aurora's room. Aurora was sitting in a lounge chair drinking coffee.

"Morning, Gran." Serena kissed her, then sat cross-legged on the bed.

"Good morning, darling. Did you sleep well?"

No, she'd had horrible dreams she wanted to forget, but she replied, "Yes, thank you."

She wondered how to bring up the subject of her mother. They never talked about Jasmine, and there were no pictures of her in Aurora's bedroom or anywhere else in the house. Serena had found the photo she had in her own room tucked away in a drawer.

"What was my father's name?" She thought that was a good place to start.

"What?" Gran frowned at her.

"I don't even know his name. My name's Farrell because you and Grandfather put it on my birth certificate for obvious reasons. His name had to be something else."

She supposed she could have researched this easily enough, but she'd never felt the need before; especially while her grandfather was still alive. And her grandparents' feelings about her father were all too evident.

"He's dead and it's best to leave him there," Aurora said in a hard tone, but it didn't stop Serena. Ethan Ramsey had opened a door in her mind, and all she could see were empty places.

"No, Gran," she said, her voice just as hard. "I want you to tell me about him—all the bad stuff. I need to know."

"Why?"

"Because he's my father."

"That's doesn't mean a thing."

Serena was taken aback by her grandmother's attitude. She'd known since she was small that her grandparents hated her father. It was one of the reasons she never asked about him, but now she had to have some answers.

"It does to me," she replied stubbornly.

Aurora took a quick breath. "His name was John Welch. Jasmine called him Johnnie. He worked as a mechanic. What attracted Jasmine to him I don't know. She was raised to be a lady, not to live in a one-room apartment above a garage. Henry and I laid down the law and forbade her to see him again, but she ran off to be with him. It almost killed us."

Serena knew this part of the story. It sounded almost rehearsed. She wanted more.

"Where is John Welch's family?"

Aurora shrugged. "I don't know and I don't care."

"Gran!"

"All right." Aurora patted her white hair. "He lived with someone in a trailer park. After he was killed, they moved away. That's the only family I knew about."

"So my father doesn't have any relatives around here?"

Aurora eyed her strangely. "Why all the questions, Serena?"

"Someone said he saw a woman who looked like me in Dallas, and it got me thinking."

"Looks like you," Aurora laughed nervously. "That's ridiculous. No one's as beautiful as you. I thought your mother was beautiful, but you've eclipsed her in every way."

Something in Aurora's voice alerted Serena. "You *have* forgiven her, haven't you, Gran?"

"Forgive? I'm not sure. A mother never gets over that kind of pain." Her hand shook as she took a sip of coffee.

"Oh, Gran." Serena rushed over and hugged her. "Jasmine gave me to you. You wouldn't have raised me if you hadn't loved her deeply."

Aurora touched her cheek. "Yes, you're the one good thing that came out of the tragedy."

Serena sat on the edge of the chair. "I wish I knew more about my father."

"He's not worth knowing. Forget about him."

Serena frowned. She'd never heard her grandmother talk with such vehemence, and it rattled her. Was there something Gran wasn't telling her?

THE DREAMS CONTINUED. She was stripping in front of men, but now Ethan was in the dream watching her with an *I knew it* expression on his face. She couldn't shake the dream and it was beginning to wear her down. She couldn't let that happen; there were too many other concerns that needed her attention.

She went to a jeweler to have the earrings appraised before hocking them—and discovered that they were worth far more than she'd ever imagined. The jeweler said the shape of the diamond was very rare, as was the box they were in. He showed her the markings on the bottom of the box and explained their significance. The information made her decision that much more difficult, but she kept reminding herself that she didn't have a choice. The jeweler made her an offer, and she accepted on condition that he'd hold the earrings for thirty days before selling them. Why, she had no idea. She just wanted an option left open to her. The jeweler also agreed to make a cheap fake pair and a similar box. He said she could pick them up in a couple of days. As she hurried out of the store, she felt as if she'd thrown away part of her heritage. But it was only a *thing,* she kept telling herself.

The next day she went to the bank and made the payment. Mr. Wylie was surprised but pleased, and she could see he was curious about where she'd gotten the money. She didn't tell him it came from the past—a past she'd probably never see again. But right now, her only feeling was relief that she wouldn't have to worry about another payment for three months.

THAT NIGHT Serena fought sleep. She couldn't tolerate another one of those nights. She had to teach in the morning. She groaned at the prospect, almost giving in to a wave of exhaustion. Why couldn't she stop thinking about the other woman? Maybe because she felt Gran wasn't telling her the whole story about her father. But what did it matter? Serena got her features from her mother's side of the family. Her father's family had nothing to do with that. Still…she'd like to know *something* about them.

Ethan Ramsey could help her. No, no, she was taking this too far. Gran wouldn't lie to her. But…she flipped on the light and went over to the trash can. His business card was still inside. She retrieved it and placed it on her nightstand. Now what? Ethan could find out about the other woman; that was the only way she was going to have any peace. Private investigators cost money, though, and she wondered how much he charged. Since she was struggling to stay afloat, hiring him was crazy to even contemplate. Absolutely crazy. She opened the drawer and dropped the card in. She had to pull herself together and stop thinking about the stripper…and Ethan Ramsey.

THINGS WERE CHANGING around the Ramsey house. Molly cleaned and cooked all week, getting ready for Travis's homecoming. Ethan even heard her singing a few times, and it did his heart good. Bruce had called Cole and Cole had talked to him, in one-word answers, but it was a start. Even though Molly was still hurting, at least she was making an effort to control her reactions. She didn't say anything when Bruce called, and that was a big improvement. She didn't even ask Cole what Bruce wanted, which Ethan considered the biggest step of all. She was letting Cole form his own opinions of his father.

Ethan was busy on the ranch, baling hay, fixing fence and clearing brush to rid his pasture of mesquite. It was a never-ending job. He'd bought a spirited horse that needed breaking. Cole was eager for the job, and Ethan figured it was a way for him to get rid of some of the tension he was carrying around. So Saturday morning, Ethan let him try his hand.

He held the horse while his nephew climbed on, then he ran to the fence as the horse started to buck. ''Ride 'em, boy. Ride 'em...''

His voice stilled when the horse managed to send Cole flying through the air. The boy hit the ground, spitting out dirt, then rolled onto his back. ''What am I doing wrong, Uncle Ethan?''

Ethan shook his head. ''You're not concentrating,'' he said from his perch on the fence.

Cole got to his feet and dusted off his jeans. ''I've concentrated so hard my head's about to explode.''

''Want to try again?'' Pop called, capturing the animal's reins.

Cole didn't answer as he stared off toward the road.

Ethan followed his gaze. A truck was coming, stirring up dust like a thundercloud.

Pop put the horse in the bigger corral and walked over to Ethan. Cole followed. ''It's Uncle Travis, isn't it?'' Cole asked excitedly.

Ethan squinted against the morning sun. ''Yep, sure looks like it.''

''Yea doggie!'' Cole shouted, then leaped over the fence and ran for the house.

Ethan jumped to the ground and winced as pain shot up his leg. Damn, he hated that weakness. But the pain in his hip was his own battle and he dealt with it privately, without complaining, without excuses.

Pop headed for his horse, tethered to the fence. ''Think I'll check on those heifers in the north pasture.''

"Pop," Ethan called.

His father turned to look at him.

"Thought you were going to make an effort—for Molly."

"Son—"

"Let's go, Pop. It's time to say hello to your youngest son."

When they reached the house, Travis and Cole were horsing around, throwing punches at each other. With an arm around Cole, Travis said, "Hi, Ethan. Pop."

"Son," Pop replied in a solemn voice. "You finally found your way home."

Ethan took a long breath and embraced Travis, not wanting to give Pop any opportunity to get more zingers in. Pop's attitude did not bode well for the weekend.

"Good to have you here," Ethan said as the front door flew open and Molly burst out.

"Travis, Travis!" she cried, and ran into his arms. He swung her round and round until all they heard was the sound of laughter.

Finally Travis set her on her feet. "You'll never believe what I have cooking in the house!" Molly paused to catch her breath. "Chicken and dressing and apple pie," she said before Travis could speak.

Travis looped an arm around her waist as they made their way into the house. "You always were my favorite sister."

"I'm your only sister." Molly giggled, and Ethan knew he'd done the right thing in asking Travis to come home. He wished Pop could see that.

The day went relatively well, considering Pop's uncommunicative mood and somber expression. That evening they sat on the front porch, and Travis played his guitar and sang. Molly joined in and Ethan and Cole clapped along. After that, they started on the gospel songs their mother used to sing. Ethan noticed that Pop was getting teary-eyed.

Suddenly Pop said, "You both got your talent from your mother. She sang like a bird."

An unwelcome tension followed.

Travis cleared his throat. "Thanks, Pop." And Molly nodded.

"I was so mad at her brother Charlie for buying you that guitar when you were twelve."

Silence again.

"Later I found out that Marie had given him the money to buy it. It was the only thing she ever kept from me." He slowly shook his head. "She knew I wouldn't like it."

Travis looked to Ethan for guidance, but Ethan didn't respond. If Pop had something to say, he needed to say it.

"I still don't like it," Pop went on. "But Ethan says you have a right to live your life the way you want. He's right, because when I hear you sing, I hear your mama and..." He stopped as his voice cracked. He got to his feet. "Think I'll turn in."

Molly threw her arms around him, and they exchanged a long hug. Then Pop looked at Travis. "Glad you're home, son," he mumbled, and walked into the house.

Ethan heaved a sigh of relief. Finally they were talking like a family. Now maybe the hurt could begin to heal.

THEY WERE STILL talking outside when the phone rang. Cole jumped up. "I'll get it."

Ethan wondered if Cole was hoping it would be his father. A minute later, he was back. "It's for you, Uncle Ethan. A woman."

"A woman?" Travis raised an eyebrow. "This is interesting.'' He grinned at Cole. ''Did she sound young and attractive?''

Cole shrugged. ''She sounded nice.''

''Nice and needs assistance from a P.I. is my guess,'' Travis stated.

Ethan stood. ''It *could* be something entirely different.''

''Yeah, right.'' Travis said with a laugh.

Ethan shook his head as the laughter followed him into the house.

He picked up the receiver. ''Hello.''

''Mr. Ethan Ramsey?''

''Yes.''

''My name is Serena Farrell. We met a week ago in a café in Fort Worth. You thought I was a…stripper. Do you remember?''

Ethan sat down on the sofa. The redhead was the last person he'd expected to call. That could only mean one thing. She needed his services, just as Travis had predicted.

''Yes, I remember. What can I do for you, Ms. Farrell?''

Silence.

''Ms. Farrell?''

''I'm not sure how to say this.''

''Don't be embarrassed. Sometimes we all do stupid things.''

''I am *not* a stripper,'' she said hotly.

''Okay, then, why are you calling me?''

''I want to know who the other woman is.''

''I see,'' he said, but he didn't, so he decided to let her do the talking.

''Do you think you can find her?'' she asked after a brief pause.

''That shouldn't be too hard.''

"How...how much do you charge?"

Ethan told her and she asked, "Do you think you can locate her in two days?"

Ethan knew where the woman worked, so the job would be easy, but he wasn't sure why Serena Farrell needed to find her. Was she telling the truth about her own identity? *Could* there actually be two of them? His curiosity was piqued, and he wanted to find out.

"I think so," he said slowly. "Can you explain what this is all about?"

"If she looks like me, we have to be related in some way. I want to know how."

Ethan accepted that, but he felt there were a lot of blanks that needed filling in. "Okay, I'll come to Fort Worth and we'll take it from there."

"I can't do it next week. I'm a schoolteacher and it's the last week of school, but the week after should be fine."

"I work alone, Ms. Farrell."

"Please, Mr. Ramsey, this is very important to me."

Something in her voice got to him. "Give me your number."

When she'd rattled off her phone number, she said, "Thanks, Mr. Ramsey. I know you think I'm lying, but I'm not."

"I'm a private investigator and I try not to judge people. If you want this woman found, then I'll find her. I'll call in a week."

Ethan hung up and stared at the phone. *The plot thickens.* Now he'd discover whether or not there were two women, and he didn't mind getting to know Ms. Serena Farrell in the process. She was either the best actress he'd ever met or a woman who genuinely needed his help. Either way, he was looking forward to the experience.

SERENA SAT until her heart stopped pounding. She'd done it. She'd called. Now she'd know. She picked up her mother's picture from the bed. They looked so much alike. Very few people had exactly that hair color together with the fair complexion. For the past few days, she'd had an awful thought, as a result of Gran's reaction to her questions. *Maybe Jasmine wasn't dead.* What if Aurora and Henry had disowned her and pretended she was dead? If her mother was alive and had another daughter—could that possibly be true? Yes, she told herself, because Gran wasn't telling her the whole story. She'd have to find out on her own—with Ethan Ramsey's help.

CHAPTER THREE

THE REST OF THE WEEKEND went smoothly, Ethan thought. Travis and Molly laughed and talked and sang, and they had their heads together most of the time. They were only three years apart in age and had always been close. Pop managed to keep his opinions to himself, but by Sunday afternoon Ethan knew something was afoot. Molly was too excited. Then she dropped her bombshell: she was returning to Dallas with Travis and singing in the club with him. Travis had cleared it with the owner. When Pop heard the news, he stomped off to the kitchen.

Molly appealed to Ethan. "Talk to him. I *have* to get away."

Ethan knew she did, but singing in a nightclub staggered him, too. His sister was more the domestic type.

Travis spoke up. "C'mon, Ethan. I'll look out for her."

"What about Cole?" Ethan said the only thing that made sense to him.

"We've already talked," Molly said. "Travis offered to get him a job with his construction company, but he wants to spend his last summer before college here on the ranch with you and Pop."

Ethan was still at a loss for words. Molly didn't need his permission, but she seemed to need his approval.

"You wanted me to get a job," she reminded him. "That's what I'm doing. I just can't stay here with Bruce getting married." Her voice wavered slightly.

Ethan put his arm around her. Molly had never been on her own. She'd gone from her parents' house to Bruce's, and needed to experience life as a single woman. He understood that. "Just take care of yourself and I'll take care of Cole."

She kissed his cheek. "Thanks. This will give Cole a chance to forge a new relationship with his father. You're right, my pain has had a bad effect on Cole. I don't want him to be bitter, and as much as Bruce has hurt me, he was always a good father to Cole. That's not easy for me to admit, but I have to go forward, as you said, and I'm trying to do that. I still have a lot of emotions to get through. This time away from everything will help me." She glanced toward the kitchen. "But what about Pop?"

"Go tell him what you just told me." Ethan knew she wanted *him* to explain, but if Molly was going to make her own choices, she had to defend them.

When she left, Travis said, "I think this is what's best for Molly right now."

"Oddly, I do, too," Ethan replied. "She has to find a life without Bruce. Singing in a club, though. That takes some getting used to."

"It's just something fun to do until she gets her bearings."

"I suppose," Ethan admitted. "I'll be in Fort Worth the week after next, and I'll drop by and catch the show."

Travis's eyes narrowed. "What will you be doing in Fort Worth?"

"A case."

"And you're not talking about it."

"Nope." He didn't talk about his cases and he definitely didn't want Travis to know he was working for the redhead. There'd be too many questions and he didn't have any answers.

Later that evening they waved goodbye to Molly and Travis. After Molly had talked to Pop, he seemed resigned to the situation. They all were, because they realized Molly was taking the first step in changing her life.

ETHAN DID a background check on Serena Farrell. He wanted to find out as much as he could. She was a schoolteacher, as she'd said. He would never have guessed that. She seemed more the executive type. Everything else was pretty much as he'd expected. She came from a wealthy family and lived in an affluent neighborhood. Polished and sophisticated—exactly as she appeared. She was unmarried and lived with her grandmother. That was a surprise, but then, he had a feeling there were going to be lots of surprises with Serena Farrell.

He called her and they made plans to get together on Saturday of the following week at the café where they'd first met. He didn't *have* to see her, he could get most of what he needed on the phone. But he had an urge to spend some time with her. Try to figure her out. Maybe get another read on the situation.

Ethan left Pop and Cole to their own devices, but he knew what they'd be doing. Cole was smitten with the Dawson girl, and after they finished work for the day, he'd drive over to her house. Pop would be playing dominoes with his buddies. He promised them both that he'd check in on Molly.

He arrived at the café early and sat watching the door—a habit that sometimes proved valuable. He saw her through the window. Her red hair was coiled at the nape of her neck. As he watched, she removed her sunglasses and put them in her purse. She wore a cream pantsuit that enhanced the red of her hair. When she entered the café and glanced around, he immediately got to his feet. She came toward him, and Ethan realized again how beautiful she was. She moved with a grace that had several men turning their heads. All of a sudden the stripper's almost-nude body flashed in his mind and he knew exactly what lay beneath the pantsuit. The vision startled him, but his body reacted instinctively—in a way it hadn't responded the night he'd seen the stripper. Damn, he was too old for this. Or did men ever get too old to respond? Especially when they were two feet away from a woman like Serena Farrell.

She offered her hand and he shook it. Her skin felt just as soft and smooth as it looked. A delicate fragrance drifted to his nostrils.

"I'm glad you came, Mr. Ramsey," she said as she sat down.

"Please call me Ethan," he invited as he resumed his seat.

"And please call me Serena."

"Well, Serena," Ethan said, "you mentioned on the phone that you want me to find the stripper."

"Yes." She set her purse on the table, then glanced at his face. "You sounded surprised when I called you, but I have my reasons."

"Do you mind sharing them with me?"

She shifted slightly in her chair. "Can I see some sort of identification?" She didn't know Ethan Ramsey and she thought it best to get some facts about him first. He had one of those faces that suggested real strength of character and she'd love to paint him, but she couldn't let feminine instincts overrule common sense. She didn't need another mistake in her life.

Ethan pulled out his wallet and PI badge and laid them on the table in front of her. He admired her astuteness. She *should* learn something about him.

"After high school I joined the army," he told her. "I got into intelligence work and liked it. After my tour of duty, I joined the FBI and was a member of a covert intelligence team. I traveled all over the world, but the time away became hard on my wife. When our son was born, I asked to be reassigned. My request was granted, and I became a special agent with the Bureau of Alcohol, Tobacco and Firearms. I was there until I was shot in the line of duty. Now I'm a private investigator. Does that answer your questions?"

"Yes," she answered slowly. He was married. She didn't understand why that bothered her. Of course he wasn't single. A man like Ethan Ramsey was hard to find—reliable, honest and straightforward. It wasn't something she really knew about him because they'd only just met, but it was something she instinctively felt. She'd sensed it that day his brother had confronted her about the stripper. In Ethan's eyes there was no judgment—just a desire to help. Studying him from beneath her lashes, she wondered where he'd been shot. It must have been in the leg. She wouldn't mention his limp; she was sure he wouldn't appreciate it.

He picked up his I.D. from the table. "So why do you want me to find the stripper?"

Daisy came to take their order, and they both asked for coffee. After she'd left, Serena said, "It's a long story, so I'll try to make it short. My parents died the day I was born. My mother had the same red hair and blue eyes as I do, and so does my maternal grandmother. It's a family trait. So when you said the stripper looked like me, I couldn't get it out of my head. I have to know who she is."

"Have you asked your grandmother?" he inquired, watching her face and trying to gauge her sincerity. So far he couldn't detect anything off. She was as sincere as they came.

"Yes, and she says it's ridiculous. That no one looks like me."

"But you have your doubts."

She waited until Daisy had placed coffee in front of them and walked away. "Yes." She touched the warm cup, then added milk and stirred it. "You wouldn't lie to me, would you? The woman does resemble me? I mean, this isn't a come-on or something? That's why I asked about your credentials. I have to be sure." What was she saying? Serena chastised herself. The man was married, but the words seemed to emerge of their own volition. In truth she didn't believe for a second that he was coming on to her.

"That happens a lot?" he asked, his eyebrow raised. "Guys coming on to you?" He startled himself with his response. For one thing, she was beautiful; of course guys came on to her. For another, this wasn't his normal interview. He didn't get personal.

"Sometimes," she admitted.

He noticed a tinge of pink in her cheeks. "Don't worry," he assured her. "This isn't a line. Like I told you before, the woman *is* a dead ringer for you."

She clasped her hands in her lap. "Then please find out who she is."

Her heartfelt words moved him, but something didn't seem quite right. Why didn't she ask where the stripper worked? She could easily find the woman herself, but then, strip clubs probably weren't to her taste. Still... He had to put his suspicions aside. For once he was anxious to see how a case turned out. If there were two of Serena Farrell, he wanted to see them both.

He got to his feet and picked up his Stetson. "I'll call when I have any information."

She grabbed her purse. "Shouldn't I pay you? You said you take a retainer."

"We'll settle up when I find the stripper." Why did he say that? He always took a retainer unless he knew the client, but nothing about this case was going according to form.

She stood. "Mr. Ramsey…I mean, Ethan." She smiled as she said his name and he felt a moment of exhilaration. "I can only afford two days."

"I'll try to get it done in that length of time," he replied, placing his hat on his head. "Good day."

Outside in his truck, Ethan took a long breath. What was wrong with him? He was acting like Cole—like a teenage boy—and he'd left those feelings behind many years ago. Serena Farrell was just another client, he told himself, but it was good to know that a beautiful woman could still move him. He wondered why the lookalike stripper didn't have that effect on him, which only triggered more confusion. *Were* Serena and the stripper the same person? Did he believe Serena's story? He honestly didn't have an answer, but he would find out—and soon.

DAISY GATHERED the coffee cups. "So you're seeing the cowboy again?"

Serena slung her purse over her shoulder. "What can I say? I like the tall, lanky Texas look."

"It's about time." Daisy laughed. "Ever since you and that fiancé broke up, I've seen guys fall all over themselves to talk to you, but you haven't been interested."

"It's hard to know who to trust these days."

"Ain't that the truth. Men can be pigs."

"I feel I can trust Ethan."

"Yeah," Daisy agreed. "He has that look about him."

"See you later," Serena called as she left. She climbed into her car, certain her instincts were right. She could trust Ethan Ramsey. And now she'd be able to get a good night's sleep.

ETHAN DROVE into Dallas and checked into a motel. He showered and changed, thinking this was probably the most bizarre case he'd ever taken. And it all had to do with Serena. In a short space of time, she'd lodged herself deep in his mind. He usually managed to keep a barrier between himself and a client, keep his emotions uninvolved. Not that his emotions *were* involved—he'd make sure of that—but he was thinking about her too much. He'd visit the club tonight and find out about the stripper, and his connection with Serena would be over. Then he'd go back to his ranch and his problems and life as it was.

He scooped up his hat and headed for the door. He planned on having supper at the club where Travis and Molly were singing. They were performing several nights a week. After that, he'd go to the strip joint.

He asked for a table at the back of the club because he didn't want to make Molly nervous. There was a small dance floor, but most of the people were eating as a trio played softly. Shortly after he'd ordered—steak and baked potato—a man stepped up to the microphone and introduced Travis and Molly. Travis came out carrying his guitar, with Molly beside him—a Molly he hardly recognized. He blinked several times. She had on a short glittery dress with tiny straps that barely concealed her breasts. Her straight dark hair was in a windswept style and her face was heavily made up.

Travis started to sing and strum his guitar, and Molly

joined him. Their voices flowed together in sweet harmony and for a moment Ethan forgot about Molly's shocking new appearance. He sat back and enjoyed the show.

They were on for thirty minutes, then took a break. Molly hurried over to his table and held out her hand. "Let me introduce myself," she said, smiling. "I'm Molly Crawford."

He stood and took her hand and pulled her into his arms for a hug. "I know who you are," he muttered. "But in that get-up..."

She drew back and twirled around. "Don't you like the new me?"

People were jostling to get by, so they sat down. "It's...different." But her eyes were sparkling and she was obviously happy. He hadn't seen her like this in a long time.

"Oh, Ethan, I'm having so much fun."

He could see that, too.

"I feel young and attractive again. A few guys have even hit on me."

"In that dress, I can imagine."

"Isn't it something? The owner picked it out for me. I wish Bruce could..."

Her whole demeanor changed as she said her ex-husband's name. Her smile disappeared, as did the light in her eyes.

She brushed at her hair with her hand. "I wish I could stop thinking about him." She took in a deep breath. "When does the pain go away?"

"I think that's up to you."

"Is it?"

"Sure, and you've made a great start. Getting away is exactly what you needed."

"What about you, Ethan?"

He was taken aback by the question. "What do you mean?"

"I mean you've been divorced for ten years now, yet you haven't even begun to live again."

He frowned. "Where's this coming from?"

"I've been doing a lot of thinking lately—without feeling sorry for myself," she added. "I'm going to survive this and have a better life. I've made up my mind. But you, Ethan, I don't think you've gotten over your divorce or Ryan's—"

"That's enough," Ethan interrupted sternly.

"No, it isn't," Molly went on. "You've spent the last few years taking care of me, Travis and Pop. But who takes care of *you?* Who listens to *your* problems?"

He shifted uncomfortably. "When I was shot, you and Pop did a damn good job of it. You almost smothered me, and you know I don't like that. I can take care of myself."

"But you need a woman in your life—someone special."

"I still don't understand where all this is coming from," he said. "I thought you were off love and marriage and all that."

"I was, but I've met someone who's making me see things differently."

Ethan was dumbstruck. She'd been here two weeks and had already met someone? This wasn't like Molly. She was deeply in love with Bruce, and she couldn't turn her feelings off this quickly. So who was the new man?

Travis tapped him on the back. "Hey, big brother."

Ethan stood and hugged Travis. A tall, suave-looking man stood beside Travis.

"Ethan, this is Rudy Boyd, owner of the club, and

Rudy, this is Ethan, our older brother.'' Travis made the introductions.

Ethan shook the man's hand and instantly disliked him. He had black hair and dark eyes, and he looked somehow familiar. Where had he seen him before? When Rudy Boyd put his arm around Molly, his dislike grew.

''Your sister's bringing in the customers,'' Rudy said. ''I'm trying to talk her into staying on. She brightens up the place.''

Molly smiled at Rudy with an infatuated expression and Ethan groaned inwardly. *This* was the man who made her feel attractive again. Couldn't she see he was a slimeball? That was what Ethan had immediately labeled him, although he hoped his instincts were wrong.

''Rudy, you're the sweetest man,'' Molly gushed, and Ethan wanted to drag her out of here and take her home. He'd begun to believe she'd put her life together again, but now he had a feeling she was sinking into something worse.

''Time to get back on stage,'' Travis said.

''Are you gonna stay?'' Molly asked Ethan.

''No, I've got some work to do.''

''Okay, see you later,'' Molly called as she and Travis walked off.

''Your sister's very special,'' Rudy remarked.

''And vulnerable,'' Ethan murmured with a hidden warning.

The two men stared at each other for a moment, then Rudy said, ''Well, nice meeting you, Ethan. Come back soon. I'm sure your sister would enjoy that.''

''I will,'' Ethan replied with forced politeness. Rudy strolled away and Ethan continued to watch him. Where had he seen that smug face before? It would drive him crazy until he figured it out, but right now he had a job to do. He headed for his truck and the strip club.

THE PLACE was the same as it had been a couple of weeks ago—dark, sleazy and packed with men. He sat down and ordered a beer just as the lights above the stage came on. The club had several cages suspended from the ceiling, and partially dressed girls were dancing in them. But now the main attraction was starting. The men gathered close to the stage—actually more of a runway. Some of them were college students and some were in their sixties and seventies, but most of the men were about his age—and looking for something to spice up their lives.

Girl after girl came onto the runway, each taking off her clothes seductively, tantalizing the men, who threw money recklessly onto the stage and tried to grab them, but the girls always escaped.

The scene was becoming monotonous and Ethan's hip began to ache, but he had to wait for the redhead. That was why he'd come to this tawdry place. A scantily clad waitress arrived at his table, asking if he wanted another beer. He hadn't touched the first one, nor did he plan to; he'd ordered it just to show that he could resist the stuff. He didn't understand why he had to do that, but he did.

He shook his head. "Can I ask you a question?"

"Sure, cowboy."

"There was a redheaded stripper here a couple of weeks ago. Is she a regular?"

"Yeah."

"Is she stripping tonight?"

"No, she used the old sick line."

"Will she be here tomorrow night?"

"I'm not her keeper," the waitress snapped. "Do you want a beer or not?"

Ethan stood and laid some bills on the table. ''No, but thanks.'' He picked up his hat and walked out.

Well, well, the old sick line. What was Serena Farrell up to? That was his thought as he went back to his motel room. But if Serena and the stripper were one and the same, why would Serena bother to hire him? It didn't make sense, and he decided to dismiss the possibility. He tended to believe her; he generally trusted his impressions of people, and he had a feeling she wasn't lying. So he just had to talk to the stripper and then everything would fall into place.

He was exhausted when he entered his room. Again, he told himself he was too old to keep these late hours. Sitting on the bed, he lifted his leg to remove his boot and was reminded of his weakness as pain shot through his hip and up his back. He jerked off the boot and threw it against the wall.

''Goddammit,'' he cursed, not at his injury but at everything crowding in on him. He squeezed his eyes shut to block the vision in his head, but to no avail. His son's laughing mischievous face was there for a brief paralyzing moment and he was caught in a vortex of that pain. Why did Molly have to say Ryan's name? She wanted him to talk, but he didn't need to talk. He had dealt with his son's death in the only way he could, just like he'd dealt with his hip injury. By himself. In private.

He stood and removed his clothes. Pulling the covers back, he crawled into bed, but his hip wouldn't let up and he couldn't get comfortable. He'd been given pills for the pain, but he'd seen all too often what drugs—including prescription painkillers, which were readily available and sometimes addictive—could do to people. He never took them unless he had no other option. He forced himself to keep the memories at bay. He couldn't think about Ryan.

He shifted his thoughts to Molly and hoped she wasn't messing up her life with Rudy Boyd. He'd check out Mr. Boyd just as soon as he could.

He moved onto his side and brought his knee up to take the pressure off his hip. That helped; the pain eased. Molly said he needed someone in his life, but he didn't. He'd tried and it hadn't worked. He was too much of a loner and he didn't share easily, and women needed men to share—especially when it came to emotions. That part of him was sealed away so tight it would never surface again, and he was satisfied with that. Or was he fooling himself? He stayed on the ranch until he became restless, then he took cases to chase away the demons that brought on those restless spells. And a woman wouldn't like that. His past was another casualty he had to live with.

As sleep drew near, Serena's face flashed in his mind. She was a woman who could ease a man's aches and pains—but not his.

CHAPTER FOUR

ONCE AGAIN Serena didn't sleep well. She kept wondering if Ethan had found the stripper. What was her name? *Did* she and this other woman have a connection? She was up early hoping Ethan would call, but he didn't. Gran had her bridge ladies over, so Serena worked in the study. She had several greeting cards to finish, and in the afternoon she was planning to work on a child's portrait. She'd already met the five-year-old girl, whose mother had brought lots of photos. That would be her routine for the summer, trying to supplement their income. She didn't know how much longer she could keep it up or what she was going to do when the money from the earrings ran out. And she still had to pay Ethan Ramsey. Again she questioned her decision in hiring him. She could definitely use the money for other necessities—like electricity and food. But for some reason, she just couldn't get the other woman out of her mind.

When she heard the cars leaving, she went into the den to talk to her grandmother.

"Are you tired, Gran?" she asked. Aurora sat in a large wing chair, eyes closed and feet propped up.

"A little."

"I'd like to talk about my mother."

Aurora's eyes flew open and she sighed. "Serena, I don't understand why you keep bringing this up."

"Because it's important to me. I'd like to know more about my parents."

"I've told you all you need to know," Aurora said in a sharp tone.

"I'm not ten years old, Gran," Serena replied just as sharply. "And I don't appreciate it when you treat me that way."

"Oh, darling, don't get upset with me," Gran pleaded. "I just don't like talking about them."

"Why?" Serena wanted to know. "Jasmine was your only child, yet there are no pictures of her in this house. It's like she never existed."

Aurora's lips tightened. "She broke my heart when she chose *that man* over me and your grandfather. I had all her things put in the attic. I didn't want any reminders."

Serena swallowed hard. "Why, Gran? Why do you hate my father so much?"

"He wasn't a nice person," came the clipped answer. "And I raised Jasmine with high standards. Standards that *he* flouted."

"What do you mean?"

"He took Jasmine from me out of spite."

Serena's eyes narrowed. Gran was talking as if she knew John Welch very well. She remembered the other conversations she'd had with her grandmother, and something here didn't ring true. "You said you didn't know anything about John Welch, yet—"

Gran cut in. "I just get angry when I think about that man and what he did to my family." Gran fingered the pearls around her neck with a nervous hand. "It's so long ago now and I'm tired of talking about them."

Gran was lying. Serena got to her feet, knowing it was useless to talk to her; Gran wasn't going to let go of years of resentment and bitterness. Still, Serena wanted to find out why. As she went back to the study, she kept thinking that maybe her mother was alive. Oh, God, *could* her mother be alive? The ringing of the phone stopped her thoughts. She immediately yanked it up. It was Ethan, and she'd never been so glad to hear anyone's voice in her life.

"Have you found her?" was all she could say.

"No," Ethan said, and her spirits sank.

"She wasn't at the strip club?"

"No, they said she was sick." He sounded put out and she wondered why.

"Then she'll be back, won't she?"

"I'm not sure. Since it was Saturday I was almost positive she'd be there." A long pause.

"What's wrong?" she asked when he didn't say anything else. There was definitely a quality in his voice that hadn't been there before.

"I believe in honesty. If clients lie to me, there's not much I can do to help them. You once asked me if I was lying. Now I'm asking you, Serena. Are you lying to me?"

Now she understood the problem—he thought that since the stripper hadn't appeared they could be one and the same person. "No, I'm not," she said earnestly. "I am not the stripper. Please believe me. But I have to know who she is."

She could almost feel his relief. "Okay, I'll go back tonight."

"Thanks, Ethan. I'll wait for your call."

Serena hung up the phone and noticed the caller I.D. Ethan was staying at a motel in Dallas. As she stared at the name, an idea formed in her head.

AFTER HEARING her voice, Ethan felt better. She wasn't lying. He believed her, and he never took a case unless he believed the client. On this one, he'd been waffling back and forth so much he was beginning to doubt his instincts. Her soft voice confused those instincts completely, something that had never happened to him before. He'd feel like a fool if he was wrong about her, but deep inside he knew he wasn't.

He decided to stake out the club to see if the redhead went in or out. He spent the afternoon watching the back entrance, but mostly saw service and delivery people. As afternoon grew into evening, a few girls trailed in, but they were blondes and brunettes, no redheads. The building was a two-story, and he glanced at the top floor. He wondered if any of the girls lived on the premises. It was certainly possible.

Bored with the inactivity, he called it quits. He'd check the club later when things were livelier. In the meantime he drove to the police station. He had a friend who worked narcotics; as far as he knew, Daniel was still on the force. He wanted to ask him some questions about Rudy Boyd, but unfortunately Daniel was out on a case. Ethan felt as if his whole day was wasted. He returned to his room, showered and changed for the evening, then drove to the nightclub to talk to Travis. Molly was getting dressed, so they had a few minutes alone.

"What do you know about Rudy Boyd?" he asked.

Travis shrugged. "Not a lot. He hired me about a year ago, but I've seen very little of him. He has clubs all over Dallas—he's a very busy man. I've seen more of him since Molly's been here than I have the whole of last year."

"What's his interest in Molly?"

"Damn, Ethan, you've been on that ranch too long. What do you *think* his interest is?"

''Be realistic, Travis. Molly's my sister and I love her, but she's thirty-five and Rudy Boyd seems more the type to go for twenty-year-olds.''

Travis shifted in his seat. ''Yeah, I thought that, too, but maybe he's tired of empty-headed twenty-year-olds. Whatever, I figure Molly's old enough to know what she's doing.''

Ethan rose to his feet. ''You just keep an eye on her, because I have a bad feeling about this.''

''Ethan, don't go looking for trouble.''

''I'm not. I'm just being cautious.''

''Too cautious, if you ask me. There's more to life than work.''

''I've got to go,'' Ethan said.

''Aren't you gonna watch the show?''

''No, I don't want Molly to think I'm spying on her.''

''Really.'' Travis raised an eyebrow. ''Where would she get an idea like that?''

Ethan gave him a piercing look and left.

AT THE STRIP CLUB, Ethan's night was a repeat of the night before. The redhead didn't appear. Tonight, though, the place was packed and there wasn't any room to sit. He stood for a long time, watching and waiting, then made his way to the bar, hoping to talk to the bartender.

''What'll you have?'' the man finally asked after serving several other men.

''A draft, light,'' Ethan said.

When the beer was placed in front of him, Ethan said conversationally, ''I was hoping the redhead would strip tonight.''

The bartender frowned. ''You got a thing for her?''

''Yeah. I'd sure like to meet her.''

"In your dreams, buster," the barman muttered.

"I'm good at dreaming," Ethan replied casually, trying to sound like a normal customer. "Any idea when she'll be here again?"

"You ask too many questions, mister."

The man was nervous. Ethan could see it in his eyes and the way he kept looking over Ethan's shoulder.

A big man pushed between Ethan and the man beside him. "What's the problem?" He spoke to the bartender.

"This one—" he nodded to Ethan "—is asking a lot of questions."

"About what?"

"The redhead."

The man scowled. "The girls are off-limits. Now get your ass out of here." As he said the last words, he grabbed Ethan by the collar. Ethan's arm came up and knocked the man's hand away.

"I wouldn't do that if I were you," Ethan said in a steely voice.

They faced each other. The other man, evidently the bouncer, was big and muscled, but Ethan was the same height and he wasn't backing down. The bouncer got the message.

"Just leave and I won't," the bouncer finally said.

Ethan stared at him for an extra second, then left the bar.

Sitting in his truck, he tried to figure out what had just happened. Questions about the redhead made everyone nervous. Why? The club's goal was to draw customers and to keep them coming back, so it made no sense to discourage their interest in any of the strippers.

Something was going on with the redhead—and it wasn't good.

THE BOUNCER stabbed out a number on a cell phone. ‘‘We got problems,’’ he said. ‘‘Someone’s asking about the redhead.’’

‘‘Who?’’ the voice on the other end asked.

‘‘Don’t know. Looks like a cop—Texas Ranger type.’’

‘‘Goddammit, where is he now?’’

‘‘I threw him out.’’

‘‘Good, and keep a close eye on her. Call me if he shows up again.’’

‘‘I will, but I don’t like this.’’

‘‘Don’t worry. Everything should be over in a few days.’’

ETHAN OPENED his motel-room door and froze. The lights were on. He’d turned them off when he left, he was positive. Slowly he inched the door wider and stepped inside. Someone came up on his blind side. He reached out an arm and grabbed the person, and they tumbled onto the bed. Ethan realized two things almost instantly. The person was a woman and the woman was Serena. He recognized that perfume. His hold loosened and his body relaxed, but Serena kicked out with her legs and knocked him to the floor—on his bad hip. Pain shot through him and for a moment he was paralyzed.

‘‘Ethan, I’m so sorry.’’ Serena fell on her knees beside him. ‘‘Did I hurt you?’’

‘‘No,’’ he lied, and struggled to his feet. If she offered to help him, he’d explode. He sank onto the bed. ‘‘What the hell are you doing here?’’

‘‘Are you okay?’’ she said quickly, avoiding his question.

‘‘What are you doing here, Serena?’’ he repeated in a tight voice.

She sat beside him—so close that he could breathe in her delicate scent. He wanted to ask her to move, to get as far away from him as possible, because he was in a mood that did not bode well for either of them.

"I just couldn't sit at home any longer, and when I saw the name of the motel on caller I.D., I decided to drive over."

How could he let something like that slip by him? "Damn, I'm getting too old for this job."

"You think you're old?" Her voice revealed surprise.

Right now he felt about ninety and her presence wasn't helping. "How did you get in here?"

"Well—" she twisted her hands. "They don't give out room numbers easily. I told the guy at the desk that I was your wife and that I wanted to surprise you. He gave me the number but no key. When I got here, the maid was putting fresh towels in the bathroom. So I just walked in. She didn't speak much English and she obviously assumed the room was mine. I didn't correct her assumption. I've been waiting for you since early evening. I was about to go crazy."

Ethan was tired and his hip was throbbing and the last thing he wanted to do was deal with Serena Farrell. Silence reigned as he tried to figure out what his next step should be.

"Ethan."

"Hmm?"

"Did you see her tonight?"

He drew a much-needed breath and turned to look at her, then wished he hadn't. Her eyes were bright with expectation. She had to be the most beautiful woman he'd ever seen—he wasn't a man who usually fell for beauty. When he was younger, beauty had attracted him first, but as he matured, honesty, faithfulness and kindness attracted him more. But looking at Serena, he didn't really care about any of those qualities. That threw him and he decided he must've been watching too many women strip. He'd *thought* he was unaffected by the performances, but clearly he'd been wrong about that.

"Ethan," she prompted when he didn't answer.

"No, I didn't see her," he said.

"Oh, no. I was hoping..."

At the anxiety in her voice, he added, "But I have a strange feeling about that place."

"Why?"

"Because everyone got real nervous when I started asking questions."

"They did?"

"Yep, and they weren't giving out any information, either."

"So, she's still there."

"That's my guess. I'll try again tomorrow night."

She fidgeted nervously. "I can't afford to pay you for another night. I suppose I could go myself, but I've never been to a strip club. The activities are probably more than my imagination will allow."

"It's not a day at Sunday school," he told her. "But don't worry about it. The next night will be on me."

"I can't let you do that," she said. "Your time is valuable."

"I want to find out what's going on in that place for reasons of my own, so we'll call it even. Now I think we should both get some sleep."

She didn't move or say anything.

"Something wrong?" he asked guardedly.

"No. I knew it would be late when I saw you, so I told my grandmother I had business in Dallas and would be spending the night. There's a No Vacancy sign outside, and I didn't want to leave in case I missed you." She should've left earlier, but she'd wanted to see Ethan. Now the thought of driving around looking for a room wasn't appealing and neither was the prospect of going home. She could stay here with Ethan. He had a big room with a sofa. As the idea crossed her mind, she wondered where it came from. It was so unlike anything she'd ever contemplated; Ethan was a stranger and male, and that alone should make her think twice about such a situation. But for some reason, she didn't fear him or worry that he'd take advantage of her.

He sighed, not wanting to think about what this meant.

"Do you mind if I stay here? I can sleep on the sofa," she offered quickly, suspecting she'd lost all common sense. She should just go home. But, somehow, she wasn't inclined to leave...and she wasn't entirely sure why. "I really don't want to drive back to Fort Worth this late. I'll explain it to your wife."

"I've been divorced for ten years." He knew he didn't have to tell her that. The fact that she thought he was married would have kept a barrier between them, but he was always honest. It was a code he lived by.

"Oh." Her eyes grew big. "Then there isn't a problem."

Yes, there is. "No" was the word that came out of his mouth.

Silence. A long, tense silence.

Ethan wasn't sure what to say. He wanted to get her out of here so he could deal with his hip, but he hated to see her on the road this late. Still, being in the same room with her all night, especially when he was in pain, was more than his nerves could take—probably more than he could take under any circumstances. But how did he say no to her? Did he even *want* to say no to her?

"Tomorrow you're going home," he said firmly. "But for tonight I guess you can stay here."

"Thanks." She smiled. "I'll go grab my bag."

He took a deep breath as she went out the door, then got to his feet. The pain was bad, but he managed a couple of steps, then several more. He hobbled into the bathroom and rummaged through his shaving kit until he found his painkillers. He hardly ever took the damn things, but this was one of those times he had no other option. He swallowed two and returned to the bedroom.

SERENA UNLOCKED her car and grabbed her overnight bag. She couldn't stop smiling. *Ethan wasn't married.* She didn't understand why that made her feel so good, but it did. She liked him—a lot. His warm eyes, his strength of character, his confident, capable manner were all very appealing. In fact, she found him appealing in every way. Except for one little flaw—his stubborn pride. He didn't want her to know he was in pain. She could tell that he was by the tightening of his jaw. She'd seen that look on her grandfather's face after his heart attack; he never wanted anyone to know he was in pain, either.

Serena winced as she recalled how she'd kicked Ethan off the bed. She hoped he'd tell her about his injury, although she doubted he'd do so willingly.

She walked back to the room feeling a sense of excitement. With Ethan's help, she knew they'd find out who the redhead was. Then all her questions and suspicions would be answered. And getting to know Ethan was a big plus…

BY THE TIME Serena reentered the room, Ethan had himself under control. "Why don't you take the bed?" he suggested. He wasn't going to sleep, anyway.

She glanced at the small sofa, then at the king-size bed. "You're joking, right? You won't fit on the sofa."

"I've slept on more uncomfortable furniture."

She bit her lip and plunged in. "But not after your injury."

His eyes caught hers. "You noticed?"

"A little." She shrugged. "And I've aggravated it by making you fall on the floor, so you don't get to be chivalrous. You get to sleep in the bed."

For the first time, Ethan found that he wasn't angry because someone had mentioned his injury. She hadn't said it to belittle or intimidate. She'd just made a statement of fact. A fact he'd grown to live with. He didn't understand why it bothered him sometimes. He was sure that, as Molly often said, it had something to do with his masculine pride. He didn't like feeling diminished.

Serena set her bag on the sofa and removed a small cosmetics case. "I'll just brush my teeth and remove my makeup, and we can get some sleep." She moved toward the bathroom.

Ethan sat down to take off his boots and realized he had a problem. He couldn't raise his leg high enough to remove his right boot. As much as he gritted his teeth, his hip was stiff and aching and wouldn't cooperate.

Serena came out of the bathroom. "I forgot my… nightgown." She glanced at Ethan and saw his tight jaw, the stress on his handsome face, and in an instant knew what was wrong.

Without a word she dropped to the floor and grabbed hold of his boot, pulling gently. She did the same with the other boot. She placed them by a chair, then stood up, retrieved her nightgown and returned to the bathroom.

Despite himself, Ethan smiled. He would've been angry if anyone else had done that, but she'd managed it in such a nonchalant way it hadn't bothered him. He liked Serena

Farrell. She was a woman after his own heart—and if he didn't watch out, he'd be giving it to her.

He realized he was dawdling. She'd be back any minute and he had to get into bed. He hadn't brought any pajamas. Slipping out of his jeans, shirt and socks, he hung them on the chair and crawled beneath the sheets as quickly as he could.

Serena emerged from the bathroom and all he could do was stare. Her red hair was hanging loose, falling midway down her back in thick, glossy waves. The stripper's hair was almost the same length and style, but…something was different and he knew with certainty that Serena and the stripper were not the same person. There was a softness about Serena that the stripper lacked, a softness that couldn't be faked.

"Mind if I steal a pillow?" she asked.

"No, and there's a blanket in the closet if the air-conditioning's too cold."

"Thanks." She took a pillow, opened the closet and found the blanket.

"Should I turn off the lights?" she inquired politely.

"Yes," he answered, his eyes never leaving her. She wore a blue nightshirt of some sort of silky material that fell just above her knees and showed off slim, smooth legs.

The room was suddenly dark and Ethan heard her settle on the sofa.

"Thanks, Serena," he said into the stillness.

"You're very welcome," she replied, knowing he was talking about her help in removing his boots. "And thank you for letting me stay."

"Didn't seem like I had much choice."

"It's odd, isn't it?" she said. "We're virtually strangers

and we're sharing a motel room. This is a new experience for me, but we're both adults and we can handle it.''

Famous last words, Ethan thought as he turned onto his side.

Serena tried to get comfortable on the sofa, but it was soft and lumpy. As she stared into the darkness, questions filled her head. Instinctively she felt that Ethan was a man who didn't like to talk. But she decided not to pay any attention to her instincts.

''What do you think the people at the strip club are nervous about?''

''It's a sleazy place, Serena,'' he answered. ''There could be all kinds of reasons.''

''But you will talk to her?''

''I'm not sure now, but I'm gonna give it my best shot.''

''Ethan?''

''Go to sleep. We'll talk in the morning.''

His voice was curt, and she knew he was still in pain. For the next half hour, she listened to him tossing and turning. Finally she couldn't take any more.

''You were shot in the hip?'' she asked quietly.

Ethan's hip was throbbing so badly he was going to have to do something—like take more pills, and he didn't want to do that. He tried to concentrate, to block out the pain, but that wasn't working, either. Her sweet voice came like a balm in the night, and instead of resisting, he found himself welcoming it. Before he even knew what he was doing, he was answering her question.

''Yeah, we got a tip that a man was storing illegal weapons. When we checked it out, the man and his friends were waiting for us. It was a setup and we had a lot of casualties that day. I was one of them.''

She wanted to say she was sorry, but she knew he

wouldn't appreciate hearing it. So she said the only thing she could. "I'm sorry I kicked you off the bed earlier. It was just a reflex action."

"Don't worry about it."

"But I do. I'm the reason you're in pain."

"Serena, go to sleep."

"Have you ever had your hip massaged?"

"No," he said in a low voice.

"Tense muscles are deprived of oxygen because blood flow is reduced. Massage improves circulation and eases the pain."

"Sounds as if you know what you're talking about."

"A little. In college I dated a guy whose sister was a professional massage therapist. She taught me some basics. My grandmother has severe headaches and I massage her neck and shoulders sometimes—she says it helps her relax. Would you like me to try with your hip?"

"No."

"I can hear you thrashing around and I know you're in a lot of pain. I can try to relax your tight muscles."

He'd bet she could. That was the problem.

"Serena—"

"We were just talking about being adults, so let's be grown-up about this. You're in pain and I'd like to help." She couldn't sleep if he couldn't. It was her fault, after all, that his pain had been exacerbated.

"I've dealt with this for a long time and—" His voice stopped as the bed moved.

Serena didn't know what possessed her, but before she could think about it, she'd left the sofa and crossed to the bed. She felt as if she'd stepped outside her body and entered a dreamlike state without her usual rules or boundaries. She followed the dictates of her heart and didn't hesitate for a minute. She just wanted to make him more comfortable.

"Turn onto your stomach," she said.

Ethan did as she ordered without a word of protest. The way he looked at it, he didn't have a thing to lose. The fact that she was his client and he didn't get involved with clients on a personal level seemed irrelevant at the moment.

Serena pulled the corners of the sheet from beneath the mattress and arranged the sheet over Ethan's backside. She didn't turn the light on. She didn't think she'd need it, and the darkness might encourage him to relax.

She knelt beside him. "I'll use long gliding strokes from your neck to the base of your spine." She wanted him to know what she was doing.

"Fine," he said into his pillow.

The moment her soft hands touched him, it truly was fine. Better than fine. At his age he hadn't thought there were any more fantasies, but one was forming so wantonly in his mind that he floated along with the rhythm of her hands. But only in his mind…

CHAPTER FIVE

ETHAN'S MUSCLES were firm. His age was hard to guess, but Serena thought somewhere in his early forties. Considering his age and his injury, he was in good shape. There wasn't any excess flab on him as she'd seen on other men his age. She stroked and kneaded until her arms began to ache, and still his muscles were taut.

Taking a long breath, she said, "I'll have to remove the sheet." She'd been trying to work around and over the sheet to keep this professional, but she could do a better job without it. Besides, Ethan wasn't interested in her in that way and she wasn't interested in him, either.

"Fine," he mumbled sleepily.

She pulled the sheet to one side. He had on briefs, so that was good. Her hands slid to his hip.

Ethan's breath lodged in his throat and he didn't know which was worse, the pain in his hip or the frustration building in him. He hated needing help, hated receiving help, but for once he wasn't fighting it.

Her fingers paused over the scar that ran along his hip, then with circular movements of her thumb and fingertips she gently massaged the area. His body still didn't release its tension.

"Try to relax," she coaxed.

"Hmm?"

"You have to relax, Ethan," she told him. "Your body is coiled tight."

She should experience this from my point of view, he thought.

''Talk to me. That might help.''

''What?''

Her fingertips pressed softly around his hip. ''Tell me about your son. Does he live with his mother?''

''No,'' he said abruptly.

''Oh.'' She was surprised. ''Then he lives with you?''

''No.''

''Oh,'' she murmured again. ''That must mean he's grown up and on his own.'' It was hard to believe he had a son that old, but it was the only explanation she could come up with.

''No, he isn't.'' His words came through the darkness like a hollow echo, and Serena didn't know what to think. But she couldn't let it go.

''Where is he, then?''

Ethan never talked about his son. Everyone in his family knew the subject was off-limits, but now from somewhere inside him the words seemed to tumble out, words he couldn't stop.

''He's dead,'' he said quietly. He couldn't ever remember saying those words out loud.

Serena's hands stilled for a second. She'd never suspected *this.* She could feel the pain in his voice, and she had to force herself to keep massaging. She'd wanted him to relax but in urging him to speak about something so intolerable, she'd only made matters worse.

''I'm so sorry. I apologize for prying.''

''He was three years old,'' Ethan added as if he hadn't heard her. ''He was a lively, curious little boy and he always loved to climb. Beth and I laughed about him being part monkey. I was away on a case and it was winter. We lived in Washington, D.C., at the time. Ryan couldn't go outside and he wanted to ride his tricycle, so Beth let him play in the garage. The phone rang then, and she went to answer it. We had boxes in the garage, things we hadn't put away from the recent move. Ryan climbed to the top of the boxes, and when he saw Beth coming, he tried to get down in a hurry and fell to the concrete floor. He…fractured his skull.'' Ethan took a ragged breath. ''He died on the way to the hospital.''

Serena just continued her massage. She didn't have anything to say. Every word was like a blow to her chest. All she could think of was the suffering he and his wife must have gone through.

The words kept coming and Ethan still couldn't halt them. It was so easy to talk here in the darkness with Serena. ''They kept him at the hospital until I arrived, and seeing my son was the hardest thing I've ever had to do.'' A long pause. ''Beth fell completely apart and we couldn't even comfort each other. I lost myself in a bottle and she found God. We slowly drifted apart, and we both knew the marriage was over.''

Silence. Absolute total silence.

Serena noticed that Ethan's muscles were finally relaxing.

Ethan couldn't believe he was talking so much. It had to be the pills. The ache in his heart had become so intense he was hardly aware of the ache in his hip. He felt winded and out of breath, as if he'd run a marathon, and he knew he had to talk about something else before his emotions completely overwhelmed him.

''Have you ever been married?'' he asked.

Even though the sudden change of subject threw Serena, she managed to find her voice. ''No, but I came close a couple of times,'' she said, her thumbs pressing gently into his hip. ''Remember the guy I mentioned in college? I was crazy about him until I discovered he was also seeing someone else. After I came back to Fort Worth, I got a job teaching and I met Brad. He's a teacher, too. We fell in love and everything was perfect until my grandfather passed away."

She was quiet for a moment. "My grandfather was heavily in debt, and the bank was expecting my grandmother and me to pay the bills. Brad wanted me to put my grandmother in a home and file bankruptcy on my grandfather's estate."

"But you didn't?"

"No, I couldn't. My grandmother's lived in our house since she and my grandfather got married. Putting her in a home was out of the question. I thought Brad would help me pay off the bills, but he didn't see that as part of our marriage deal. I saw a side to Brad I didn't like and I broke the engagement."

"How are you managing to make ends meet?"

"I do greeting cards and paint portraits on the side, but it's not enough. I finally had to hock the earrings my grandfather gave Gran on their wedding day. The jeweler at the Diamond Room said he'd hold them for thirty days in case I changed my mind, but that's not likely to happen. It hurt so much to sell them. They belonged to my grandfather's mother, and Grandfather said they'd be mine on my wedding day. Since the wedding was off, I felt I had a right to use them to save our home." What was she doing? She'd promised herself that she wouldn't tell anyone what she'd done. The darkness and the intimate conversation—or was it Ethan?—were getting to her.

"So what made you hire me?" he asked.

Her fingertips ran along his hip in smooth circular strokes. What was that old saying—In for a penny, in for a pound? "Talking to my grandmother, I got the feeling she wasn't telling me the whole story about my parents. You see, my mother ran off when she was eighteen and married a boy they disapproved of, and they wouldn't have anything to do with her after that. When my mother and father were killed in a car accident, my grandparents agreed to raise me, but I don't think my grandmother ever truly forgave my mother. I don't know anything about my father's family, and my mother was an only child. So if there's someone who looks like me, I have to know who she is.''

Ethan suddenly understood why finding the other woman was so important to her. She needed answers about her birth, her parents and most of all herself. He would find them for her and he wouldn't charge her a dime. His mind was becoming clouded from the pills, and her hands had worked magic on his body. He was floating in a world where only he and Serena existed. And he liked it. He liked it a lot.

Ethan's body was now completely at ease and Serena was glad. Her arms were almost numb. ''Ethan?'' she called softly.

No response.

He was asleep.

Serena sat back on her heels and tucked her hair behind her ears. Thank God. He was finally out of pain enough to sleep. She slowly returned to the sofa. Picking up her pillow, she glanced at the bed. Why not? she asked herself. She'd done so many crazy, different things tonight, it seemed almost natural. Besides, the bed was comfortable and the sofa was not. She walked back to the bed and lay down, then spread the sheet over both of them and curled up on her side. Ethan might be upset that she'd taken it upon herself to sleep in his bed, but she knew he wouldn't do anything. She trusted him completely. She had from the first moment she'd set eyes on him. Drifting into sleep, she felt her features relax into a soft smile.

AS SOON AS Ethan woke up, he noticed that his hip wasn't hurting, and he let himself revel in that freedom from pain. A moment later the night's events came rushing back. Serena, her hands touching him with gentle strokes until he revealed his emotions in a way he never had before. He'd talked about Ryan and he didn't feel as if he was coming apart at the seams. For the first time it felt good to share his pain with someone.

He turned over—and his breathing stopped as he saw Serena sleeping beside him. Her red hair was everywhere and there was a peaceful look on her beautiful face. He tried to remember what had happened after they'd talked, but he drew a blank. Then he knew. He'd fallen asleep. The pills—they always eventually knocked him for a loop. That was why he never took them. He liked to have his head clear.

So what was she doing in his bed? The sofa must be a nightmare to sleep on, he reasoned, and she'd opted for a more comfortable place. That said a lot about the way she felt toward him—as a man. He was older and she probably trusted him, probably thought of him as fatherly. Oh, yeah, that was just how he wanted her to think of him.

He eased out of bed, careful not to wake her. His hip felt fine; that massage had worked a miracle. He glanced at Serena, observing that the sheet was tangled and her blue shirt had ridden up, revealing more of her long legs. Just looking at her created emotions in him he hadn't felt in years. Something about her attracted him deeply, and it wasn't just her looks. It was her gentleness, her caring, her honesty and her openness. She'd been straight with him from the start, and he felt she always would be.

He collected jeans and a shirt from the closet and found underwear and socks in his carryall. A shower, clean clothes, and he'd be ready to face the day…and Serena.

THE SOUND of running water woke Serena. Ethan was in the shower, she realized. She hoped his hip was better and wondered what he'd thought when he saw her in his bed. Evidently not much, since he didn't wake her. They were both old enough not to worry about something so trivial. She reached for her pillow and hugged it. At least her virtue wasn't compromised, she told herself with a quick grin. So far, she wasn't even aware that Ethan had noticed her virtue—or anything else.

She remembered what he'd told her last night. Losing a child had to be a horrific experience. She wasn't sure how anyone overcame that or lived with the memory, but Ethan had. That was why she saw that somber look in his eyes at times. Life had dealt him a blow that was hard to overcome. From the beginning, she'd sensed Ethan's strength, and she was sure it was what kept him sane.

Her financial problems seemed petty compared to what he'd been through. If necessary, her problems could be solved by selling their house, although she couldn't bring herself to do that. It was Gran's home and it would be devastating for her to leave. Serena would figure out a way to keep them there. She had to. Chasing the stripper seemed petty, too. Finding her wasn't going to change anything, though it might tell Serena something about her mother. That one tiny hope made it seem worthwhile.

Ethan came out of the bathroom fully dressed except for his boots. He wore his usual jeans and a white shirt. His hair was neatly combed back and his face clean-shaven. She felt an unexpected tingling in the pit of her stomach.

"Good morning," he said as he sat in a chair to put on his boots.

"Good morning," she answered. "I hope you're not upset about me sharing your bed."

He smiled at her as he shoved his foot into a boot without any difficulty. "What man would be upset about a pretty woman sharing his bed? I would've suggested it, but I didn't think you'd agree."

"Oh."

As color stained her cheeks, he wished he could take the words back. He didn't even know why he'd said such a thing. Maybe he'd been subconsciously thinking it, or maybe the sight of her sitting in the middle of the bed looking like a photograph in a Victoria Secret's catalog triggered the thought. Whatever, he had to ease the awkwardness he'd just created with those casually spoken words.

"Don't worry, Serena. I'm forty-three, way too old to be tempted by a woman who's twelve years younger than I am."

Her eyes narrowed. "How do you know my age?"

"I did a background check."

At her startled expression, he added, "I do that with every case. I don't like surprises."

She barely heard what he said. She was still focused on his earlier remarks. Ethan was as straitlaced as they came, and if he'd shown any signs of wanting to share a bed, they'd completely escaped her.

He raised an eyebrow. "Having second thoughts about last night?"

"No." She shook her head, feeling a little out of her element as new emotions surged forth. "It's just..." she hesitated.

"Just a little uncomfortable in the light of day."

"I'm not uncomfortable," she insisted. "Last night I knew I was doing the right thing. But now...I'm wondering what you must think of me. It's not my practice to ask to stay in a man's motel room or to offer him a massage."

She brushed her hair over her shoulder and he watched as if mesmerized. "I think you're a headstrong, determined woman with a caring, impulsive nature." He paused and jammed his foot into the other boot. "That's all."

They stared at each other for an endless second, then she rushed into speech to dispel the tension that suddenly enveloped them. "Your hip must be better. You put your boots on without a problem."

"Yeah." He stood. "I may have to look you up from time to time to get a massage. You have a magic touch."

"It's a deal."

Their eyes locked again, and something passed between them that neither was willing to fully accept. Ethan was the first to look away. He reached for his hat.

"Are you going somewhere?" she asked.

"Yes, to get coffee."

She pointed to a small coffeepot on a table. "There's coffee here."

"It only makes two cups. I need more and some food to go with it. I'm going across the street. I'll be back in a minute." He disappeared out the door.

SERENA SQUEEZED the pillow more tightly. She'd said they were adults and could handle the situation. What had happened to that logic? Bridget, her massage therapist friend, had told her that in order to give a good massage she'd have to acquaint herself with the subject's body by touch. Without even realizing it, she'd done that last night with Ethan. Her fingertips could still feel the hard texture of his muscles. From touching his body, she'd learned he was strong, active and very proud. But massages had nothing to do with why she was here, she thought in sudden panic. She shouldn't have any interest in him beyond the job she'd hired him to do. And after Ethan found the stripper, she'd never see him again—but she'd always remember this interlude in a motel room and the things he'd told her. He was a good man and a kind one, and she couldn't help responding to that.

She noticed the clock and saw it was past nine. She picked up the phone and called home, since Gran would be up by now.

"Hi, Gran," she said as her grandmother answered.

"Serena, darling, are you having a good time?"

Serena was thrown for a second. She'd told her grandmother she had to go to Dallas on business. It seemed as if Gran thought she was doing something else. Before she could think of a suitable reply, Gran added, "I probably let the cat out of the bag, but I'm so happy you and Brad are trying to work on your relationship. A weekend together is what you both need."

Serena frowned. "Gran, what are you talking about?"

"I saw Brad's mother yesterday and she said Brad was in Dallas. I'm not a rocket scientist, but I can put two and two together."

"I hate to disappoint you, but I'm not here with Brad."

"If you want to keep it a secret, then—"

"I'm not here with Brad, Gran, and I'm not lying or trying to keep it a secret."

"Oh." Her grandmother's voice was puzzled. "Then what are you doing there?"

"I'm here on business." She crossed her fingers behind her back. "I'll be home sometime today, so don't worry."

"Okay, darling," Gran replied. "Drive carefully."

As she hung up, Ethan came back in with two brown paper bags. He set them on the nightstand and removed a large container of coffee, which he handed to her, along with a napkin and two doughnuts.

"Thank you," she said as she took them. The container had to hold at least four cups. "When you drink coffee, you mean business."

"Yeah," he answered as he sat and sipped on his. "It gives me a jumpstart in the mornings. There's cream and sugar if you want it."

"Thanks." She rummaged in the bag until she found the cream. She opened two of the tiny creamers and dumped the contents in her coffee. As she sipped, she studied the doughnuts on the napkin.

She looked up and saw that Ethan had finished one and was starting on his second. She ran her finger across the sugary icing and tasted it. Doughnuts were her one food weakness. The café where she got a muffin and juice before work received them fresh every morning, the smell alone was a test to her willpower. Daisy tempted her all the time, but Serena didn't indulge her weakness too often. She was becoming more conscious of health issues as she grew older, and doughnuts, unfortunately, were nothing but fat, sugar and refined flour.

Ethan eyed her for a moment. "Are you gonna play with it or eat it?"

She met his gaze. "That depends."

"On what?"

"Whether my willpower or my appetite wins."

Ethan shook his head, finished off his doughnut and peered at her over the rim of his coffee. "I'd say you were a natural beauty, and if you're worried about your weight or your looks, then you're wasting your time."

Despite herself, she smiled. It never hurt to hear a man say that, and she had to admit his flattery warmed her.

"Eat the doughnut, Serena. You need a sugar boost."

She nodded and took a big bite, and watched him smile.

"Feel better?" he asked.

"Mmm" was all that came out of her mouth.

He continued to watch her as she ate the doughnut, then licked her fingers with a sensuality that was better than the doughnuts he'd just had.

"Sorry," she muttered. "I guess I have to justify eating one of those."

He shook his head again.

"What?" she asked.

"Women. I'll never understand them."

Her tone was thoughtful as she said, "We're like a puzzle with many different parts, but most of us have a central theme—love, family and happiness. If a man's lucky, he can put the pieces together without a problem, but the majority don't have a clue."

"You're right about that," he said. "A woman is definitely a puzzle and I'm not sure *any* man's ever figured one out."

Serena laughed and leaned back against the headboard, hardly able to believe she was sitting in a motel room with this wonderful man and talking nonsense...happy nonsense.

A comfortable silence stretched between them and any awkwardness that had been there earlier was completely gone. Ethan relaxed and finished drinking his coffee.

"Ethan?"

"Uh-huh?"

"What happened to your wife?"

When he didn't respond, she wanted to take the words

back—and yet, she wanted to know all she could about him.

Slowly his words came. ''Beth remarried—he's a minister—and now has two children. They live in Arizona.''

''Then you still hear from her?''

''Occasionally. We once shared someone special and it's hard to let go of that bond.''

There was probably more to it than that on Beth's part, Serena thought. It was probably equally hard to let go of Ethan. She lifted her head. ''You said you lost yourself in a bottle. Were you an alcoholic?''

He stood, crushed the cup in his hand and threw it in the trash. ''You ask a lot of questions.''

''I'm curious about you,'' she said openly. ''You don't seem like the type of person, if there is one, to become an alcoholic.''

''We all have our dark sides,'' he muttered. ''I'm not an alcoholic, but I was on the verge of becoming one.''

She took a quick breath and dove in. ''So what made you stop drinking?''

His eyes met hers with a chilling look, and she braced herself for a sharp retort. Instead, he sat down, elbows on his knees, hands clasped together. ''My family came to be with us during that terrible time. After the funeral I told them they didn't have to stay, that Beth and I were fine, although we weren't. She wanted to talk but I couldn't. So she talked to a minister and I found if I drank enough, I could forget completely. Travis, my brother, stayed on and tried to talk sense into me, but I wasn't hearing anything back then.''

He swallowed and she waited, almost afraid to breathe in case he stopped talking. ''I guess it was about six weeks later that I woke up one morning in my truck—which had veered sideways into a ditch. I didn't know where I was or where I was going. All I could think was that I could've killed someone. I wasn't worried about myself. At that point, death was preferable to the living hell. As the sun broke through the clouds, it all came down on me and I cried and cried. Up until that moment I hadn't shed a tear.'' He paused. ''I've been a lawman, sworn to uphold the law and help others, for most of my life. If you're a good lawman, you live by a certain code of ethics. I realized I was breaking every oath I'd ever taken. I was driving drunk, endangering lives, instead of saving them. That wasn't a very good memorial to my son. I stopped drinking that day, cleaned up my act and went back to work. Unfortunately, Beth and I couldn't recapture what we once had. We'd both been hurt too badly.''

''Oh, Ethan, I am so sorry.'' All she wanted to do was comfort him. ''Thanks for telling me,'' she whispered, moved by his trust in her.

He lifted an eyebrow. ''Any more questions?''

She shook her head. Every emotion, except her compassion for Ethan Ramsey, was blocked out.

Ethan felt ten pounds lighter, and he knew an enormous weight had been lifted from his shoulders. He'd carried it around for a long time, and he'd never intended to share his burden with anyone. But here he was, talking to this woman, pouring out his heart. He wasn't sure why talking to Serena was so easy. He'd never told a living soul why he'd stopped drinking. Molly, Travis and Pop had all tried to get him to talk, but he couldn't share that part of himself. So why was it so easy with *her?*

He stood. ''I've got work to do and you should go back to Fort Worth.''

She pleated a seam in the pillowcase, gaining courage. ''I could stay and go with you.'' The more time she spent with Ethan, the more she wanted to stay with him—to be there when he found the stripper.

"No," he said emphatically. "I told you before, I work alone."

She stared at him. "Please, Ethan. I want to see her."

Her face was an enchanting picture framed by her burnished-copper hair, but it was the distressed look in her eyes that got to him. "I'll ask her." That was the most he could guarantee.

"Why can't I just go with you?" she asked boldly. "I promise to be cooperative."

That conjured up all kinds of images in his head, which he quickly stopped. She had a way of getting around him, and he had to put a stop to that, too. "You can be cooperative by doing as I ask and going home. I let you stay last night only because it was late. Don't read more into it than that."

She frowned. "Like what?"

"Like I'm a pushover for a pretty face."

"Where would I get that idea?" she snapped sarcastically, trying to control her temper.

He ignored her words and picked up his hat, setting it on his head. "I'll call when I have some news."

"Ethan," she said before he walked out. "I'm not trying to be difficult, but I *have* to see her."

"I know," he said, not looking at her. "Let me do my job first and then we'll take it from there."

"Okay," she replied unenthusiastically.

He glanced back at her. "And no more surprise visits. Understand?"

She bit her tongue. She couldn't promise that, and she was glad when he didn't seem to expect a response.

"I'll find her, Serena," he added more softly. "But don't expect too much."

"I don't," she assured him. "All I expect is the truth."

CHAPTER SIX

OUTSIDE THE ROOM Ethan paused for a moment. This situation had the potential to get out of control. He'd been around beautiful women before, but for some reason, Serena affected him more strongly than most. He could control it, though. And he would.

He drove straight to Travis's apartment. He had to talk to Molly, then he planned to visit his police friend before paying the strip club another visit. Considering her late night, he hoped Molly was up.

Ethan was taken aback for a second when Molly opened the door fully dressed and ready to go out. "I thought you might be sleeping in," he said as he stepped inside. The apartment was immaculate—very different from the last time he'd been here.

"I have a date." She smiled brightly.

Ethan was hoping she'd met someone besides Rudy Boyd, but her next words dispelled that. "Rudy's taking me to his place for lunch."

Ethan removed his hat and sat on the sofa. "What do you know about Rudy Boyd?"

Molly frowned. "Don't start, Ethan. Rudy is nice to me and he makes me feel like an attractive woman."

He nodded, gesturing at her outfit. "Is that the reason for the new look?" She wore a short white skirt and a yellow tank top with a yellow sweater tied around her neck. Her hair was in its windswept style. She looked attractive and happy, and he hated the feelings he had about Boyd.

"Yes." She twirled around and held out her arms. "What do you think?"

"You look wonderful."

"I feel wonderful." Her face dimmed a little. "So please pull in your FBI antennae and let me have some fun." She shrugged. "I mean, there's no way Rudy could be a bigger creep than Bruce."

"That's just it, sis. I don't want to see you get hurt again."

She sank down beside him. "I'm just having fun—fun that's way overdue." She paused. "Have you talked to Pop?"

"I talked to him last night. They're fine."

"I know. I talked to Cole this morning. He's so involved with his girlfriend I don't think he even misses me. I'm afraid he might do something stupid."

"Like what?"

"Like get her pregnant."

Ethan raised an eyebrow. "You think that's a possibility?"

"He's seventeen, Ethan. Of course it's a possibility. Don't you remember what it was like to be that age?"

He thought about Serena back in his motel room and all the feelings she brought to life in him. "Vaguely." He grinned.

"I don't want Cole to be caught in the trap that Bruce and I were. I want him to have a better life."

Then you need to be at home guiding him with a mother's wisdom, instead of trying to recapture your own youth.

The words hovered on his tongue, but he wouldn't say them. They'd only hurt her and he refused to do that. But he wished he had a magic formula to turn her life around—one that didn't involve Boyd.

"Cole has a good head on his shoulders," was all he said.

She stood up and retrieved her purse from a chair. "He said he's talked to Bruce a couple of times. I think he just wanted to get my reaction. You'd be very proud of me, Ethan. I told him that was great and he seemed relieved."

"I'm sure he was," Ethan commented, knowing that Cole was deeply loyal to his mother, yet loved his father, too.

Rummaging in her big bag, she pulled out a tube of lipstick and stared at Ethan. "You seem different today."

"How?"

"I don't know. You don't have that tenseness around your eyes."

It was massaged away by a beautiful redhead.

"I'm sorry if I upset you by mentioning Ryan last night, but it's okay to talk about him, Ethan. It might even be good for you."

He rubbed his hands together. "I know you believe I haven't come to terms with his death, but I have, as much as possible."

Her eyes opened wide.

"What?"

"You've never said that before."

"What?"

"That Ryan is dead."

"Yeah, I didn't want to admit it for a long time and you're right, it's okay to talk about him. But frankly, I'd rather not. It's too painful."

She leaned over and hugged him. "Oh, Ethan. I'm so sorry."

"I know."

Straightening, she said, ''No more maudlin thoughts,'' and applied lipstick to her already red lips.

''Too much makeup?'' she asked.

Yes.

''It's more than you normally wear, but if you like it...''

''I do,'' she replied pulling at the short skirt. ''Is my skirt too tight?''

Yes.

''How does it feel to you?''

''Sexy.''

Ethan swallowed. ''Then it's fine.''

She smiled. ''You don't lie very well, but I love you for trying. Now I've got to run.''

''Isn't Boyd picking you up?'' Ethan followed her to the door.

''No, I'm taking a taxi to his place, then he's bringing me home after lunch.'' She waved. ''See you later.''

Ethan drove to the police station to talk to Daniel, who he hoped might be able to give him some answers about Boyd. He wondered if Serena was headed back to Fort Worth yet. He wasn't bending his rules for her, he told himself again. Tonight if all went well, he would locate the stripper and his association with Serena Farrell would be over. He'd go back to Junction Flat and his family problems, and she'd sort through her financial difficulties. They'd probably never meet again.

He felt a certain sadness at the thought.

AT THE MOTEL Serena changed, then packed her overnight bag. Soon she was driving toward Fort Worth. She wasn't going because Ethan had told her to, but because she'd realized it was plain stupid to follow him around looking for the stripper. Besides, she had a portrait to paint and obligations at home, and Ethan didn't need her help or require her presence. That made her feel very alone, and she had to acknowledge that she was thinking too much about Ethan. She was just a client to him, and wasn't looking for any type of involvement. Neither was she.

She parked in her driveway and for a moment stared at the huge, stately house. It was redbrick with white trim and had large white columns adorning the front portico. This place was way too large for two people, she thought, and the trim would soon need painting. How could she afford that? The only solution was to move into a smaller place. But she couldn't do that, either. It would break Gran's heart. There was one thing she *could* do, though. She'd call Ethan and tell him to stop searching for the stripper, even though he'd said he'd give her a day's work free. It was pointless. If her mother was out there, she hadn't looked for Serena in all these years. Anyway, the chances were very unlikely. She'd just overreacted to the idea of someone looking like her; in reality, the resemblance probably wasn't all that remarkable. She'd just needed a moment to escape from her problems and Ethan had provided a pleasant distraction. She ran her hand over the steering wheel, remembering the feel of his body. A *most* pleasant distraction.

Serena walked into the kitchen and stopped short. Myrtle, the cleaning lady she'd let go, was polishing the silver.

"What are you doing here, Myrtle?"

"Your grandmother called me."

Serena closed her eyes in frustration. "Myrtle, we can't afford to pay you. I thought I made that very clear."

Myrtle wiped her hands nervously on her apron. "But your grandmother keeps calling me. She says you're being overcautious and that she'll pay me."

"Has Gran paid you?" Gran never carried cash, just credit cards, and Serena knew Myrtle didn't take credit.

"No, but…"

Serena opened her purse, took out some money and laid it on the counter. "Finish up for today, but if Gran calls again, please don't come back, because I can't pay you."

"I'm sorry, Serena."

"It's not your fault." She glanced around. "Where's Gran?"

"She went shopping."

"Oh, no," Serena groaned.

"Is something wrong?" Myrtle asked.

"No, Myrtle," Serena assured her. "Don't worry about it." She walked into the den and sank into a chair.

Memories from her childhood flashed through her mind. Memories she'd apparently forgotten. But suddenly she remembered arguments between her grandparents, remembered her grandfather pleading with Gran to curb her spending. Gran loved expensive clothes, jewels, cars, furnishings and parties. As much as her grandfather tried, Gran had never listened to him, just as she wasn't listening to Serena now.

Serena was ashamed to admit that a lot of money had been spent on her. Gran insisted she have the best of everything and Serena realized now that the cost was more than Grandfather could afford. Gran was willfully blind to their financial situation, and Grandfather didn't have the heart to force the issue. Now Serena would have to. Like her grandfather, she'd been putting it off, but she couldn't do that any longer.

It was useless to try to figure out why certain patterns of behavior had developed. All she could do was deal with the present. But—the spending had to stop.

She went into her study to work on the painting, but

she couldn't concentrate. The skin tone wasn't right, so she wiped it off and tried again, then just gave up. There was too much on her mind to give the portrait her best. She'd work later. As she washed her brushes, the phone rang. It was Mr. Hudson, the jeweler who'd bought her grandmother's earrings. He said he was having a problem reproducing the design, and she told him to forget it—she wouldn't need them, after all. It was time to tell Gran the truth.

Serena heard thunder and walked over to the window to stare at the June rain. Water streamed down the windowpane, and Serena watched as if enthralled. Then, just as suddenly as it had started, the rain stopped. Serena looked for a rainbow as she had so often when she was a child. She couldn't see one. *There are no rainbows, Grandfather.* Just life—real life. And she wished she was more equipped to handle it...and Gran.

As she removed her smock and laid it on the counter, she heard voices. Gran was home—without packages, she hoped.

She stared at the phone and knew what she had to do. If Gran had to stop spending, then so did she. She had to call Ethan. She'd made that decision earlier, but had done nothing about it. After all her importuning, all her talk about needing to see this woman she resembled, Ethan would be shocked at this turn of events. But she had no choice, and as it was, she owed him for two days' work. His cell-phone number was in her purse. It took her a while, but she found it.

Poking out his number, she felt a loss she couldn't describe. She liked Ethan and wanted to know him better, but now that wasn't going to happen.

The phone rang several times, then his voice mail came on. Damn. Where was he? She didn't want to leave a message, but now she had to. The beep sounded and she said, "Ethan, it's Serena. I've changed my mind. Please stop looking for the stripper. It doesn't matter anymore. Send me a bill and I'll mail you a check. I just…I just… Goodbye, Ethan."

Hanging up, she swallowed the constriction in her throat. *Goodbye, Ethan.* She stood for a moment, realizing that in the few hours she'd known Ethan, she had connected with him in a special way—in a way she'd never connected with Brad or any other man. Maybe someday the reasons for that would be clearer to her, but now too many other problems took precedence.

Serena inhaled deeply and hurried upstairs. In Gran's room, she came to an abrupt halt. The bed was covered with shopping bags. As she tried to control her temper, Aurora turned from placing her purse on the settee.

"Oh, Serena," she said nervously. "I…I didn't know you were home."

"Obviously not," Serena replied coolly, waving a hand toward the bags. "What's all this?"

"Now, darling, don't get angry, but we're having the bridge tournament next week and I needed something new to wear."

Serena stalked to the huge closet with its double doors and flung them open. The inside was crammed with clothes. "What's wrong with these?"

"Darling, the ladies have seen them all. I need something new. It's expected of me."

Serena shook her head. She hated to be hard, but she had no choice if they were going to survive. "Not this time, Gran," she said, and gathered up the bags.

"What are you doing?" Gran spoke sharply.

"Taking these things back."

"No! I absolutely forbid it."

Serena saw the fear in her eyes. It wasn't a fear of being penniless or homeless. It was a fear of not being the perfectly coiffed, well-dressed lady in front of her friends. She was beginning to think she didn't really know her grandmother. Gran couldn't be this insensitive, could she? Serena dropped the bags and crossed to the settee. Lowering herself onto it, she said, "We need to talk."

Aurora sat beside her. "Darling, you're blowing this out of proportion. It's just a few outfits. I'm sure we can afford it."

Serena stared at her. Did she not grasp their situation at all?

"No, Gran, we're broke and you can't call Myrtle anymore, either. I'll do the cleaning."

"That's nonsense. I've always had a cleaning lady. Henry saw to that."

"Gran, we're broke," she said again in a patient voice.

"You keep saying that, but Henry's family owned a big company and I'm sure there's plenty of money."

Serena took a calming breath. "Listen to me. Grandfather sold his share of the company. All he had was a job, for which he was paid a salary. When he died, that money ended. I've already explained this to you."

"I'm sure it's not true. Henry never mentioned a word." Serena was equally sure that her grandfather had, but Gran had a way of ignoring unpleasant things.

"It's true," Serena said sternly. "Grandfather even took out a second mortgage on this house. A mortgage I can't pay."

"Serena, you're making all this up," Aurora said in dismissive tones.

Serena knew of only one way to convince her. She went straight to her room to find all the letters from the bank.

She carried them back to Aurora and placed them in her lap. ‘‘Read these.’’

Aurora’s skin turned a pasty white. ‘‘They’re…going to foreclose on our home.’’

Finally Gran seemed to recognize their dire situation. Serena felt a moment of relief. Now she had to tell her grandmother what she’d done…. She sat down again. ‘‘We won’t have to worry about that for a while. I sold the diamond earrings Grandfather gave you on your wedding day.’’

‘‘What!’’

‘‘I didn’t have much of a choice.’’

‘‘Those earrings belonged to me! You had no right.’’

Serena was taken aback at the venom in her grandmother’s voice. ‘‘Would you rather be homeless?’’

Aurora straightened. ‘‘I am Henry Farrell’s widow. They wouldn’t dare do such a thing.’’

‘‘They don’t care who you are,’’ Serena told her. ‘‘The bank wants its money.’’

Aurora put a hand to her head. ‘‘I’m tired, darling. Would you get me a cup of tea, please?’’

Aurora lived in her own little world of wealth and privilege, and she intended to stay there, closing her eyes to everything around her. Serena had to resort to drastic measures. She picked up Aurora’s purse and removed the credit cards from her wallet.

‘‘What are you doing?’’ Aurora asked immediately.

‘‘Taking your credit cards.’’ She then gathered up the bags on the bed. ‘‘And I’m returning all this stuff.’’

‘‘Stop being so mean.’’

‘‘I’m not. I’m just being realistic. These are unnecessary purchases we can live without. I’m sorry if that’s hard for you to understand.’’

Aurora’s eyes narrowed. ‘‘Henry wasn’t like this.

You're just like *her*. I never thought you were, but you are."

"Like who?" Serena asked.

"Your mother, that's who," Aurora said coldly. "We gave her everything and she threw it back in our faces. Expensive clothes hung in her closet, but she wouldn't wear them. There were diamonds in her jewelry box, but she wore rhinestones. A Corvette sat in the garage, but she wouldn't drive it. It was too flashy—unnecessary, she said. Materialistic. That was her constant insult to us. I never understood Jasmine. She was my daughter, but we were so different. She said she wanted love and happiness, not material things. When she ran away, I was almost relieved. I was tired of all the arguing and fighting. Henry wanted to go after her, but I told him to let her go. She'd find out what life was really like. And she did. John Welch wasn't her dream come true."

Serena had trouble breathing. Gran's words were tearing her heart out. "You don't mean what you're saying." Serena heard her own voice and hadn't even realized she'd spoken the words aloud.

"Yes, I do," Gran told her. "Jasmine hurt me just like you're hurting me. I should have let *her* raise you."

"Her?" Serena echoed. "Who are you talking about?"

"Your father's family. They wanted you."

Serena swallowed. "They wanted me."

"Yes, but I wouldn't let them have you."

Serena swallowed again, this time more painfully. "You kept me out of spite?"

"Yes," Aurora said without even pausing.

As Serena's world caved in on her, her body trembled and her breath locked in her throat. The shopping bags fell to the floor, as did the credit cards. She looked down at the clutter at her feet and raised her eyes to her grandmother.

"Goodbye, Gran," she said, and walked out of the room.

"Come back, Serena!" Aurora called. "I didn't mean it. Oh, darling, I'm sorry."

Serena didn't hear her. Her mind had completely shut down. She grabbed her purse and the overnight bag she hadn't unpacked. Within minutes she was in her car, driving without any destination. All she knew was that she had to get away from her grandmother, as far away as possible.

ETHAN DROVE to the police station where his friend Daniel Garrett worked. The big room with its rows of desks, filing cabinets, technical equipment and the constant ringing of phones was a poignant reminder of the days he'd spent in law enforcement.

Still wearing his shoulder holster, Daniel sat at a desk cluttered with paper, his sleeves rolled up as he read a document. He glanced up and saw Ethan.

He leaped to his feet, a smile on his handsome face. Daniel was somewhere in his thirties with dark hair that tended to curl. "Well, I'll be damned. If it ain't Ethan Ramsey." They shook hands vigorously. "Haven't seen you since we worked that case together. How you doing?"

"Fine," Ethan replied.

"You look great—after taking a bullet like that." Daniel waved toward a vinyl chair. "Have a seat."

Ethan sat down, hoping Daniel didn't want to talk about the shooting. It was a subject he wasn't comfortable with.

"What brings you to my neck of the woods?"

"I need information about someone in Dallas."

"Sure." Daniel tipped back his chair. "Who is it?"

"Rudy Boyd. Ever heard of him?"

Daniel leaned forward with a scowl on his face. "Why are you looking for him?"

"I'm not looking for him. I know where he is. My brother and sister sing in one of his clubs. I just have a...feeling about him. I was hoping you could fill me in."

"He's bad news. I know he's moving drugs in and out of those clubs, but I can't prove it. We've done surprise raids on several clubs, even his home, but we always come up empty. He's slick. Knows how to cover his tracks."

Ethan was right, but he didn't take any pleasure from that. He had to know more. "He looks familiar. Has he been involved in anything else?"

"Remember Roscoe Myers?"

"Sure, we got him for selling illegal firearms."

"Boyd was also questioned at that time. The FBI thought he was involved."

"Now I remember. Johnson handled that part of the case. I knew I'd seen Boyd's face somewhere."

"He has a rap sheet as long as my arm, but he's never been convicted of anything. He was in a gang as a kid and he uses the old story of a street kid turning his life around. He talks big about giving back to the community, and claims to be deterring kids from a life of crime through sports and so forth. He's given speeches for the Chamber of Commerce, the mayor and city council. But what Boyd's putting back into the community would turn their hair gray."

"Sounds like a smooth operator."

"You bet, but I'll get him," Daniel vowed. "No matter how long it takes."

"Then you have a good lead?"

"I did," Daniel admitted. "Had a cop, Greg Larson, working undercover at one of the strip clubs we believe is owned by Boyd but fronted by someone else. My officer disappeared a month ago and we found traces of blood in his apartment."

"What did the DNA show?"

"The blood is Greg's," Daniel said. "Doesn't look good."

"No, it doesn't," Ethan agreed. "Which strip club was he at?"

"Teasers."

Ethan's expression hardened.

"Something wrong?" Daniel asked.

"I've been to Teasers a few times."

"Damn, Ethan, I didn't know you favored strip joints."

Ethan gave him a tolerant glance. "Don't be cute. I'm on a case and looking for a stripper who works there."

"Did you find her?"

"No, and whenever I ask questions, everyone gets a little nervous."

"Who's the girl?"

"I don't know her name. That's what I'm trying to find out. All I know is that she's a very attractive redhead."

Daniel's eyes narrowed. "Greg was infatuated with a redhead who worked in that club, but she was a waitress. Are you sure the girl's a stripper?"

"Most definitely. I've seen her take it all off."

Daniel shifted restlessly. "I should have a comeback for that, but right now I'm thinking this can't be a coincidence. Greg was on to something that would tie Boyd to these clubs. He said he'd call me the next day. I never heard from him again. Somehow the redhead is connected to this."

"But you said he was interested in a waitress," Ethan reminded him.

"That's the only part that doesn't make sense. Greg said she hated the job but was a waitress because she needed the tips. She was working her way through grad school."

"Did Greg give you a name?"

"He always called her Red, and I never asked anything else. I just told him he'd better keep his head on straight and stop fooling around with her. He was there to do a job, not lay some waitress."

Ethan stood. "Guess your next step is to locate the redhead."

"Yeah." Daniel also stood. "She might know something, she might not. At this point I'll take anything I can get." He quickly scribbled a number on a piece of paper and handed it to Ethan. "That's my cell phone. You can reach me anytime—day or night."

"If I find her, I'll let you know."

"And I'll use whatever means I have to track her down. I have to know what happened to Greg. He's a good cop and I hope he's still alive."

They shook hands again. "I hope so, too," Ethan replied, but they both knew there was only a slim chance. The cop bond was too strong to admit it, though.

AFTER LEAVING DANIEL, Ethan sat in his truck going over the information he'd learned about Boyd. His gut instinct had been right. But how did he tell Molly? With facts. He had to have concrete evidence to show her, but how could he manage that when the FBI and the Dallas police couldn't get anything on him? He'd better think of *something,* he thought grimly, because Molly had to end her relationship with Boyd. No question about that.

His next thought was to wonder what Boyd wanted with Molly. It was more than sex, he was sure of that much. But what?

He glanced at his cell phone and saw that he had a message. He pushed the buttons to access it, and his whole body tightened as he heard her voice. ''Ethan, it's Serena. I've changed my mind. Please stop looking for the stripper. It doesn't matter anymore. Send me a bill and I'll mail you a check. I just…I just…Goodbye, Ethan.''

He pushed the ''end'' button and stared off into space. What the hell did that mean? This morning she'd been so adamant about finding her. What had changed? He didn't know, but he sensed something was wrong.

As he started his truck, her words resounded in his head. ''Goodbye, Ethan.'' It was final. She didn't intend to see him again.

CHAPTER SEVEN

SERENA DROVE and drove. She didn't know where she was going, barely paid attention to the streets or neighborhoods. She just kept driving. Afternoon turned into evening and darkness fell. Still she kept driving. She wouldn't think. Didn't dare. It was too painful.

When she stopped, she was at the curb outside the motel where Ethan was staying. Why had she come here? She'd been driving for hours, so how had she ended up here? Had it subconsciously been her destination all along? She didn't know, didn't care. She rested her forehead on the steering wheel. Her skin felt clammy; her whole body felt as if she was suffering from a pain too deep to assuage. She raised her head. "Okay," she said. "Enough." She could deal with this. She had to pull herself together.

Her grandmother had never before spoken or acted the way she had today. Did Gran really mean all those things? Of course not; she'd even said she didn't. Gran was just upset and angry with Serena—still, she must've been harboring those feelings if they'd come out so easily. Serena knew she should've stayed and talked to her grandmother, but she was hurting too much to do that just yet.

Her father's family had wanted to raise her. She had to let herself think about that and what it meant—for her. She'd never given her father or his background much thought; asking questions about him only upset her grandparents. But now she knew she had another family out there, and apparently they'd wanted her, maybe still did. She closed her eyes, trying to sort through the rush of emotions.

When she opened her eyes, she saw Ethan walk to his door and insert his key into the lock. As she watched his strong, sure movements, she understood exactly why she was here. She needed Ethan and the strength that was such a part of him. He was almost a stranger and she'd always been strong enough to cope with anything—even losing her grandfather and facing all his financial problems. But now…

Serena grabbed her purse, climbed out of the car and hurried toward him. "Ethan," she called softly.

Her voice startled him and he turned swiftly. "Why are you always sneaking up on…" His voice trailed off when he saw her face. Her eyes were red and he could tell she'd been crying. He reached for her arm and pulled her into the room.

"What's wrong?" he asked once they were inside.

She sank onto the sofa and burst into tears, hating herself for that feminine weakness.

Ethan yanked some tissues out of a box on the nightstand and poked them into her hands. She wiped her eyes, still sobbing. He gave her a minute.

"I'm sorry," she said, hiccuping. "I'm not usually this weepy."

Ethan sat beside her. "Tell me what's wrong," he said calmly.

Unable to stop herself, she told him everything—the hurt her grandmother's words had caused her, the confusion and sense of betrayal.

"That's why you left the message about ending the search?"

"No, this happened afterward." She sniffed. "I can't be spending money on something so silly. If I expect Gran to stop spending, then I have to stop, too." She looked into his eyes. "I'm sorry I got you involved in this and wasted your time."

Any time he spent with her wasn't wasted.

Despite the self-control he was so proud of, he finally had to admit he wasn't in control around Serena.

"Don't worry about it," he said, clasping his hands together. "In my experience, men tend to use force when they get angry and women use words—and often say things they don't mean. I'm sure that's what happened with your grandmother. She was just angry at you for taking away something that's obviously important to her—shopping. She's probably sitting at home waiting for your call—to apologize for the awful things she said."

Serena shook her head. "I can't talk to her."

"Sure you can." He picked up her purse, pulled out her cell phone and placed it in her hand. "When you hear her voice, the words will come. Trust me."

Trust me.

Her mouth felt dry and she really didn't want to talk to her grandmother. But…she trusted Ethan. She punched out the number.

It rang once and Gran's voice came on. "Serena, is that you?"

She glanced at Ethan. He was right; Gran was waiting for her to call. She brought her concentration to Aurora's voice.

"Yes."

"I'm so sorry, darling. Please come home so we can talk. I didn't mean any of those things I said. I loved your mother and I love you—that's why I raised you. No other reason."

Serena swallowed. "I know, Gran, but I'm...hurting right now. I need some time."

"Oh, Serena, I'm just a spoiled, pampered old lady and I guess it took your walking out to make me come to my senses."

"What do you mean?"

"I returned the clothes and I put the credit cards in your room."

Serena sat up straight. "You did?"

"Yes, and I called Mr. Wylie at home and arranged a meeting with him. It's not fair for you to handle this financial crisis alone. Whenever your grandfather mentioned money problems, I just ignored them and he made them go away. I was doing the same thing with you, but I have to stop burying my head in the sand. I have to face this. Together we'll get through it."

Serena was dumbfounded. For weeks she'd been trying to get Gran to acknowledge their crisis, and now she had. Something good had come out of their confrontation. But...it wasn't enough. She wanted more information about her mother.

"Thanks, Gran. That makes me very happy, but..." She knew what she needed to say, but she found it difficult to actually say the words.

"But what, darling?"

"We need to talk about my mother. I want to know everything about her—the good and the bad."

A pause.

"That's not easy for me, Serena," Gran eventually said.

"I know, but I'm old enough to accept whatever happened back then."

Another long pause.

"Gran," Serena prompted.

"You may not like what you hear."

"That's okay," Serena assured her. "I want the truth. No more secrets."

"Okay, darling. Just come home."

Serena looked over at Ethan, who sat staring at his hands. "I will, Gran, but first I need some time to figure things out. Don't worry, though. I'll be back."

"I love you, Serena," Gran said.

"Love you, too," Serena replied. "I'll be home soon."

Serena hung up and gave him a wobbly grin.

"Feeling better?" Ethan asked.

Her grin broadened. "Much. Gran's sorry, just like you said she'd be, and she took all the clothes back. *And* she's agreed to tell me about my mother. I've had this feeling that she's been keeping something from me."

"Like what?"

She tucked a stray tendril behind her ear. "That my mother may still be alive."

"What makes you think that?"

"It seems my mother and grandmother were always arguing, until my mother finally ran away. Maybe my grandparents pretended she was dead so they wouldn't have to face what they'd done. My grandmother's good at not facing reality. But that doesn't explain how they ended up with me—unless my mother got pregnant and didn't want a baby, so my grandparents took me. Gran said I wouldn't like what I heard. That could be it."

"There's an easy way to find out."

"How?"

"Courthouse records. Your mother's death would be recorded."

"Oh, Ethan, I never thought of that! Is it hard to do?"

"No," he answered. "A close relative can get the information or—" he smiled slightly "—a very good P.I."

She lifted an eyebrow. "I know one of those."

"Do you?"

The heat between them was building and Serena could feel its warmth. "But I can't ask anything else of you," she said quickly. "I've taken up enough of your time."

Ethan ignored her words. "You think the redhead at the strip club is connected to your mother?"

"Yes." She bit her lip. "Do you think that's crazy?"

"No, it could be the reason you resemble each other so much."

She linked her fingers together. "I'll have to wait and talk to Gran, then I'll know how likely that is."

Ethan frowned at his watch. "Damn, I've got to get moving." He stood up as he spoke.

"Where are you going?"

"To the strip club."

"But, Ethan, I can't afford to pay you."

"Forget the money, Serena," he said. "I told you I wouldn't charge for this. Besides, I have my own reasons for doing it." He described his visit with Daniel Garrett.

"Then the redhead could be involved in the cop's disappearance?"

"Yes, or at least know something about it."

"Let me go with you."

"Serena..." He sighed, not hiding his frustration.

"Ethan—"

"No, Serena." He walked to his carryall and removed a T-shirt. "You can stay here for a while, but it would be best for you to go home to your grandmother tonight and talk things out." Saying that, he went into the bathroom.

No, she wasn't going home. Not yet. She and Gran both needed time before dredging up the past. The stripper was here in Dallas, and the possibility that she might have a chance to see her was just too tempting. But how did she convince Ethan?

Ethan came out wearing sneakers, a baseball cap and a T-shirt that said Dallas Cowboys.

She studied him curiously. "Why are you dressed like that?"

"Disguise. I don't want the bouncer to recognize me."

"Oh." Then it occurred to her. "A woman draped all over you would be a better disguise."

He shook his head. "That's not gonna work. You look so much like the redhead everyone will think you're her."

"Okay." She took a stabilizing breath as her mind tripped over itself thinking of solutions. Her eyes grew bright. "I've got it! I'll wear a wig—a black one."

He waved a hand at her black slacks and white linen top.

She glanced down at herself. "What's wrong with my clothes?"

"You're dressed like a lady, and ladies don't go to strip clubs."

"For heaven's sake, I can change that in a heartbeat. Some tight clothes and flashy jewelry will do the trick."

"Do you have those kinds of things with you?"

"Of course not, but I can easily buy them."

His eyes narrowed. "Isn't that what you and your grandmother argued about—spending money frivolously?"

She felt deflated by the question, but he was right. Still, there had to be some way… Since Ethan was discussing it, that must mean he was at least considering her plan. She had to persist.

"I could get stuff at a thrift shop. It wouldn't cost much at all."

"You'd wear clothes someone else has worn?" His voice was filled with skepticism.

She wrinkled her nose. "They do wash them, don't they?"

His mouth twitched. "I certainly hope so."

"Okay, let's do it."

"You assume I'm going along with this."

"I'm just hoping you might like my company."

They stared at each other. *The club is dangerous. No place for a lady. She doesn't need to get involved.* Ethan said all these things to himself, but they didn't seem to matter. Maybe it was the glow on her face or the hope in her eyes that was making him take her suggestion seriously.

"Ethan, please?"

Two softly spoken words, and any doubts he had vanished. They could get into the club undetected, see the redhead, find out who she was and end all this tonight.

He pointed a finger at her. "You must do exactly as I tell you."

She tried to curb the excitement rising in her and failed. "Yes," she answered earnestly. "Without question."

"I think I want that in writing."

"I promise, Ethan," she said solemnly.

He stared into the blue of her eyes and felt weak from the contact. "Let's go," he said.

"Thank you, Ethan." Without deliberation, she threw her arms around him and hugged him tightly. His body stiffened and she backed away with a knowing look on her face. "I guess that's a no-no."

"Yes," he said. "Let's keep this on a business level."

She started to remind him of last night and how they'd gone way beyond business, but she'd just promised to do what he told her, so she gave in without a whimper.

"Okay," she answered. "I just got a little carried away. Sorry."

Before he could respond, she grabbed the phone book off the nightstand. "What are you doing?"

She flipped through the Yellow Pages. "Looking for a thrift shop that's close to the motel."

Ethan heaved a sigh, glad of a moment's reprieve. Resisting her was going to be one of the hardest things he'd ever had to do. But despite any feelings he might have for Serena, he had nothing to offer a woman like her. His fate had been sealed a long time ago.

"There's one about three blocks from here and it closes at ten, so we'd better hurry."

Ethan opened the motel-room door and she slung her purse over her shoulder. He led the way to his truck, unlocked it and they both climbed in. It was a white four-door Chevy cab with a tan leather interior. He started the engine and the radio came on. A country-music station.

"Very nice," she said as she buckled her seat belt. "I like trucks. I used to date a guy who drove one."

He backed out of the parking lot. "You seemed to have dated a lot of guys."

"Not as many as you might think."

But more than he wanted to.

Out of the corner of his eye, he saw her reach for the knob on the radio. "What are you doing?"

"Changing to a rock station."

"It stays on country."

"It's not hard rock. They play Sheryl Crow, Rod Stewart, Celine Dion— people like that."

"It stays on country."

"Why do men have to be so stubborn?"

"Let's not get into that."

"You should learn to share, Ethan."

He glanced at her. ''Against my better judgment, I'm letting you come with me tonight. That's all the sharing I'm willing to do.''

''Fine,'' she snapped, yet she couldn't help smiling. They were arguing over a radio station like two teenagers. This felt good after the day she'd had. Being with Ethan felt good, even if he was the stubbornest man she'd ever met.

Since it was late, Ethan found a parking spot close to the thrift shop. Serena unbuckled her seat belt and noticed that he didn't. ''Aren't you coming with me?''

''No.''

''Why not?''

''Because you'll ask my opinion, and I don't give opinions on women's clothes. I hate shopping.''

She shook her head. ''Ethan Ramsey, you're a typical male. Didn't you ever go shopping with your wife?''

''No, she knew how to shop all by herself.''

Serena bit her tongue, then said, ''Fine, but don't say one word about what I buy.''

''I won't,'' he assured her.

She got out and slammed the door harder than necessary.

He watched her walk into the shop, feeling a tightness in his gut. He was being testy for no reason. Well, he did have a reason. To resist Serena, he had to erect a barrier between them, and if she thought he was an insensitive jerk, then that could only help. As long as he maintained some distance between them, he would manage.

Ten minutes later, Serena was back with a bag. ''Did you get what you wanted?'' he asked.

She had the urge not to answer him, but that would be petty. ''Everything except a wig, and at this hour all the shops are going to be closed. I'll have to put some sort of color on my hair."

"We don't have time for you to color your hair."

"Pull into that Wal-Mart." She pointed. "I know what I'm doing."

Without another word Ethan did as she said. Serena collected the bag and her purse and ran into the store.

Ethan waited and waited. Fifteen minutes, twenty, twenty-five... He kept glancing at his watch. What was taking her so long? He was about to go look for her when he saw a black-haired woman leave the store. She wore a black miniskirt and a red tank top, both very tight and revealing. Long silver earrings dangled from her ears and her dark hair was in disarray around her face. She tottered on red high heels.

She walked to his truck and opened the passenger door. "Can I get a lift, mister?"

Ethan smiled. "Anytime, ma'am."

Serena slid into the truck. "What do you think?"

"I think you make a damn good hooker."

"Ooh, is that good or bad?"

"For tonight it's good," he said, starting the engine. "I wondered why you were in there so long."

"I knew they have rest rooms, so that made it easy."

"How did you do the hair?"

"With a spray, and I'll probably have a hell of a time getting it out."

"I hope this is all worth it."

"Me, too."

They drove to an area of Dallas Serena had never visited before. At an intersection she saw a sign that read Harry Hines Boulevard and Northwest Highway. Flashing neon signs of naked women seemed to be everywhere, as were strip joints, bars and adult-video stores. Unsavory-looking characters walked the streets and women who were dressed much like her strolled along, waiting for customers. She remembered Ethan saying this wasn't a day at Sunday school and it certainly wasn't. Suddenly she questioned her judgment in coming here, but she had to see the other woman. She had to get this settled, this doubt and confusion about her family.

Ethan parked the truck and turned to look at her. "Ready?" Serena with her red hair and blue eyes was stunning, but this black-haired Serena was just as stunning, too, in a different way. This one was bolder, more overtly sensual, daring.

"Yes," she replied, pushing her aversion to the area aside.

Ethan hesitated. "For tonight," he said slowly, "we have to act like lovers."

She shrugged nonchalantly. "I don't have a problem with that. Do you?"

"Just trying to keep things on—"

"A business level," she finished for him. "You've already said that."

"I don't want you to feel—"

"I won't," she replied. "You have an honorable streak a mile wide."

"One of my faults."

"Yeah, I'm beginning to see it that way, too."

They stared at each other, and for a brief moment Serena could see a rainbow in the warmth of his brown eyes. But it was pure fantasy, and so was this entire night. She'd been in the drama club in high school, and they'd put on plays in which she had to act, become another person. That was what she'd do tonight. As she felt the adrenaline pump through her veins, she knew that with Ethan beside her, she'd give the performance of her life.

Ethan lowered his eyes. "Let's go," he said.

Serena clambered out and walked to his side of the truck. Her role started now. She slid an arm around his waist, pressing her body into his.

Ethan didn't stiffen or move away. Instead, he reciprocated. Her softness rekindled a familiar, almost forgotten, ache in his limbs, but he ignored the feeling as they walked into the club.

The place was packed. Ethan noticed one empty table and he forced his way through the crowd toward it, towing Serena behind him. The bouncer was nearby, but he didn't spare them a second look. The disguise was working. They sat at the table close together, his arm draped loosely around her shoulders. Serena hadn't said a word and he stole a glance at her face. It was white as a sheet.

Serena had trouble believing her eyes. She was trying very hard to be blasé and pretend this was all normal to her, but she suspected she wasn't pulling it off. Her acting skills didn't extend this far. Loud rock music played as women wearing nothing but G-strings danced in cages. Half-naked women waited on tables and the leers on the men's faces turned her stomach. The place smelled like stale tobacco, whiskey and disgust. Not only did *she* feel disgusted with what she saw, she couldn't help thinking that while these men might desire the women displayed before them, they had contempt for them, too. And the women themselves seemed numb, empty…and scornful of their audience. She knew disgust didn't have a smell, but for her it did now. From now on, she would always associate the word *disgust* with this place.

Ethan's arm tightened around her. "Want to leave?"

She shook her head. "No, I'm fine. It's just so…"

A waitress came over to take their order. "Draft beer, light," Ethan said, and looked at Serena.

"Ah...the same."

The waitress eyed her. "You're new. I haven't seen you in here before, but you look kind of familiar."

Serena swallowed. "Yeah, I'm new." Whatever that meant.

"Keep bringin' your johns in here, honey. We'll treat you good," the waitress said as she walked away.

"Oh, my God," Serena breathed painfully. "She thinks I'm a hooker." Maybe her acting was better than she'd thought.

"And she thinks I'm a john, so which is worse?"

She smiled—and as long as Ethan could make her smile, she'd get through this. But she was worried about something.

"Ethan, do you still drink?"

"No, I just order it as a reminder that I don't need it. Anyway, it's expected in places like this, so don't worry," he told her as the waitress set two foaming beers in front of them.

She did worry, though. She didn't want to cause Ethan any difficulty or unpleasantness, but she'd already done that by asking questions about his personal life. Still, he'd seemed fine with that. She knew instinctively that Ethan could handle just about anything.

Suddenly he pulled her closer. "Talk into my ear," he said urgently.

"Why?" she asked against his face.

"Because the bouncer's coming this way and I don't want him to get suspicious."

"Oh, I'm supposed to act like a hooker."

"Yes."

Instead of talking, Serena stroked his ear with her tongue and rained tantalizing kisses along his jaw. Her hand played with the hair at his nape. "How's that?" she whispered, realizing the acting part had gone right out of her head. Her actions felt natural—and very exciting.

Ethan's breath was locked in his chest in exquisite torture. Her touch was driving him crazy, and he wasn't even aware when the bouncer walked by them. He was too wrapped up in Serena.

"Ethan?"

"Hmm?"

"You didn't answer."

He let out a breath, trying to remember what she'd asked. "Yes, yes, it worked. He's gone."

Before he could say anything else, the music stopped and a man strode onto the stage with a microphone. A spotlight was centered on him.

"All right, guys. It's time for the main attraction, so sit back, relax and enjoy the ladies. And please be generous. The ladies deserve it."

The music started with an upbeat dance tempo, and the first woman came out dressed as a secretary, carrying a pad and pen. Seductively she began to take off her clothes, and the men went wild with whistles and catcalls. They threw money onto the stage and the stripper leaned over repeatedly to let men tuck money into her G-string. Each woman who came out was dressed as a different profession—nurse, teacher, cocktail waitress.

Serena stared with her mouth open; she couldn't seem to close it. She couldn't imagine why a woman would degrade herself like this. But she had to put that out of her mind. She was here for a reason. *Where was the redhead?*

"Do you think she'll show?" she whispered to Ethan

"We'll just have to wait."

The next woman came out, swathed from head to toe

in flowing purple robes. ''The mother of all professions—the madam,'' the MC announced.

Ethan recognized her from the way she moved. ''Watch closely,'' he said. ''This is her.''

''Are you sure?''

''Just watch.''

The woman slowly removed the cloth from around her head, and her red hair fell sensuously around her. Serena gasped and Ethan reached for her hand. She gripped it tightly.

The woman tossed her hair and with the same slowness she began to remove the cloth. Whistles and yells filled the room as with each movement the men grew more frantic, more excited.

It was like looking in a mirror. Ethan wasn't lying or exaggerating when he'd said the woman was her double. She was.

The last piece of cloth gone, she swung her hair and rotated her hips boldly one way, then the other. Serena closed her eyes. She couldn't watch anymore. It was too painful, too humiliating. Like those dreams she'd had. She didn't even know the woman, but Serena felt as if she was on that stage—naked—in front of these men. Her skin crawled with revulsion.

Her body grew hot and she thought she might throw up.

Finally the woman ran off the stage. Without even knowing what she was doing, Serena pushed back her chair and went after her.

CHAPTER EIGHT

SERENA MOVED so fast she caught Ethan off guard. He made a grab for her, but she was headed for the stripper, shoving her way through the crowd. He immediately followed. She went through the double doors that led to the back of the club. A big man stepped in front of her.

"Backstage is off-limits," he said in a gruff voice.

"Please, I have to talk to her."

The man laughed. "We've had lots of men trying to get to that stripper, but you're the first woman."

"Please, I..." She stopped as she saw the redhead standing some distance away, tying the belt on a black robe. Two men stood beside her. The stripper raised her head and their eyes met. Serena saw the fear Ethan was talking about and felt it echo through her own body. The woman was frightened of something—or someone. Suddenly the men whisked her away.

Serena tried to follow, but the man blocked her path again. "I don't want to have to tell you twice. Get out of here."

An arm slipped around her waist. "C'mon, honey." It was Ethan.

The man gave him a sly smirk. "If I were you, I'd get her head checked. She was chasing the stripper."

"Sorry about that," Ethan said. "She's very friendly."

"Sure, if that's what you wanna call it."

Ethan led Serena away, resisting the urge to punch the guy in the mouth. He knew when he was outnumbered.

''Ethan, we can't go,'' Serena protested. ''She's back there! I have to talk to her.''

''Didn't you see all the guards? We won't get anywhere near her tonight, but at least we know she's still here.'' All the while he was leading her toward the front door.

Outside Serena pulled free of him and sucked air into her lungs. Nausea churned in her stomach and she fought the weak feeling inside her.

Ethan walked her to his truck and helped her in. ''You okay?'' he asked quietly as he settled into his own seat.

She didn't answer. Instead, she said, ''She looks just like me. She really is my double. She even has a sprinkling of freckles across her breasts like I do. Who is she?''

''I don't know, but I'll find out.'' He reached for his cell phone and punched out a number.

''Daniel, it's Ethan. I'm at Teasers and I just saw the stripper. She's here, but she's being guarded by several big burly guys.'' Pause. ''Okay, I'll be at my motel.''

When he hung up, Serena asked, ''Will the cops come here?''

''Yeah, Daniel's gonna pay the club a surprise visit.''

''So that means he'll get to talk to her?''

''Yep. Now we just have to wait.'' He started the truck and drove toward the motel.

''I don't understand why they're guarding her so heavily.''

''We'll find that out, too,'' Ethan replied.

The rest of the drive took place in silence. There seemed nothing more to say.

As soon as they reached the motel, Serena jumped out and ran to her car for her overnight bag. She met Ethan at the door. ''Hurry! I have to get out of these clothes. I feel so dirty.''

He opened the door and Serena sprinted for the bathroom. *Well,* Ethan thought, *that must mean she's staying the night. Now what?* Should he ask her to leave? He removed his baseball cap and threw it on the bed, then sat in a nearby chair. He had a few minutes to decide what to do. She'd probably be in there a while. He listened to the sound of running water and didn't understand why this was so difficult for him. She didn't seem to mind his crippled hip, and she had a softness that complemented the hardness in him. So what was the problem? Oh, he knew what it was, all right. He just didn't want to think about it.

''Ethan?'' he heard her call.

He walked to the bathroom door. ''Yes?''

''I need more shampoo. I can't get this crap out of my hair.''

''I'll see if they have any at the front desk.''

''Thanks.''

The motel office was around the corner and empty at this time of night except for a woman in her sixties reading a mystery novel.

''Can I help you?'' she asked as she pushed her glasses up on her nose.

''Do you have any shampoo?''

''Isn't there some in your room?''

''Yes, but my…girlfriend needs more.''

''I see,'' she said in an impatient tone. She got up, heaving a loud sigh, and went into the back room. She returned minutes later with a small plastic bottle.

Ethan stared at it. ''I don't think that's gonna be enough. You see, she has long thick hair.''

Without a word, the woman stomped into the room

again and this time came out with a handful. "Will *this* be enough?" He didn't miss the irritation in her voice.

"Yes, thanks," he said as he took them from her. He turned to leave, then stopped. "Do you have any vacancies?"

She tapped the sign in front of her with one long fingernail. It said, No Vacancy.

"Sorry, didn't see that." He hadn't seen it because his mind was preoccupied with thoughts of Serena and the night ahead. He quickly made his exit. Outside he had the urge to laugh, but didn't. He felt ridiculous, as though he'd been trying to wrestle condoms, not shampoo, from the desk clerk.

Back in the room, he tapped on the bathroom door. Serena, a towel wrapped around her head and one around her body, opened it a crack. He handed her the shampoo. "This had better be enough because I'm not asking for more," he told her. "The woman thinks we're clean freaks or worse."

"Poor Ethan," she cooed as she closed the door.

He kicked off his shoes and sank into the chair again. His hip throbbed a little, so he propped his feet on the bed. He glanced at the phone and wondered if Daniel had his search warrant yet. Since a missing cop was involved, Daniel shouldn't have a problem getting the warrant. Were they at the club?

He'd been involved in a lot of unusual situations in his career, but tonight had been…surreal. He'd seen Serena sitting beside him, yet he could look at the stage and see her there—totally nude. His hand went to his left ear. Serena's touch was more tantalizing, more memorable, than anything the stripper had done. And he knew Serena was awakening parts of him that had been dormant—

needed to be dormant because that was how he'd been able to endure, to survive. But now…

Serena came out of the bathroom in the blue silk nightshirt. She was rubbing her hair vigorously.

"Did you get it out?" he asked.

"Yes, finally." She crawled onto the bed and sat cross-legged as she continued to rub her hair.

Her hands suddenly stilled. "I can't get over how much she looks like me. You said she was a dead ringer, but I didn't expect her to be my exact double. We *have* to be related."

"Through your mother?"

"Yes."

"What was your mother's name?"

"Jasmine Aurora Farrell."

"Where was she born and where did she die?"

"In Fort Worth."

"What's her married name?"

"Welch."

"First thing in the morning I'll check it out at the Tarrant County clerk's office. Then we'll know for sure if she's dead or alive."

Serena smoothed the towel across her thigh. "I won't talk to my grandmother until afterward." She stared down at the coarse white towel. "This sounds terrible, but I'd like to have proof if she lies to me."

"Yeah. It might also be a way to get a lead on the stripper."

She raised her head, the damp strands framing her face. "Do you go to strip clubs often?"

He was taken aback for a second, but answered readily. "No."

"You went a couple of weeks ago with your brother." She shouldn't be prying into his private life, but she didn't

HARLEQUIN®
Live the emotion™
Visit us online at
www.eHarlequin.com

want Ethan to be one of those guys she'd seen in the club. Her heart had already told her he wasn't, and yet...she had to hear him say it.

"That was a forced situation. I was trying to get Travis home for a visit. He's a musician and he's into the nightlife. I'm not."

"Then you don't get turned on by naked women prancing around in front of you?"

He watched her serious expression. "What are you getting at, Serena?"

Her eyes met his. "When you saw *her* nude body, did you think about her or me?"

"What?"

"Since we look so much alike, did you wonder if I was the same underneath my clothes?" She couldn't believe she'd asked that question. It wasn't like her to be so personal, but she had to admit she wasn't herself tonight.

Ethan removed his feet from the bed. "I think it's time for me to take a shower." Come hell or high water, he wasn't answering *that* question. He realized it was constantly on his mind—and it shouldn't be. "While I was in the office, I checked into vacancies," he added.

"Ethan, please, I don't want to spend tonight alone." There was a wealth of meaning in her words, and her voice was low with an appeal that sent a warmth pulsing through Ethan's stomach. As he tried to gather his wits, she spoke again. "Tonight when we were at the club and I was nuzzling your ear, I felt something happening between us. Was I wrong?"

God, no, you're not wrong.

"Serena." He thrust a hand through his hair. "We've known each other a very short time. You're fresh out of a broken engagement and dealing with a lot of complicated emotions. You're very vulnerable. I won't take advantage of that."

"My life may be a little crazy right now and I may not have known you long, but I'm very certain that you'd never intentionally hurt me. We're two consenting adults and I like you. I like you a lot." She paused. "Please let me stay here."

"There aren't any vacancies," he murmured and watched her eyes light up. In that instant he accepted the fact that he was fighting a losing battle. He hadn't even kissed her, but he wanted her in a way he hadn't wanted anyone in so many years that he'd almost forgotten the feeling.

"I'd rather not sleep on the sofa," she informed him with the same honesty. He recognized the risk she'd taken in revealing her attraction, knew that being truthful in these situations was always a risk. She was willing to admit that she was on emotional overload, but it didn't deter her. It only made her feelings that much stronger.

"Last night I was in pain and things were different. Tonight..." His voice drifted off as he stared into her eyes.

"Tonight will be different, too."

"Time for my shower," he said, and got to his feet, not quite able to accept what he was seeing in her eyes.

"Wait!" she called, and scrambled off the bed. "There's a hair dryer in the bathroom. I need it." She retrieved the dryer and then Ethan disappeared into the bathroom.

Serena quickly removed the bedspread, folded it and laid it on the sofa, smiling all the while. She plugged in the dryer and began to dry her hair. Was she crazy? If so, it was the best craziness she'd ever felt. She'd never been this honest before, this...brazen. She was the one always saying no, claiming she needed more time, but with Ethan it was easy. No indecision. No doubting thoughts. She knew what she wanted—Ethan. That shocked her a bit, but it didn't change her mind. She'd known girls who'd slept with guys after one date. She'd never understood that, but now she was seeing things quite differently. She had no idea what tomorrow would bring—a mother? A sister? Heartache? Pain? But tonight would be hers and Ethan's, and she'd be refreshed to cope with the unknown.

Ethan showered and tried to keep his mind a blank, but he couldn't. The situation was emotionally volatile and he'd been in volatile situations before, but not like this, not where his pride was involved. He had to allow himself to admit what was really bothering him, what he'd pushed to the farthest corner of his mind. He thrust his face under the cold water and let it spray down his body, cooling the turmoil inside him. *He hadn't had sex since he was shot five years ago.* It wasn't a conscious decision; it had just turned out that way. He didn't know if his pride could take it if a woman was turned off by his hip injury. And he didn't even know if he could perform.... He was suddenly overcome by doubt.

Maybe he was blowing this out of proportion, he told himself. Maybe he was seeing things in Serena's eyes that weren't really there. But he knew he wasn't. He felt a surge of confidence—and hope. Here he was in a motel room with the sexiest redhead he'd ever seen in his life, and his body was telling him he was ready to experience the part of his nature he'd been denying—his passionate side.

He quickly dried and slipped into clean underwear. He didn't have a robe or pajamas, so this was it. The sound of a hair dryer filled his ears as he opened the door, and he saw Serena bent over, her hair falling over her face to the floor as she dried it. He stared at her a moment before he slipped between the sheets. Leaning against the headboard, he watched her.

She straightened and slung her hair back. Her movements were more sensual, more real and much more arousing to him than the stripper's. Watching the other woman, he'd felt pity because he sensed she was stripping against her will. But with Serena he felt all male, with a male's needs, and he—

"Oh, you're out of the bathroom," she said when she noticed him. She flipped off the dryer. "That's as dry as it's gonna get. Want me to turn off the light?"

"Sure," he replied.

The room was plunged into darkness and he felt the bed move as she crept in.

He turned away from her, his confidence fading. "Good night." As much as he wanted her, he couldn't do it. He remembered last night and how her fingers had paused over the scar that ran along his hip. He'd been half-drugged, but he knew she was shocked and he didn't want to know any more than that. It was better to leave things the way they were.

"Ethan."

"Go to sleep, Serena."

He had his back to her and it felt as though he'd erected a wall to shut her out. Why? Because he was an honorable man. She already knew that. It was one of the things she loved about— Wait! She couldn't fall in love that quickly. Her emotions were just bruised and sensitive and she needed someone—and Ethan was here with his great big heart and… All of Ethan's good qualities ran through her mind and she realized that in a short amount of time he'd come to mean a lot to her. That was why she found it was so easy to be herself with him.

Damn, Ethan cursed as he turned onto his back. His hip was throbbing from lying on his right side. He moved his legs to get more comfortable.

Serena sat up. "Does your hip hurt?"

"No," he lied.

"You're lying," she said.

"Go to sleep, Serena," he muttered again.

"No. If you're hurting, I can help." She knelt beside him, prepared to begin massaging his injured hip.

"Don't touch me." The words were fierce.

She sat back on her heels. What was wrong with him? Was he just in pain? No, it was more than that—he really didn't want her to touch him. Why? He sounded almost afraid, but what could he possibly be afraid of? There was only one way to find out.

"Why are you afraid to let me touch you?" she asked point-blank.

Ethan tensed. "Go to sleep," was all he said.

"No," she replied. "Stop saying that."

"Earlier you said you'd do as I asked. I'm asking you to go to sleep."

"That was while we were in the club, not here in this room, alone."

He didn't say anything. He couldn't.

"You've been keeping a barrier between us since we met. At first I thought you weren't attracted to me, but I know that's not true. So what is it?"

"Why do you have to keep pushing?" His voice was low and rough.

"Because something besides your hip is hurting you." She couldn't have said how she knew that, but she did. "And I want to help," she added quietly.

Ethan swallowed the lump in his throat, and his pride wavered on a line that didn't make a lot of sense. It had before, but not now—not with Serena and her softness all around him.

"Ethan..."

"You can help me by going to sleep."

"Ethan..."

"If you touch me tonight, we'll..."

"Make love," she finished for him. She already knew that and accepted it with an excitement that astonished her. When he didn't say anything, she murmured, "I'm well aware of that, so you're not taking advantage of me."

"Serena, you don't understand."

"No, I don't, but—"

"I haven't had sex since I was shot in the hip." The words tumbled out and mingled with the darkness. The silence stretched as taut as his nerves, but at least now maybe she'd stop torturing him.

Serena was shocked, not by what he'd said but by the agony in his voice. Oh, God, she'd never dreamed of anything like this. He was so virile, so strong. Now it was clear why he'd placed a barrier between them. Probably between himself and all women. *Oh, Ethan.* All she wanted was to help him, and to do that she needed more information.

She licked her dry lips. "Is it that you physically can't or is it something else?"

She felt the answering silence all the way to her heart, and she didn't know where she got the courage to ask such a question. Maybe it was these newly discovered feelings she had for him. It didn't matter, though, because she wasn't giving up.

"I can," he said at last, "but I just haven't."

Relief tiptoed through her. "Why?"

"I don't want to talk about this."

But *she* did...very much. She ran both hands through

her hair and tried to figure out the situation. Why hadn't he had sex? she asked herself. It had to be his pride. She was becoming well acquainted with that pride of his. He didn't feel like the man he once was and he didn't want to be reminded of that in the bedroom. She remembered the jagged feel of the scar and the indentation in his flesh where the bullet must have entered. He didn't want a woman to see that because he didn't know how she'd react.

"Men can be stupid sometimes," she said.

"Excuse me?"

"You haven't had sex because you're scared a woman might be repulsed by your injury. Give women some credit! Most of us aren't heartless."

"When you touched my scar last night, you went still, as if it took you a moment to get used to what you were feeling. I was half out of it, but I remember that."

She took a breath. "When I touched your scar, all I could think about was the pain and suffering you must have endured. You have such an aura of strength I never realized you were injured that badly."

Her words were soothing, comforting—but what had he expected her to say? He shook his head. He had to stop being negative; he had to trust what he was feeling inside. He had to trust Serena. He'd trusted her when it had seemed she might be lying to him, and his instincts had been confirmed. Now could he—

"I'm not repulsed by your injury."

Silence. Stubborn male silence.

"Okay, I'll prove it," she said. "Turn over and take off your underwear." As she spoke, she left the bed.

"Where are you going?"

"To get lotion," she answered. "I'm going to give you the massage of your life—and you're *not* falling asleep."

"Serena."

"Do it, Ethan."

Without a second thought, he pulled off his underwear and rolled onto his stomach. He was tired of resisting, tired of fighting something he wanted with all his heart—and body. He didn't know where this would end, but he was ready to experience it...with Serena.

The bed dipped as she climbed back on. "This lotion will be cold, so I'll warm it up in my hands," she said as she squeezed some into her palm.

"What's that smell?" he asked.

"It's the lotion—lavender-scented."

"Ah, Serena, I don't want to smell like that."

"What *do* you want to smell like? Wood? Leather? Spice?"

"I'd rather not smell at all."

"Well, tonight it's lavender and rosemary," she said, resisting the urge to laugh. The humor had relieved some of the tension—but not all of it.

She rubbed the lotion in her hands, trying to think of a way to make him relax, to make him understand that she wasn't doing this out of pity or anything but the way she felt about him.

"Isn't there a country song about needing help to make it through the night?"

"Yes."

"That's the way I'm looking at tonight. I'm not certain what tomorrow will bring, but I want this night for you...and me."

God, he did, too. Even he had to smell like lavender.

She pulled the sheet away and touched his back with her warm hands. He didn't tense and she began to stroke his firm flesh. Her hands, silky smooth from the lotion, slid over his back, buttocks and to his scar. She'd never seduced a man before, but tonight she was giving it all she had. Her senses were supercharged from touching him, and she knew she had to do more.

She turned on the lamp.

He raised his head slightly. ''Why'd you do that?'' His eyes were glazed with passion.

''Because I want to see you and I want you to see me.'' She bent her head and rained kisses down his back to his hipbone, to his scar.

Her hair brushed erotically against his skin. Ethan thought he'd died and gone to heaven, and Serena was surely the paradise he'd always heard about. His body was hard and ready, and he didn't know how much longer he could wait to experience her. Her lips trailed to his waist and he reached out his arm and pulled her up to him.

''Serena,'' he murmured hoarsely, their breaths mingling. His tongue stroked her lower lip and he groaned as he took her lips in gentle, aching need.

Serena moaned and opened her mouth, giving herself up to Ethan. Her arms locked around his neck and he gathered her close, so close she felt every throbbing muscle. He definitely didn't have a physical problem.

Their tongues played, tasted, explored with excited haste until they were both trembling from the explosion of their senses.

Finally he rested his face against hers. ''Ah, Serena,'' he muttered. ''I've wanted to do that for so long.''

''Me, too,'' she whispered, and caught her breath as his hand slid from her throat to her breast.

''One of us has too many clothes on,'' he said as he unfastened the buttons on her shirt one by one. Slowly he eased the shirt from her shoulders, then cupped her breasts and stroked until a purring sound left her throat. She'd never felt like this before, wanting only to please and be pleased. All that mattered now were these emotions, these unequaled sensations....

His tongue and mouth toyed with each nipple, then moved to her navel and below. Her panties were gone with one easy movement, and his lips and fingers tantalized until her body quivered with a need that had her reaching for him.

She caressed his chest—and lower—with eager movements, wanting to feel every part of him. When her hand touched him, he caught it and held it tightly, gazing into her desire-filled eyes. She understood that look. He wanted to take it slow. His lips were on hers again, and for a moment they enjoyed the feel of skin against skin, their hearts beating in unison to a tempo they both recognized.

Serena knew they were close to an ultimate conclusion, and she had to ask something before all conscious thought left her. "Ethan, this won't hurt your hip, will it?"

"Let's find out," he whispered.

CHAPTER NINE

A LONG TIME LATER, their sweat-bathed bodies lay entwined. Serena's leg rested between his, and her body was half on him and half off. He cradled her head on his chest, one hand beneath her hair, his other resting lightly against her arm.

Serena felt as if she'd been to the moon on a rocketship and it was the best experience of her life—everything she'd wanted it to be and more. Maybe it was because Ethan was so gentle, so caring that her body responded with such intensity. Whatever it was, she wanted to hang on to it as long as she could. A lifetime sounded about right. In a matter of two days, she had fallen madly in love, to the point that it was difficult to even think about her problems.

With Brad it had been different. They'd met at school and she hadn't particularly liked him at first. She'd thought he was too self-absorbed, but she'd grown to like him, then love him. It was months, though, before she'd slept with him—as if she'd had to work herself up to it. With Ethan, she didn't have to *think* about anything. It was all emotion and it came from her heart.

She had wanted to make this night special for him, but she was ashamed to admit that she'd totally forgotten about his hip as his hands and lips touched her in places that were meant just for him. All reason had abandoned her and she simply acted on her feelings. She knew it was the same for Ethan. If he had a problem with his hip, he'd forgotten about it, too, as stronger, more powerful dictates took over.

"Ethan..." she said as she lazily drew circles on his chest with one finger.

"Mmm?" Ethan was floating among the clouds without a parachute, without a thing except the feelings Serena brought to life in him. And he didn't want to come down. It was a wild, dizzying sensation and he'd missed it. He hadn't realized that until now—until Serena touched him. He'd forgotten about his hip, forgotten both his pain and his self-consciousness. He couldn't believe that. It was so constantly on his mind, but his scars didn't matter to her and suddenly they didn't matter to him. Everything else came naturally and he felt as if this was the first time for him, felt as if his body had experienced something he wanted to do over and over again—but only with Serena. *Now she had to make love to him for the rest of his life.* Damn! Where did that come from? He hadn't thought beyond tonight, but now... His feelings for her were deeper than anything he'd ever imagined, and not merely sexual. How that had happened he wasn't sure—and he wasn't sure where they went from here.

"Was it...okay?" she finally asked.

He smiled and rubbed her arm. "Better than okay. Better than anything I ever remember."

"Really? Then your hip wasn't a problem. It was all in your mind."

"Yeah." He nodded. "Thank you."

"For what?"

"For understanding and for breaking through my defenses until you gave me no choice."

She raised her head and grinned sleepily. "Are you saying I seduced you?"

"Very nicely, too." He kissed her softly.

She snuggled against him. "I can't believe you waited this long."

"I never found anyone I cared enough about."

She raised her head again. "Until now?"

"Until now." His eyes were dark with passion and something else she longed to name. Was it love or was she simply seeing what she wanted to?

The ringing of the phone broke the moment. Ethan reached for it. "Hello," he mumbled. "Damn." Then, "Okay, I'll be in touch tomorrow."

"The police?" she asked.

"Yes, Daniel and his guys went to the club, but they didn't find the redhead. Anthony Carzoni, the manager, said he didn't know who she was or where she lived. She comes in and strips when she wants to make money, and since she's so popular he lets her."

"Do you believe that?"

"Not for a minute. If it was true, there'd be no reason to guard her like they were."

"Will Daniel continue looking?" She was disappointed they hadn't found the stripper, but with these new feelings the setback didn't overwhelm her.

"Oh, yeah. Tomorrow's another day and we *will* find out what's going on, but right now I don't want to think about anything else besides us."

She didn't, either. The stripper had been uppermost in her mind for days, but now Ethan took center stage, and all she wanted was to be with him. Tomorrow would come soon enough.

He pulled her up to him and they kissed deeply. She slid onto him and let herself indulge in pure pleasure. She felt his hardness and a bubble of excitement ran through her.

Drawing her lips away, she said in a teasing voice, "Didn't you tell me you were too old to be tempted by a woman my age?"

"Yeah." He grinned.

"Then what I'm feeling against my leg is a figment of my overactive imagination?"

He laughed out loud and rolled her onto her back. It was the first time she'd heard him laugh, and it warmed her through and through. He definitely needed to laugh more.

Ethan kissed the sprinkling of light freckles across her nose, then his lips glided down to her breasts and tasted the freckles there. Continuing the journey lower, his mouth tantalized and teased, and soon her pleasure began to spiral out of control.

He lifted his head and gazed deeply into her dreamy eyes. They stared at each other for several seconds, then he slid into her. "How does that feel?" he asked in a raspy voice.

She took a quick breath. "Ah...perfect."

"Oh, Serena," he groaned as his lips took hers with a fierce need that was echoed in every nerve in her body. He started to move and she met each thrust until they soared higher and higher.... Spasms of pleasure shuddered through her as Ethan moaned his release a moment later.

Neither thought about his hip.

Ethan held her close, thinking of so many things, but especially his gratitude. Gratitude for Serena Farrell. Gratitude that she'd given him back an essential part of himself—his manhood. Another world waited outside the motel room, but he decided it could wait. For now he would just think about the beautiful woman in his arms.

He reached up to turn off the light. "Go to sleep, sweet Serena," he murmured.

I love you, Ethan.

"I'll always remember this time with you," he said.

Everything in her froze. Ethan's words meant he wasn't looking beyond tonight. That hurt. She'd told him earlier that they were two adults who could handle the consequences. Now she was wondering if she could.

When they'd made love the first time, Ethan had asked if she was protected. She'd told him she was and she hadn't lied, but she now knew Ethan didn't want any little surprises in the future. Did that mean he didn't envision her in his future? Probably not. She closed her eyes, but all she could see was Ethan. All she could feel was Ethan. It would be different tomorrow, she told herself. Her problems would resume, and Ethan would be nothing but a pleasant memory.

Try as she might, she couldn't make herself believe it. Love didn't disappear that easily. At least not for her.

ETHAN AWOKE feeling refreshed and young again. His hip didn't ache. He'd never felt so damn good in his life, and it was all because of the woman lying in his arms. His right leg lay across hers and his arm rested against her waist. His left arm was underneath her and had gone numb, but he didn't care, not one bit. It occurred to him that he wouldn't mind waking up like this for the rest of his life. He was getting in so deep that he suddenly had trouble breathing. He didn't mind that, either.

Ethan had the rest of his life all planned out. He would live on his ranch and continue to help his family, taking the odd case when the restlessness drove him. He figured he'd already lived his life and now all he needed was peace and tranquillity. Looking at Serena, he felt like a completely different man, as if his life was just starting. He'd only known her a few days, but she was changing his way of thinking, his way of feeling. He wondered what she'd say if he told her that. They hadn't talked about commitment or the future; it was too soon. Or was it? It had been so long since he'd had these kinds of emotions that he felt as insecure as a sixteen-year-old boy.

He'd take one day at a time, he decided, and see where the future took them. Other than that, there wasn't much he could do but be there for her, which he intended to do.

For a moment he watched her sleep, studying each feature—the silky skin, pert nose, fine reddish-brown eyebrows and eyelashes and those adorable freckles. The copper hair that lay everywhere was breathtaking. Unable to resist, he pushed the hair away from her face and gently kissed the freckles on her nose.

"Ethan," she murmured sleepily, as if she was used to waking up to his kisses.

"Go back to sleep," he said. "I'm going to the county clerk's office to check for your mom's death certificate."

She rubbed her head against him. "I want to go, too."

"There's nothing you can do, so get some rest. You had a very active night."

"Mmm." A smile tugged at her lips.

"I'll be back before you know it." He kissed her again and crawled out of bed. Within minutes he was dressed and headed for his truck.

IT DIDN'T TAKE Ethan long to reach the clerk's office. It was early, so the traffic wasn't bad and he had to wait for the office to open. The county clerk was out, which meant he had to deal with an assistant. She was very cooperative after he showed her his P.I. badge and explained the case he was working on. In short order, he had the information in hand, but he had to dig deeper. Something wasn't making sense.

Thirty minutes later the mystery was solved, and it was so simple it should've occurred to him sooner. Now he had to tell Serena. He didn't have to wonder how she'd take it. He knew—with courage and determination.

On the way back to the motel, he picked up coffee and doughnuts. He'd been so eager to get to the clerk's office that he hadn't even taken time for coffee. Now he'd have it with Serena. He smiled. She'd have to talk herself into eating a doughnut and he'd enjoy every second.

SERENA SCRAMBLED out of bed feeling lonely. She missed Ethan. She missed everything about him—his touch, his warmth, his stubbornness. How could this have happened so quickly? She'd asked herself that same question last night and she still had no answer. It didn't matter anymore. The way she felt was all that mattered.

The future was a blur, uncertain, but her feelings for Ethan were real and she would hold on to that. His words of last night came back to her. *I'll always remember this time with you.* She pushed them away, determined not to let them destroy her happiness.

She'd think about her mother, her grandmother and the mysterious red-haired stripper later. Now she just wanted to enjoy whatever time she had with the man she loved. *Hurry back, Ethan.*

ETHAN OPENED the motel-room door and paused, looking around. The bed was empty and everything was quiet. He removed his hat and set the coffee and doughnuts in a chair. Had Serena left? His heart raced alarmingly.

Suddenly she came out of the bathroom fully dressed, her hair pinned up, and he let out a sigh of relief. They stared at each other, the morning after a little awkward for a moment, then Serena ran across the room and into his arms. They kissed until their breathing became labored.

"You were gone too long," she murmured, trying to catch her breath.

"But I brought coffee and doughnuts," he said, wanting a little more time before he had to tell her the truth.

"Just what I was wishing for."

He reluctantly moved away to get the coffee and handed her a cup. "It already has cream in it."

"Thank you." She sat on the bed and sipped it, delighted by his thoughtfulness but not surprised—because her heart had already told her Ethan was that kind of man.

He offered her a doughnut. "Eat it and don't think about the calories." His eyes darkened. "We'll work them off later."

She met his gaze. "I like that idea."

He did, too, but he wasn't sure it was going to happen. Everything would change when he told her what had taken place all those years ago. He was wondering why she hadn't asked yet.

She finished off the doughnut and licked her fingers, eyeing him with a sheepish grin. "How's the hip?"

When anyone else asked that question, he became tense and frustrated, but with her he couldn't object. With her he didn't seem to have any defenses left.

He looked into her eyes. "Great. Better than ever."

"I'm glad."

Ethan watched her provocative movements as she continued to lick her fingers. All he could think about was tasting each finger, then slowly kissing the rest of her body. But he forced his mind elsewhere. Other things took precedence. He got up and threw his cup in the trash then he sat beside her, needing to be close when he told her.

"You have something to tell me, don't you?" she asked guardedly.

"Yes."

She swallowed. "Is my mother dead or alive?" She'd been afraid to ask, but now she couldn't avoid it.

"She's dead," he answered. "She died from injuries she received in that car accident, just like your grandmother told you."

She bit her lip. "Somehow...I guess...I was hoping she was alive. It would explain the stripper, but now..."

Ethan had grown very still beside her and she knew there was more. "What is it?"

"Your grandmother didn't tell you the whole truth."

"She didn't?"

"No, your mother wasn't married. Jasmine Farrell is the name on the death certificate and there's no record of her marriage."

"Oh." She hadn't expected this, but she should have. Gran was a stickler for propriety and probably couldn't stand the idea of Jasmine living with John Welch, so she'd told everyone Jasmine had married him. "I guess that was something else Gran couldn't face."

"Maybe, but I searched a little deeper and found—"

"What?"

"Jasmine Farrell gave birth to twin girls."

"What!"

She leapt to her feet and began to pace. *Twin girls.* She knew the woman was her double, and a small part of her had known there was only one way they could look so much alike. They were twins—had to be. But she didn't want to let herself believe that because it meant her grandmother had lied to her, deceived her. She had to say the words out loud. "That means the stripper's my sister. My twin. Oh, God, where has she been all these years? Why would my grandmother keep that a secret?''

''My guess is that Sarah was raised by the Welches.''

Her eyes jerked to his. ''Sarah?''

''Yes, her name is Sarah Welch. It's on the birth certificate. Your grandparents gave you their name, and the Welches obviously did the same with Sarah.''

She sank down beside Ethan. ''Hold me, please.'' The plea in her voice tied his stomach in knots and he slipped his arms around her. She rested her head on his shoulder.

''Serena and Sarah,'' she murmured as if in a daze.

He kissed her forehead. ''I think you have to talk to your grandmother now.''

''Yes.'' She raised her head. ''She has to tell me the truth, but I can't understand why they separated us and kept it a secret.''

''I'm sure they had a good reason, or at least what sounded good to them at the time.''

''No.'' Serena jerked to her feet. ''No reason was good enough to separate us.''

''Don't overreact,'' he warned.

''It's hard not to.'' She started to pace again. ''Can you imagine what kind of life Sarah has to be living as a stripper?''

''Well, I've thought from the start that she's being forced to strip. She has a fear in her eyes that doesn't come from exposing herself.'' He stood and caught Serena by her forearms. ''You go home and maybe you can straighten all this out with your grandmother. In the meantime I'll get with Daniel and do a check on Sarah and the Welches. That should give us an address—and a lot more.''

''Okay,'' she said without much enthusiasm.

''You have my cell number?''

''Yes.''

"And I have yours."

The incredible news she'd just heard was overshadowed by the thought that her time with Ethan was ending. Why did that hurt so much more? She knew the answer: because she couldn't change the past, and the future stretched endlessly before her—without Ethan.

Ethan reached for his hat and stepped toward the door. He wanted to kiss her, wanted to turn back the clock and leave their problems outside this room. That wasn't realistic, though; once he walked through that door, things would be different. For her, for him, for whatever they had together. But life was about changes, he told himself, and how you dealt with them.

A lump formed in Serena's throat as he opened the door. "Goodbye, Ethan." The words slipped out. They weren't the words she wanted to say, but they were the words that came from her throat, not her heart.

Goodbye. They would talk on the phone until the situation about Sarah was resolved, but he knew that now they'd go their separate ways. His chest felt tight, and against his will he looked back at her, then wished he hadn't. Her blue eyes were watery, and his chest grew tighter. *Say goodbye and get it over with.* But he couldn't. He wouldn't. All he could do was walk quietly out the door.

ETHAN SOON GOT his emotions under control. He *would* see her again. He was determined about that, but... He called Daniel Garrett to get his mind on something else. Daniel wasn't expected in for another hour, so Ethan decided to stop by Travis's and see Molly. He didn't like her involvement with Boyd and he couldn't wait any longer to tell her what he'd learned.

When he arrived at Travis's door, it swung open and Bruce walked out. Ethan was taken aback. "What are you doing here?'' he asked, unable to keep the surprise out of his voice.

Bruce scowled. ''Trying to talk some sense into Molly.''

''Oh?''

''She has a seventeen-year-old son to raise and she's left him with Pop while she's busy singing in a nightclub. That's absurd! And have you seen the way she looks? She doesn't even look like herself anymore.''

Ethan held up his hand. ''That's enough. You're the one who left Molly, and if you're not happy with how she's living her life, then that's your problem. As for your son, he's a big boy and needs little supervision. Besides, Molly talks to him every day. I think this break has been good for Molly and Cole.''

''I guess you're right,'' Bruce admitted grudgingly. ''At least Cole's talking to me again.'' His face suddenly crumpled. ''I want my son back. I want…''

Ethan watched him for a moment. ''I don't think you know what you want.''

Bruce glanced off at the bright blue sky. ''I thought I did, but now… I want my son not to hate me.''

This was like the old Bruce, and Ethan found he was more sympathetic than angry with him. ''Give it time. It takes time for wounds to heal.''

''Yeah, if they ever do,'' Bruce said.

Ethan walked into the apartment expecting to find Molly in tears, her usual reaction when she was around Bruce. But she was dressed, not a tear in sight. She slung her purse over her shoulder.

''Ethan, I thought I heard your voice.'' She stood on tiptoe to kiss his cheek.

''I met Bruce outside,'' he said, waiting for her reaction. None came.

''He's upset that I'm singing in a club. Can you believe

that? And of course, he talked about Cole. He wants him at the wedding. I told him that's Cole decision, not mine."

"You're taking this very well."

"I'm not crying over Bruce anymore," was her response. "For so long he was my whole world, but I've found there's another world out there. I'm still young, reasonably attractive, and I plan to enjoy my life without constantly thinking about Bruce."

He raised an eyebrow. "Did you come to this conclusion all by yourself?"

"Rudy had a lot to do with it."

That's what I was afraid of. Nevertheless he had to tell her. It was going to break her heart and he didn't know if he could stand that. Still...

"Oh." She glanced at the clock on the wall. "I've got to run."

"Where're you going?"

"I promised Rudy I'd do an errand for him and I don't want to be late."

"An errand?"

"Yeah, he's very involved with one of the boys' clubs. They helped turn his life around when he was a kid and he wants to repay them for that. So he provides new sports equipment every once in a while. He's buying baseball uniforms, balls, bats and gloves for everyone, and I promised to pick them up."

"Really?"

"The plane lands in thirty minutes and I need to be there."

Ethan frowned. "Plane? Where are the uniforms coming from?"

Molly shrugged. "I don't know, but he had them specially made. Isn't he wonderful?"

Ethan couldn't answer that. He was trying to take in

what she'd said. A plane? That immediately raised suspicions.

"I really need to talk to you," Ethan said quickly as Molly moved to the door.

She turned. "I'm fine. I can even see Bruce without getting upset. You don't have to worry about me." Before he could respond, she was gone.

He *was* worried about her, he couldn't help it. His instincts told him something about Boyd wasn't right. Now he had to figure out exactly what that something was.

SERENA PURPOSEFULLY PACKED her bag, refusing to think about Ethan. She thought, instead, about what she'd learned. She had a sister. A twin. Why had her grandmother lied to her? She had to find out, she had to have answers.

With her bag in the car, she glanced back at the motel. It represented a moment out of time that would always be with her. She felt tears gather in her eyes again. "Goodbye, Ethan," she whispered, and backed out of the parking lot.

As she waited in traffic, she dreaded the coming confrontation with her grandmother. She also dreaded whatever else she might learn. Gran had done her a terrible injustice and she had to find out why. But most of all, Serena wanted to see her sister, talk to her, hear her story.

Why not? she asked herself. She knew where she worked and maybe, just maybe, when the manager saw that they were obviously sisters, he might tell her how to find Sarah. Yes, she'd do it. At this time of day the club should be empty and she'd have a good chance of talking to the manager. And Sarah.

As she drove toward the club, she wondered if she should call Ethan. No, she had to do this on her own.

She hoped he'd understand.

CHAPTER TEN

IT DIDN'T TAKE Ethan long to explain the situation to Daniel. He also told him about Molly and Boyd.

"Damn, Ethan, your sister's involved with him?"

"I wouldn't say 'involved.' He just has her snowed at the moment."

"He's good at that." Daniel leaned back in his chair. "I've got my ass in a sling on this. My superiors are talking about pulling me off the case. Too many man-hours, too much money, not enough results. Although they've given me more time since a cop's life is on the line… I thought if I could just find the redhead, it might give me a much-needed clue. That raid was another dead end. They've got her well hidden. So I came back here last night and put the screws to my computer expert. This is what he found." Daniel picked up a folder and placed it in front of Ethan. "Does anything jump out at you?"

Ethan opened the file. Inside was a list of corporations and their directors. The corporations were owners of a lot of strip clubs and adult video stores.

"Look at the director's name at the top."

Joseph Rudolph Boydardi. Ethan glanced up. "Rudy Boyd. He shortened his name."

"Yeah, and changed it around. Joseph Rudolph is a director of one company, as is J. R. Boydar and Rudolph Dardi, but they're the same person—alias Rudy Boyd, and no telling how many others."

‘‘Then Boyd owns all these strip clubs?’’

Daniel pointed to a name on the paper. ‘‘Yes, and he owns Teasers.’’

‘‘Good God.’’

‘‘My guess is that Greg found out he owned these clubs, and Boyd silenced him. I just have to prove it. The redhead—Sarah Welch—is my only hope.’’

‘‘Why does Boyd want to keep this a secret?’’

‘‘Because he’s Mr. Upstanding Citizen. He’s big with the mayor and the city council and known for his generosity. I know he’s pushing drugs through these clubs, because I’ve busted too many small-time pushers who say that’s where they get their supply, but no one will testify against Boyd. Everyone’s frightened of him. They keep saying they don’t know who he is. Now I can connect him to the clubs—and, I hope, a whole lot more.’’

Ethan closed the folder. ‘‘The first step is still to find Sarah Welch.’’

‘‘Yeah.’’ Daniel yanked up the phone and barked out a few orders, then turned back to Ethan. ‘‘Jimmy, my computer guy, will have everything we need in a few minutes.’’ He fingered the file. ‘‘I have to do this, Ethan, before they pull the plug. I have to find Greg. He was a good cop. He just got mixed up with the wrong woman.’’

‘‘I think Sarah Welch might be a victim, too.’’

‘‘Why?’’

‘‘She doesn’t seem like a typical stripper. She’s afraid. I could see it in her eyes. And there’s a group of men guarding her. That doesn’t add up.’’

Before Daniel could say anything, a young man who couldn’t be more than twenty walked up and brought Daniel some papers. ‘‘Thanks, Jimmy, and keep digging up whatever you can on Boyd. Time’s running out.’’

‘‘You got it,’’ Jimmy said, and ambled away.

Daniel glanced through the papers and handed them to Ethan. "There's everything you want to know about Sarah Welch, but it doesn't tell us why she's stripping at Teasers."

Ethan read the report. She didn't have a record—not even a traffic ticket. But everything else, from her birth to her schooldays in Oklahoma and Arizona to college attendance, was listed. She attended Southern Methodist University, where she obtained a psychology degree. She had several jobs as a waitress, obviously paying her own way through college, since it took her several years. She was now working on her masters. Celia Welch was listed as next of kin, and her address was noted. Sarah had the same address.

What Ethan had suspected was true—different grandparents had raised Serena and Sarah. Why? That still had to be answered. He wondered if Serena was talking to her grandmother yet. Maybe she already knew the answer.

Ethan slowly laid the papers down. "This is a profile of a hardworking young woman."

"Doesn't fit what we know about her, does it."

"No," Ethan agreed. "Let's pay grandmother Welch a visit. She might be able to tell us where her granddaughter is."

Daniel grabbed his jacket and spoke to the man who occupied the desk behind him. "Hey, Ron. Call me if anything happens."

The man mumbled his assent, and they walked out to Daniel's car. The Welch address was in a Dallas suburb less than thirty minutes from Fort Worth. Ethan shook his head at the irony of it—Serena and Sarah lived so close, yet they'd never met. Now they would.

Daniel was familiar with the area. Soon they turned

down a street of compact brick houses all jammed together with small yards.

They stopped at the Welch address. "Let me do the talking," Daniel said. "This is police business."

"I never interfere with police business," Ethan replied smugly.

"Yeah, right." Daniel laughed.

They made their way to the front door. "How's your hip?" Daniel asked.

For once Ethan didn't feel his insides caving in when someone asked that question. Since last night, he had a whole new perspective on his hip—and on everything else—because of Serena. "Not troubling me too much," Ethan answered, trying not to smile. "Thanks for asking."

Daniel knocked loudly on the door.

"Who is it?" a woman's voice called.

"Police," Daniel yelled.

The door swung open immediately. A plump woman in her seventies stood there. Medium height, gray hair. A flowered housedress and slippers. "Is this about Sarah?"

"May we come in, please?" Daniel asked politely.

"Oh, yes, yes, where're my manners." She moved aside and they entered the main room of the house.

Ethan glanced around. Shabby furniture, worn carpet. Bric-a-brac cluttering every available space. There were parakeets in a cage by a window, and their chirping softened the room. He figured from the evidence around him that Celia Welch had a hard time making ends meet. His eyes froze on a couple of pictures on the wall. Red hair, blue eyes, same gorgeous skin as Serena, but it wasn't Serena. It was her twin—Sarah.

Daniel pulled out his badge. "I'm Daniel Garrett with the Dallas Police Department and this is Ethan Ramsey, a private investigator. We'd like to speak with Sarah."

Celia put her hands on her hips. "So would I!"

"She's not here?"

"No, she moved in with that boyfriend of hers. I told her not to. She's only known him a few months, but she wouldn't listen to me. Stubborn, just like her mother. You can't tell her a thing."

"Her mother?" Ethan couldn't help it. It just slipped out. The only sign that Daniel disapproved was the muscle working in his jaw.

Celia waved a hand. "Forget it. I don't know why I said that. Jasmine's dead, but Sarah reminds me so much of her with her finicky ways. Nothing's ever good enough for her. She just had to go to college, even though I couldn't afford it. She works as a waitress and goes to school part-time. She's been going for years and she's still not through. What good is a degree when you're living on pennies? That's what I tell her, but does she listen? No."

"Is your husband here?" Daniel asked.

"Good heavens, no. He died years ago. It's just me and Sarah, and we've managed to survive. I'm a damn good waitress and Sarah learned that from me. Not something I wanted her to do, but as I said, you can't tell her anything."

Ethan got a glimpse into Sarah's life and he knew where the hardness came from. Her life hadn't been easy, whereas Serena's had been storybook perfect—until now. How would each deal with what had been done to them?

"Mrs. Welch, we need to find Sarah. It's very important," Daniel said urgently.

"Find her boyfriend and you'll find her."

"What's his name?"

"Greg something. She said she'd call and give me the address and phone number, but I haven't heard from her."

At the mention of Greg's name, the muscle in Daniel's jaw picked up speed, and Ethan knew Daniel was hoping his cop was alive.

Daniel removed a card from his pocket and passed it to her. "If she contacts you, call me immediately. As I said, it's very important."

Celia took the card. "What kind of trouble is she in?"

"We're just looking for her boyfriend."

"Why?"

"Just call me," Daniel answered.

"She is okay, isn't she? We argue a lot because we're so different, but she's all I have and I love her."

No, you have another granddaughter, Mrs. Welch, and you know it. How can you forget about her?

"If I find out anything, ma'am, I'll get in touch."

"Oh, please do that. I'll worry until I hear something."

"Thanks for your help," Daniel said as they left.

Outside, he remarked, "For a moment there, I thought you were gonna mention the other twin."

"I almost did. I can't understand how she can just wipe another granddaughter from her mind—a blood granddaughter."

"Beats me, but I got other things to worry about. Damn, another dead end." Daniel hit the top of the car with his fist. "There were some women's clothes in Greg's apartment. I'll have another look at them. The stripper has to be *somewhere.*"

"The best way to find her is to stake out the club."

"Yeah." Daniel glanced at Ethan over the top of the car. "I'll have men on it tonight and I'll also put a watch on Mrs. Welch. Just in case she's not telling the truth."

They got into the car. "I think Mrs. Welch knows as much as we do—nothing."

“It's so damn frustrating—and all the while, Boyd goes on with his illegal activities.”

“But not for long.” Ethan sighed. “Hopefully not for long.”

SERENA FOUND the strip club without a problem, but it was locked. The windows were all dark, so she couldn't see through them. She ran to her car, noticing that everything was dead around here at this time of day. She drove as far as the next corner, took a right and came up a backstreet. There *had* to be a way into the club. Her heart started to race as she saw people coming and going through a rear entrancc. A beer truck was backed in, obviously delivering beer. A cleaning-service van was parked to the side. She stopped behind the van and got out before she could change her mind. There were businesspeople here, so what could happen? She'd simply ask about Sarah and then leave.

Approaching the entrance, she met the beer-delivery man. He held the door and winked at her. “Thank you,” she said, trying to ignore that look in his eyes—the same look she'd seen on those men last night.

In the hallway she saw boxes stacked along the wall. A dressing room with women's clothes all over the place was to the right. A cleaning woman was hanging up the clothes and dusting. Good. At least someone not directly involved with the club was here. To the left was a hall with several doors and a staircase. Then she spotted the double doors that led to the inside of the club. Maybe someone there could help her.

She pushed open the door. Three men were talking at the bar, and when they saw her, they fell quiet. The man in the middle, the one she'd encountered last night, came over to her with a scowl on his face.

"How the hell did you get out of that room?" He grabbed her by the arm and shoved her through the door, still holding on to her.

"Let go of me," she shouted, and tried to pull away, but his thick fingers held her tight.

"Listen, bitch." His black eyes bored into her. "You don't give orders around here, and I want a damn good explanation from Ric on how you escaped." He yanked her toward the stairs.

It suddenly hit her that he thought she was Sarah. That was both good and bad—good that he was possibly taking her to Sarah, and bad that she was in the hands of these despicable people. At the moment there wasn't anything she could do about either.

"You're hurting me," she said as she tripped on a couple of the stairs.

"Be glad I don't wring that pretty neck of yours. You've been nothing but trouble since we brought you here. So shut up."

On the landing he dragged her along to where a guy was sitting in a chair, asleep.

Her captor said a profane word and knocked the second man from the chair with one blow while still holding Serena. The felled man stumbled to his feet. "Wh-what?"

"You bastard." The first man shoved Serena forward. "Look who I found downstairs."

The man rubbed his jaw, muttering, "I swear, Anthony, she didn't come out of the room." He was clearly afraid.

"How would *you* know? You've been asleep. The boss'll have your ass for this. She could've gotten away. She was just too stupid to find her way out. Now open the damn door."

The man fumbled for a key and quickly opened the door. Anthony pushed her inside. "If you know what's good for you, you'll stay put,'' he said, slamming and relocking the door.

Serena heard a gasp and whirled around. Sarah stood a few feet away wearing the same black robe she'd had on last night, her red hair in disarray and the hands at her cheeks shaking. ''Oh, God!'' Sarah cried. ''Now I'm seeing things. I'm losing my mind.''

Serena's breath froze in her throat. It was so...surreal, like looking at her own image, yet knowing it wasn't her. She had the urge to pinch herself to make sure. Swallowing hard, she moved toward Sarah, wanting to relieve her twin's distress.

''You're not seeing things,'' she told her. ''I'm real.''

''Then why do you look like me?''

''I'm—''

Sarah broke in. ''Go away and leave me alone! I can't take any more.''

Serena wasn't sure what to do—to blurt out who she was or try to talk calmly to her. Clearly Sarah was close to the edge.

Serena went with her instincts, knowing they had to face the truth. She held out her hand. ''Touch me,'' she invited. ''I'm real.''

Sarah watched her for a moment, then tentatively reached out one finger and touched Serena. ''You *are* real,'' Sarah said in a breathless voice.

''Yes.'' Serena linked her hand with Sarah's, and led her to the sofa. ''Let's sit here and talk.'' Glancing around, Serena noticed the place was a small apartment with a living area, bedroom and bath.

''Who are you?'' Sarah asked in that same breathless voice.

''My name is Serena Farrell.''

"Farrell?" Sarah frowned. "That's my mother's name. Are we related?"

"Yes." Serena took a deep breath. "My parents were Jasmine Farrell and John Welch."

"That's my..." Sarah's voice trailed off and her eyes grew big.

"We're twins. Identical twins." Serena said the words she knew Sarah was trying to say.

"But...how? Celia never mentioned I had a twin."

"Celia?"

"Celia Welch, my grandmother," Sarah answered.

"Oh, Henry and Aurora Farrell raised me, and they never mentioned you, either."

"Who are they?"

"They're Jasmine's parents. My—our grandparents," Serena explained.

"How did that happen?"

"I'm not sure, but they must have separated us at birth."

"But why?"

"I don't know. We'll have to ask our grandparents that."

"I don't understand. If your grandparents didn't tell you, how did you find out about me?"

"It's a long story, but I'll shorten it. A private investigator saw you stripping." Sarah's face turned pink when she said that, and Serena could see she was embarrassed, but she continued. "Then the next day he saw me in a café in Fort Worth and thought I was you. I told him I wasn't, but he assumed I was lying because he said we looked identical. I couldn't get that out of my head. My grandparents refused to talk about my father, so I knew nothing about him. When I asked my grandmother a little while ago, she told me things that didn't make sense and

I knew she was lying. You see, Jasmine and Gran didn't get along and Jasmine ran away to be with my—I mean, our father. I thought maybe she wasn't really dead, and maybe they lied about that, too. So I hired the detective to find you. Ethan, the detective, said you were stripping against your will, and you are, aren't you?''

A noise outside the door prevented Sarah from answering. ''Serena, you have to get out of here,'' she said nervously.

''Why are you locked in this room?''

''It's an even longer story, and I don't have time to tell you.''

Serena looked at the bars on the windows, then at the door. ''I'm locked in here with you. When I came in, this guy named Anthony thought I was you and literally dragged me up here. What's going on?''

Sarah jumped to her feet and ran to the door, listening. ''It's just service people. Thank God.''

''What's going on?'' Serena asked again.

Sarah pushed her hands through her hair. ''It's awful. Just awful.'' She returned to sit beside Serena. ''I wanted to help Greg, plus get information for the psychology thesis I was writing.''

''Greg, the cop?''

''Yes. Do you know him?''

''No, but I know the police are looking for him.''

Sarah's hands shook. ''They'll never find him.'' She paused, then added, ''I met Greg at the restaurant where I used to work. We fell instantly in love and we were so happy. He told me he was going undercover and the police department was renting him a new place so his identity couldn't be easily traced. He wasn't supposed to have contact with anyone besides his boss. The narcotics team he works with were after this thug, and they needed some hard evidence. Greg wasn't supposed to tell me, but he said he'd be going to a strip club as a patron. I told him I could work there as a waitress. I'd be able to get inside information on a stripper's life—what makes her do it, what motivates her, that kind of thing. It would be great research. I could also keep my eyes open.... Greg was against it at first, but we didn't want to be apart, so he agreed. I moved into the apartment with him. I got the job without a problem, but I wasn't prepared for the sleazy atmosphere. Still, everything was going okay until..." She paused.

"Until what?" Serena prompted.

"Until *he* took an interest in me."

"Who?"

"Rudy Boyd."

Serena remembered Ethan mentioning that name and how the police were after him. "Does he own this place?"

"Oh, yeah, and a bunch of others. Greg finally put it together." She gave a long, shuddering sigh. "Rudy comes to the club late at night through a back entrance. He has a room up here where he can watch everything downstairs. He finds a woman he wants and has Anthony send her up. One night Anthony said the boss wanted to see me upstairs. I knew what that meant and I told him I wasn't interested. He said I'd lose my job, but no one fired me. The next night it happened again, and Greg said it was time for me to get out. I was packing my things to go back to Celia's when there was a knock at the door." Sarah paused again and tightened the belt on her robe with trembling fingers.

"It was Anthony, two of his men and Boyd. That was the first time I'd seen him. I'd only heard about him from the other waitresses. I didn't know his name until that night. I only knew him as the boss. The men grabbed me, and Boyd told Greg that he'd found out he was a cop trying to nail him. He said nobody nails him. I didn't even see the gun until he raised it and fired. He...he shot Greg like a helpless animal. He didn't stand a...'' Sarah brushed away a tear.

Serena murmured soothing words and stroked Sarah's arm until she could continue.

''I screamed and screamed and I thought they were gonna kill me, too,'' she said in a stark voice, ''but they put tape over my mouth and injected something into my arm. I woke up in a room. I don't know where. Boyd was there and he had a disk from my computer. He knew I was writing about the strippers. He said I was working with the cop and I'd pay for that, but he seemed angrier that I'd turned him down. He said no woman turns him down and if I was so interested in strippers, I could get the information firsthand. I told him I'd never do such a thing and that he turned my stomach. He hit me. I've being living in fear ever since. I keep seeing Greg's face just before he...''

Serena placed a hand over Sarah's. ''Try not to think about it.'' Silence ensued for a few moments, then Serena asked, ''How did Boyd make you strip?''

''He said if I didn't, he'd slit my throat.'' Sarah shivered. ''Sometimes I think that's preferable to what I've been going through, but I keep thinking I can get away eventually and go to the cops and tell them what happened to Greg. But, so far, Boyd's men guard me day and night.''

''I saw you last night.''

''You did?''

''Yes, Ethan and I came to the club to see you. I was the woman with black hair trying to talk to you.''

''I remember, and if I'd known your detective friend

was with you, I would've screamed my head off.'' Sarah briefly closed her eyes. ''I can't take any more. He forces me to strip in front of him and it makes me sick to my stomach.''

Serena took a painful breath and had to ask, ''Has he…forced himself on you?''

Sarah shook her head. ''Not yet, but it's just a matter of time. If that happens I'll— He makes me physically ill.''

''It won't happen,'' Serena assured her. ''All I have to do is call Ethan and he'll get us out of here. I should've done that earlier.'' She turned and reached for her purse, but it wasn't there. ''Damn! No, no, no.''

''What?'' Sarah asked.

''I left my purse in the car. How could I do something so stupid? I was just in such a hurry to see you, I forgot everything else. I didn't even lock my car.'' Serena let out a breath. ''Don't worry. The police are checking this place. It won't be long before they find us.'' Serena was trying desperately to convince Sarah, but she felt a spasm of fear.

''The police were here last night,'' she added. ''But they couldn't find you.''

''Boyd moves me around,'' Sarah said. ''He knows the police are looking for me.''

''Oh,'' Serena answered, feeling more than a little hopeless.

She and Sarah stared at each other and suddenly their plight didn't seem so bad.

''I have a sister,'' Sarah said.

''So do I.'' Serena smiled.

They embraced and held each other tight. ''Trust me, Sarah, we'll get out of this.''

Sarah drew back and wiped away tears with her sleeve. ''You're very optimistic.''

''I am because I know Ethan, and once he finds out

I'm not at my grandmother's like I'm supposed to be, he'll come looking for me.''

She didn't tell Sarah that Ethan might not call her. That he might assume she'd made up with her grandmother and everything was fine.

Oh, Ethan, don't do the typical male thing and not call. I need you. Please call. Please, Ethan.

CHAPTER ELEVEN

ETHAN LEFT DANIEL at the police station. Now it was a waiting game. The redhead—Sarah Welch—would show eventually, and when she did, the police would be there. He took out his cell phone to call Serena, to tell her about Celia, but then wondered if maybe he should give her more time. That conversation with her grandmother couldn't have been an easy one. He set the phone down and stared at it. But he needed to hear her voice. She'd reached his heart and opened up a whole new— He grabbed the phone and hit the speed-dial for her number. It rang and rang, and then her voice mail came on. He clicked off, not leaving a message; he'd try again later.

He called Molly next. He had to talk to her. In fact, he should've done it this morning. Now he had no choice. Boyd was going down one way or the other, and Ethan didn't want Molly anywhere near him when that happened. She picked up on the second ring.

"Molly, I have to talk to you."

"Ethan, I'm real busy. I just got the uniforms and I'm going to the boys' club to deliver them, then I'm meeting Rudy. Why don't you come tonight before our set and we'll chat?"

"This can't wait. It's important."

"What is it?"

"It's about Boyd."

"Oh, Ethan, stop looking for problems."

"I've checked him out, Molly, and he's into all sorts of illegal activities."

"I know about his past," she said to his surprise. "He had a record as a teenager. He was in a gang and involved with drugs, but he's straightened out his life and I admire that."

Ethan sighed irritably. "Molly, when you've delivered the uniforms, go to the apartment and wait there until you hear from me."

"I will not!" she snapped. "I'm not fifteen years old and you can't order me around."

He took a breath. "Have I ever steered you wrong?"

"No."

"I'm not now. Just do as I ask. Please."

Silence.

"Molly?"

"I'll think about it," she finally said.

"Molly..."

She hung up.

Damn. Why did she have to be so pigheaded? He started to call her back, but knew it was pointless. He remembered when she was a teenager and their parents had tried to warn her about getting too serious with Bruce. She hadn't listened. Molly rarely listened to anyone; she did exactly what she wanted. That could have been part of the problem between her and Bruce. He'd never thought of that before, hadn't allowed himself to think anything negative about his sister. Well, he couldn't worry about that right now; he only hoped she'd listen to him.

He called Serena again. Still no answer. He tried two more times and finally left a message. Still nothing. By late afternoon, he knew something was wrong. He got

Aurora Farrell's number from Directory Assistance and called.

"May I speak to Serena, please?"

"She's not here. Who's calling?"

"Ethan Ramsey. I'm a friend of hers."

"She's never mentioned you."

"We met just a few days ago."

"Oh."

"Mrs. Farrell, have you seen Serena today?"

"No, she was supposed to come home, but she hasn't and I'm getting worried."

Me, too. God, Serena where are you?

"I'm sure she's fine," he muttered, trying to sound reassuring.

"Yes, yes of course she is. But if you see her, will you have her call me? I've tried her cell phone, but she doesn't answer."

"I will, and thanks, Mrs. Farrell."

A hard ball of fear formed in his stomach. Where did Serena go after leaving the motel? Why didn't she go home to talk to her grandmother? *Sarah.* It had to have something to do with Sarah.

A thought crossed his mind, but he pushed it away. No, she wouldn't. Would she? *Oh, God, Serena, please don't tell me you went to the strip club to find Sarah.*

"YOU NEED TO GET over here and quick," Anthony said into the phone.

"What the hell for? You know I'm busy today."

"The redhead got out of the room. I found her downstairs."

"Goddammit, Anthony! How did that happen?"

"Doesn't matter. She's trouble. I told you we should've gotten rid of her long ago. She could bring us all down."

''I'll be over there as soon as I can to teach her a lesson, and, Anthony, you'd better make damn sure she stays locked in that room.''

SERENA AND SARAH moved to the bedroom in case someone came in. They didn't want anyone to see both of them. They sat on the bed and talked; that was all they could do and it helped keep the fear at bay. Serena learned that Sarah lived with Celia Welch and that Celia hadn't liked Jasmine.

Sarah's life was hard because of money problems. After her husband's death, Celia worked as a waitress and made just enough money for them to get by. John Welch had numerous affairs, but Celia always took him back. Serena found it hard to believe that these people were her grandparents. Sarah had a serious romantic relationship in high school and had briefly thought about running away to get married, but she didn't want to make the same mistake Jasmine had. John Welch had died years ago, and Serena told Sarah about Henry Farrell's death a few months earlier. Serena felt guilty about her private schools and the life of luxury she'd lived, so it was easy—and more comfortable—to talk about her financial difficulties and her relationship with Aurora.

Serena and Sarah couldn't figure out why their grandparents had chosen to keep the other twin's existence a secret. They decided to confront their grandmothers together and learn the truth.

''You're so much prettier than me,'' Sarah said, studying Serena.

Serena lifted an eyebrow. ''I don't think so. We're identical.''

''But you have a polished edge that I don't.''

"I know exactly how much that cost. I have the bills at home to prove it."

They laughed together.

"Seriously," Serena mused, "you have an earthiness and a sensuality that I don't."

"Yeah, that'll get you stripping in a joint like this," Sarah said sarcastically.

"Don't be bitter."

"I can't help it. If he touches me one more time, I'll die. I'll just die. If I don't get away soon, I'll lose my mind."

"You're stronger than me," Serena said gently. "I could never strip in front of all those men. That takes courage."

"I, ah…the first time was just horrible." Sarah blinked away a tear. "I was scared and humiliated, but… Boyd stood in the back with a knife in his hand, so I played this game in my head where I shut everything out and pretended I was alone. Greg's face was all I'd allow myself to see. It worked and kept me from falling apart." Sarah's voice stilled. "I…I just want justice for Greg. Otherwise I'd never have been able to do it. Still, it's awful and…"

Serena held Sarah's trembling body. "It's going to be okay. What time do they come for you to strip?"

"Between midnight and one," Sarah muttered.

"That gives us time. Ethan will find us. I know he will. Just stay strong."

Ethan, where are you?

AS SOON AS Ethan drove to the club, he saw Serena's car parked in the back. His fear became a palpable thing that almost choked him. Why would she do this? he thought again. He knew the answer. To see Sarah.

He got out and walked to her car. The door wasn't locked, so that meant she'd left in a hurry. When he opened it, a familiar fragrance greeted him. Lavender... *Serena.* His feelings for her were deep. So very deep. *He loved her.* He could finally admit it, and the air rushed from his lungs in a sigh of relief. He'd sworn he'd never fall in love again, but now... He realized that love didn't give a man much choice and he was no longer sure he *wanted* a choice. He just wanted to find her.

Her purse lay on the seat; as he expected, her cell phone was inside. Another sign that she'd left in a hurry. He glanced toward the club—she had to be in there. But how long? And what was happening? There was only one way to find out; he had to go in. He needed a way of doing that without being recognized.

Looking around, he saw an Apex Plumbing truck parked near the back door. Ethan hurried over to it and peered through a window. A shirt lay draped over the seat. He surveyed the street—empty—then opened the unlocked door and grabbed the shirt. "Apex" was embroidered on the pocket, along with the name "Bill." That would work. Fortunately the back of the van was also unlocked, and Ethan removed a small toolbox. He'd return both items later.

At his own truck he removed his hat and changed shirts. The shirt fit well enough, a little loose, but that was okay. He took off his boots and put on some old sneakers he had under the seat. Then he opened the glove compartment and retrieved his gun, placing it in the toolbox. He was ready, but first he had to call Daniel. His friend answered immediately.

"Daniel, it's Ethan."

"I was just fixing to call you."

"Why?"

"I got a payroll list of employees at Teasers. Sarah Welch is listed as a waitress."

"So why'd she go from being a waitress to a stripper?"

"That'll be interesting to find out."

"I'm at Teasers now," Ethan said abruptly.

"What are you doing there?"

"I found Serena's car here. Something's wrong. I'm going in, so get here as fast as you can."

"Dammit, Ethan! I'm way across town. It'll take me a while."

"Just get here and bring some backup."

"Ethan."

"What?"

"Be careful. These guys play for keeps."

ETHAN SAW a baseball cap in his glove compartment and took it out. It was one of Cole's and a little the worse for wear. He straightened it out as much as he could and fitted it on his head. He picked up the toolbox and made his way to the door, where a guard was standing just inside. Ethan held his breath.

The guard pointed down the hall. "To the right, and get the damn thing fixed before we have to open."

"Yes, sir," Ethan said, and walked away quickly doing his best not to limp.

A bathroom door was open and Ethan could hear plumbers talking inside. He slipped up the stairs before anyone saw him. On the landing he saw several doors and a man sitting in a chair reading a magazine, apparently guarding one of the doors. Ethan had to get in that room, and he had to do it fast. He pulled the bill of his cap low and strolled toward the man.

"What the hell are you doing up here?" the guard wanted to know.

"I was told to check the bathrooms—make sure they're working properly."

The man got to his feet with a scowl. ''I better talk to Anthony. He doesn't want anyone up here.''

''Sure.''

As the man made to walk off, Ethan set the toolbox down and caught him around the neck. He knew how much pressure to apply and where. When the man went limp, Ethan lowered his body to the floor, then hurriedly opened several doors until he found a closet. He dragged the unconscious man inside. Finding a bedsheet on a shelf, he ripped it into several pieces and tied his hands and feet and gagged his mouth. He searched the man's pockets until he found the key.

Quietly closing the closet door, he headed for the locked room. The man was guarding it for a reason—and Ethan hoped Sarah was the reason. With a little luck Serena would be in there, too.

Ethan collected the toolbox and inserted the key. He stepped into the room, locked the door and saw that this was a living area and very quiet. Suddenly a redheaded woman in a black robe stepped out of the bedroom.

''Sarah?''

''Who are you?'' she asked weakly.

He didn't have time to respond as Serena poked her head around the door. ''Ethan,'' she breathed, and ran to him.

He caught her, just holding her for a precious second. ''What are you doing here?'' he asked, then held his finger to his lips. ''We have to be quiet.''

She drew back. ''Don't be upset,'' she whispered. ''I just had to see Sarah, but when I came in, they thought I was her and locked me in here, too.''

''You've been in here most of the day?''

''Yes, and we've talked and talked, but, Ethan, you

have to help us.'' In a low voice she told him most of the things Sarah had told her.

He looked over her shoulder at Sarah. ''You saw Boyd shoot Greg?''

''Yes.''

''He's dead?''

''Y-yes.''

Ethan knew Daniel had been hoping to find Greg alive. Now that hope was gone, but he had to let it go and concentrate on getting the women out of here. Which meant he also had to ignore his own reactions to having both Serena and Sarah in the same room. They were so alike, yet so different. It was downright eerie.

He cleared his throat. ''The cops are on their way. We have to wait…and pray that nothing breaks before they get here.''

Serena fingered his collar. ''Where'd you find this get-up?''

''I—'' Voices outside stopped him cold.

Sarah shuddered. ''It's him. I know his voice.''

Ethan did, too. He opened the toolbox and took out his gun. ''Get into the closet,'' he ordered. ''Maybe he won't look there.''

Sarah was trembling so badly that Ethan had to literally drag her inside. He reached for Serena, but she pulled back.

''No, Ethan, if Sarah's not here, they'll search and find us, and they'll kill us before the cops arrive. I can be Sarah. She's in no condition.''

''No, Serena—''

A key turned in the lock, and he made another grab for her, but she evaded his hands and shut the closet door. Sarah sank to her knees, her body trembling severely. Ethan removed his cap and knelt beside her. ''Hang on.

It's almost over.'' She just shook her head, unable to speak. Rage filled Ethan. Whatever Boyd had done to her, he had completely shattered her spirit.

He checked the clip in his gun, then shoved it in place. He stood with his ear to the door, gun ready.

Serena quickly took the pins out of her hair and shook it loose around her. She undid two buttons on her blouse and kicked off her shoes a moment before a man entered the room, a man with dark hair and eyes. She knew from Sarah's description that it was Rudy Boyd and her stomach churned.

''You see the trouble I go through to come and see you,'' he remarked as he locked the door.

''Then don't come.''

His eyes opened wide at that. It probably wasn't something Sarah would say. She had to be careful.

''But when you pull a stunt like you did today, I have to teach you a lesson.''

Serena knew he was talking about the man discovering her downstairs. Boyd assumed Sarah had been trying to escape, and Serena had no idea what he had in mind for her sister now. She just had to stall.

He walked farther into the room and glanced around. ''Is Ric in here?''

''No.'' Serena shook her head.

''That bastard,'' Boyd growled. ''He left the door unguarded, but I'll take care of him later.'' Boyd sat on the sofa and his gaze slid over her; it was all Serena could do not to shudder. ''See you're feeling better. No headache or nausea today.''

''No.''

''Just an urge to run, huh?''

''You can't keep me locked up forever.''

He laughed cruelly. ''Sarah, baby, I can do whatever I

please, and for the moment it pleases me to have you at my disposal.'' The way he said *disposal* sent a shiver up her spine.

He watched her for a moment. ''Since you're feeling so spunky, you can strip tonight, then later you and I will have some private time together. And after that, you'll never run away again.''

Serena bit her lip to still its trembling. ''No, I don't want to.''

He rested his arms along the back of the sofa. ''Ah, Sarah, baby, don't you know by now that you don't get a choice?''

''Please, just let me go!'' she blurted.

He laughed that cruel way again, and it turned her stomach even more. ''So you can run to the cops and tell them how I shot your lover cop? That's never gonna happen, baby. You're not going anywhere until I'm through with you—and the only place that'll be is the morgue.''

An involuntary gasp erupted from her throat. The man was vile as Sarah had said, but she had to keep stalling for time. *Where were the cops?*

He crossed his legs. ''Now, I'd like some entertainment. I've had a very harrowing day. Strip. Show me that beautiful body and all the moves you'll make tonight.''

''I...I...'' She froze, unsure of what to do.

''Just a taste. It'll be much more fun with your clothes on. You're usually in your bathrobe moping around, hoping to reach my compassionate side. Baby, I don't have a compassionate side. Unfasten your blouse before I lose my patience.''

''No, I'm not stripping,'' she said, knowing there was no way she'd take a stitch off in front of him.

Slowly he got to his feet. ''What did you say?'' His eyes were black with anger.

She swallowed. "I'm not removing my clothes."

"I hate sassy bitches." He hit her across the face and she fell to the floor. "Get up, bitch!" he shouted. "No woman refuses me."

At that moment Ethan kicked the door open and came out with his right arm straight, gun in his hand. It was pointed at Boyd. "Don't touch her again." His voice was razor-sharp.

Boyd jerked up. "What the…" His voice trailed off as he noticed Sarah huddled in the closet. Boyd glanced from Sarah to Serena.

"Yup, there's two of 'em, Boyd," Ethan enlightened him. "Serena, are you all right?"

"Yes," she answered. Sarah was crying openly and Serena crawled to her on hands and knees. "Shh," she soothed. "Everything's going to be fine.

Boyd gathered himself, shaking his head. "What are you doing here, Ethan?"

"Glad to see you remember me, Boyd. To answer your question, I'm here to nail a slimeball."

"C'mon, Ethan. I know this looks bad, but—"

"Save it. I was in the closet. I heard every word you said."

Boyd's demeanor changed. "You won't get out of here alive. The place is full of my men."

"The police are on the way and they'll take care of *your* men. It's over, Boyd, and where you're going, there won't be a strip club in sight."

Boyd smiled a crooked smile. "If you think you're holding all the cards, think again."

Ethan frowned. "What are you talking about?"

"If you want to see your sister alive, you put the gun down."

Ethan kept his face blank and his gun pointed at Boyd,

but fear burned his insides like acid. ''What's Molly got to do with this?''

''Well, she became a little too curious, asking questions, and I don't like questions, especially from a woman. I gave her something to calm her down—heroin, to be exact. My man will either inject her with more heroin or release her. He's just waiting for my call.''

''You're lying.'' But Ethan knew he wasn't. He was well acquainted with creeps like Boyd. He also knew that Boyd had just played his ace and it was a good one. *Damn, Molly, why couldn't you have done as I asked?*

''You can either believe me or not. It's up to you.'' Boyd was calm; he obviously thought he had Ethan backed into a corner.

''I need proof.''

''Sure,'' Boyd said, and reached for his shirt pocket.

''Don't!'' Ethan commanded.

''It's just my cell phone.''

''Okay, take it out slowly.''

Boyd removed the phone. ''All I have to do is call and you can hear her voice.''

''Do it, and don't pull any tricks, because I'd just as soon shoot you as look at you.''

Boyd poked out a number, then snapped, ''Get her on the phone, dammit. Wake her up.''

''Serena,'' Ethan said, ''get the phone and bring it to me.''

Serena scrambled to her feet and took the phone from Boyd, then held it to Ethan's ear. Ethan never took his eyes off Boyd.

Ethan waited until her voice came. ''E-Eth-an, h-help me.''

His blood ran cold. ''You bastard,'' he hissed.

Serena lowered the phone and moved away.

Boyd raised both hands. ''All I have to do is say the word and they'll release her. It's up to you. Just let me walk out of here. That's all *you* have to do. Once the police arrive, your sister's a dead woman.''

Ethan didn't have many options, but he'd learned a long time ago never to make deals with people like Boyd. He'd also learned that there was always a way to beat an ace. Now he had to gamble—and gamble big.

''Where's Molly?'' he asked, his voice as calm as Boyd's.

''I'm not giving you that information until you let me leave. You got one minute. It's your choice.''

''Where's Molly?'' he asked again, losing some of his calm.

Boyd's lips thinned to a sneer.

''There's ten bullets in this clip,'' Ethan said. ''I can place each one in a different part of your body. That's *your* choice. Now where's Molly?''

''Hey, Ethan—''

Aiming the gun over Boyd's left shoulder, Ethan pulled the trigger. Boyd jumped and someone started beating on the door. ''Rudy, what's going on?'' Evidently they had orders not to come in.

''Tell them to back off or I'll put a bullet through your heart,'' Ethan said.

''It's okay!'' Rudy yelled.

''Serena,'' Ethan said. ''Pull that big chair in front of the door.''

Serena immediately did as he instructed. At this point, she was just reacting, not thinking.

''You won't get out of here alive, Ethan,'' Boyd said. ''So give it up. Let me go.''

Ethan fired several more shots around Boyd. ''Where's Molly?''

Boyd didn't answer.

Ethan fired again and again, the sound deafening in the confines of the small room. "Where's Molly?"

Boyd flinched, but he didn't respond.

"There's one or two bullets left in the clip. I wasn't counting, but I'm positive I can put one of 'em right in the center of your empty heart."

"You won't kill me," Boyd said smugly. "It's the end of Molly if you do."

"Look me in the eye, Boyd. I'm dead serious."

They stared at each other and Ethan didn't blink or move.

"You're crazy!" the other man bit out.

"You've got five seconds to tell me where Molly is. One, two…" He began to count.

Boyd swallowed noticeably, and Serena saw he was afraid. She fell down by Sarah and held her tight, waiting for Ethan to pull the trigger, waiting for the sound to echo through her brain.

CHAPTER TWELVE

"THREE, FOUR..."

Gunshots echoed in the hall and suddenly the door was rammed open and police officers surged into the room.

Serena let out a long sigh of relief. "It's over, Sarah. The police are here." *Thank God.*

Ethan slowly lowered his arm as they handcuffed Boyd. For the first time he realized his stomach was curled into a hard knot. He took an agonizing breath.

"You'll never find her, Ethan. You just signed her death certificate," Boyd snarled.

The knot in his stomach solidified into a burning rage. He grabbed Boyd by the collar and jerked him forward. *"Where is she?"*

"Dead, Ethan, dead." Boyd laughed.

Daniel caught Ethan around the chest and pulled him back. "Cool off, Ethan."

"You can't make anything stick, Garrett," Boyd snarled. "You got nothing on me."

"How about murder and kidnapping, for starters," Ethan said.

Daniel swung his head toward Ethan. Ethan hadn't meant it to come out this way. "I'm sorry," he said. "Greg's dead. Boyd shot him, and Sarah saw the whole thing. That's why he's had her locked away."

"It's all right Ethan. I figured as much. I was just hoping.'' Daniel turned to one of the other officers. ''Read him his rights.''

''My lawyers will have me out before dark,'' Boyd boasted.

''Keep dreaming,'' Daniel replied.

Boyd grinned at Ethan. ''You'd better hurry up and look for your sister. I'm through with her. She was very useful. She did exactly what I wanted her to, like a good little girl.''

Ethan made a dive for him, but Daniel blocked his path. ''Get Boyd out of here,'' Daniel shouted to his men. They could hear Boyd laughing as he went down the hall.

Ethan jammed both hands through his hair, trying to calm down, trying to think. He quickly told Daniel about Molly.

''Ethan,'' Serena screamed from the closet, ''call an ambulance! I don't think Sarah's breathing.''

''There's one on the way,'' Daniel said as he and Ethan lifted Sarah from the closet and laid her on the floor. Daniel felt the pulse in her neck. ''Damn, I can't find it.'' Daniel opened her robe, exposing her breasts, but he didn't seem to notice. He rested the side of his face against her chest. ''Her heart's beating and she's breathing. It's shallow, but...''

Ethan stood and took Serena in his arms. ''Ethan!'' she cried. ''I...she...''

''Shh,'' he said. ''She passed out, that's all. She'll be fine.''

They heard the ambulance a moment later. Daniel covered Sarah before the paramedics came through the door, and then he gave them details of her condition. ''She's been severely traumatized,'' he finished, and they loaded Sarah onto the stretcher taking her vitals and giving her oxygen.

"I'm going with her," Serena said to Ethan.

"I've got to find Molly," he told her. "I'll meet you at the hospital later."

"Okay." She hugged him and kissed him lightly. "Good luck!" She hurried after the paramedics.

Daniel stared at Ethan. "Where do we even start?"

"Let me think." He closed his eyes, but he was so worried that his mind was a blank. The instant he opened his eyes, he saw Boyd's phone. He snatched it up and pushed "redial." The last number appeared on the small screen. He showed it to Daniel.

"Boyd called this number. Find out who it belongs to and we'll find Molly."

Daniel reached for the phone on his hip and gave succinct instructions. Ethan was already out the door and Daniel followed. Outside they went immediately to Daniel's car. "This could take a—" His phone buzzed.

Daniel answered, then scribbled an address on a piece of paper. "That's the same street as the boys' club."

"That's it!" Ethan said, and told Daniel about Molly's "errand." Daniel put the siren on and they raced through traffic. "You know, Daniel, I don't think Boyd's moving drugs through his clubs. He probably sells them there, but I feel his shipments are going through the boys' club. *That's* why he needed Molly. Unknowingly, she probably picked up drugs for him. God, can't you go faster?"

"I'm breaking the speed limit now."

She has to be okay, Ethan kept thinking. He didn't know what he'd do if she wasn't.

Daniel switched off the siren as he turned onto the street. The address was a house down from the boys' club; it had apparently been converted into apartment units. Daniel caught Ethan before he could jump out. "We can't just go barging in. They'll kill her. We have to have a plan."

Ethan tried to calm down and noticed he still had the Apex Plumbing shirt on. He tapped the name sticker. "I'll pretend to be a plumber again. Just give me back up and make sure there's an ambulance ready."

"It would be best if one of my men or I went in. You're not on the force."

Ethan's eyes darkened. "She's *my* sister and I'm going in."

They glared at each other. "Damn, Ethan, you're making me break the rules."

"So?"

Tense silence, then, "I'm probably gonna regret this. Be careful, okay?"

As Ethan started to get out, he stopped abruptly. "I left my gun and the toolbox back at the strip club." He cursed.

"I have something that might help," Daniel said as he left the car and opened the trunk. Inside was a toolbox, which he handed to Ethan. "I keep it for emergencies." He motioned to the officers arriving behind them, and one came running up. "I need a weapon." The officer produced a pistol and Daniel placed it in the box. Daniel and Ethan met each other's eyes before Ethan headed for the building. He went up the front steps, and knocked at the door. *Be okay, Molly. Please be okay.*

"Who is it?" a man yelled.

"Apex Plumbing," Ethan shouted back.

"Didn't call no plumbing company."

Ethan swallowed. "I got a message to come to this address. It was called in by, let me see—" he took a moment "—Rudy Boyd. That you?"

The door swung open and a jeans-clad man stood there.

He had to be in his early twenties, but there was a lot of hard living on his young face. Ethan didn't see anyone else.

"Ain't got no plumbing problems. Don't know why Rudy called."

"You sure? Have you checked everything? I mean, I'm here and I don't want to have to come back."

"Stay there. I gotta call Rudy. He owns the place."

"Sure," Ethan said, and the man closed the door. Ethan waited, knowing Boyd wouldn't be answering.

The man came back. "He don't answer. Anthony don't, either. That's strange." He seemed to be talking to himself.

"I'm on the clock, kid, so make up your mind. If the owner called, then there has to be a problem."

"Maybe. I guess it won't hurt to check." He opened the door wider and Ethan stepped into the small seedy apartment.

"The kitchen's right there—" he pointed "—and the bathroom's next to it. Make it fast."

Ethan noticed that the bedroom door was closed and there was no one else in the living area or kitchen. But how many people were in the bedroom? He walked into the kitchen, set the toolbox down and opened the doors beneath the sink, all the while keeping an eye on the young man. He had turned up the TV and sunk into a chair to watch a movie, some action film; that told Ethan the kid was probably alone—except for Molly. He saw two officers through the grimy back-door window. It was time. He removed the gun from the toolbox and nodded at them. With the gun behind his back, he moved toward the kid, who was so engrossed in the movie that he didn't even notice Ethan until the gun barrel was placed against his temple.

"Movie's over," Ethan said.

"What the—" the kid tried to jump up, but Ethan pushed him back down as two officers stormed through the back entrance, and Daniel and the others came through the front.

"Who's in the bedroom?" Ethan asked.

"Nobody!" the boy snapped angrily.

Ethan walked toward the door, Daniel behind him. With one blow an officer broke through the door, and Ethan and Daniel charged in, guns ready. And just as Ethan had guessed, the room was empty except for Molly, lying inert on the bed. Ethan ran to her and checked her pulse. She was alive.

"Molly, can you hear me? It's Ethan."

"E-than." She moved her head.

"Hold on, sis, an ambulance'll be here soon." He glanced at Daniel. "Where the hell is it?"

Daniel was on the phone. "There's been an accident. They're having to take a different route, but it shouldn't be much longer."

"Molly," Ethan said gently, but she was unconscious. He noticed a bruise on her face and touched it gently. "That bastard."

"Stay calm, Ethan," Daniel said. "We've got him now."

Ethan stood and curled his hands into fists. "God, I could..." He stopped as he saw two large suitcases with a Spanish name on the side. He walked over, opened one of the suitcases and jerked out a stack of folded baseball uniforms, each wrapped in heavy plastic. He tore the plastic and began pulling out uniform after uniform.

"Ethan, what are you doing?" Daniel demanded.

"There's drugs somewhere in these uniforms, I know it. That's why that bastard had Molly pick them up."

Daniel stared at the pile on the floor. ''It's just uniforms. I think you're on overload.''

Ethan didn't hear him. He kept digging through the suitcase, then yanked out a package near the middle. ''This one's heavier.'' He ripped the plastic and drew back sharply.

''What is it?'' Daniel asked.

''Smell that.'' He shoved the uniform under Daniel's nose.

Daniel's eyes lit up. ''It's opium.''

''Yeah, the fabric is soaked with opium.''

''Well, I'll be a son of a bitch.'' Daniel dropped to his knees and began to go through the uniforms more carefully. When they finished, they had eighteen soaked uniforms. ''I've heard this was done up north, but this is the first I've seen here. After processing, it's probably close to a million dollars' worth of heroin. I've been busting my ass on those strip clubs of his, and all the while he was using the boys' club to get the drugs into the country. And using kids and women like Molly. He's a sorry bastard, and I hope I'm there when they put him away.''

A siren sounded and Ethan went back to Molly. ''The ambulance is here,'' he told her, but she was out, really out, and fear gripped him.

Within minutes the paramedics had Molly on a stretcher; Ethan followed. ''I'm going in the ambulance with her,'' he told Daniel.

''Okay. I've got to stay here and take care of this.'' Daniel patted Ethan on the shoulder. ''Thanks.''

Ethan held Molly's hand in the ambulance, but she remained unconscious. Once they'd taken her into emergency, Ethan called Travis and told him as much as he could. Then he sat tensely in the waiting area. He wondered how Serena was coping and wished he could go find her and be with her, but realized he had to wait. God, he needed to hold her. He could acknowledge that now—he *needed* Serena Farrell.

It wasn't long before Travis strode into the waiting area. "How is she?" he asked anxiously.

"They're flushing out her system. They checked her pupils and respiration and said they thought she'd be fine. They want to observe her for several hours, so she'll be staying the night."

"I can't believe this." Travis sank into a chair.

"He hit her, too," Ethan added. "Her face is bruised."

Travis's features tightened in anger. "God, Ethan, I should have listened to you. You *knew* something wasn't right about Boyd."

"I doubt we could've stopped her from getting involved with him."

"I could have," Travis muttered dejectedly.

"How?"

"By not bringing her here in the first place."

Ethan sighed tiredly. "We all thought it was good for her, and if we're placing blame, I'm equally guilty. I'm the one who told her Boyd was involved in illegal activities. She started asking him questions and that made him angry. If I'd kept my mouth shut, it probably wouldn't have happened. There's enough blame to go around, but let's just concentrate on getting her better and back home."

Travis didn't say anything for a while. Eventually he asked, "What does the redhead have to do with all this? You said there's two of them."

"Yeah, the stripper, Sarah, saw Boyd shoot her boyfriend, who was a cop. So Boyd was keeping her captive and forcing her to strip."

"Then, you were right about that. She *was* doing it unwillingly."

"Yes, and the woman in Fort Worth, Serena, is her identical twin. They were separated at birth. Neither knew she had a sister."

"What a story!"

Ethan stood up. "They'll be taking Molly to a room in a little while. Stay with her. I'm going upstairs to check on Serena and Sarah. I'll meet you in Molly's room."

"Ethan?"

"What?"

"Have you called Pop?"

"No, I'll wait until Molly's better to do that. I don't want him to worry."

"I guess that's best."

"Yeah, see you upstairs."

ETHAN GOT OFF the elevator and walked toward the nurses' station to ask for Sarah's room number, but then he saw Serena in a waiting area. She was sitting on a vinyl-covered chair, leaning forward, her arms wrapped around her waist. Her hair fell forward, partially covering her face. She looked very alone, and his heart twisted with a new kind of pain. The kind that came from loving someone and wanting to shield her from heartache. He knew Serena had more harrowing realities to confront, and what tore him up inside was the knowledge that he might add to her pain.

She raised her head and immediately jumped up and ran to him. She went into his arms as if she belonged there. "Oh, Ethan, I've been so scared. Did you find Molly?"

"Yes, she's in the ER."

"How is she?"

"The doctor says she'll be fine."

"Thank God."

He took her arm and led her back to the chairs. They both sat. "How's Sarah?" he asked.

"They've sedated her and she's resting. The doctor said the same thing Daniel did—that she's been severely traumatized, emotionally, as well as physically, and it will take her a while to get over it."

He brushed back her hair. "And you? How are you?"

"I feel as if I'm watching a horror movie—and at the same time, I'm in it. I keep wanting to turn it off, but I can't. I thought my life couldn't get any worse, but suddenly it's beyond anything I've ever imagined."

He touched the bruise on her cheek. "Boyd's good at hitting women. He also hit Molly. Her face is black and blue."

Serena shuddered. "He's evil, Ethan."

"He won't be hitting another woman—not where he's going."

"He put Sarah through hell. I wish I could help her, but I don't know what to do."

"Just be there for her."

After a brief silence Ethan asked, "Have you called your grandmother?"

"No, I'm not feeling too kindly toward her at the moment."

"She's an old lady, Serena, and she's worried about you."

Her lips curved slightly. "You had to remind me of that, huh?"

"Mmm." He gazed into her eyes. "I met Celia, your other grandmother."

"What's she like?"

"Well, I'd say another concerned grandmother, but one

with attitude. She lives in a Dallas suburb and obviously depends on social security. From the things she said, I gather life has been rough for her and Sarah.''

''I feel so guilty. My life's been so different.''

''You had nothing to do with that,'' he was quick to tell her.

''No.'' She chewed the inside of her lip in thought. ''Now we have to confront our grandmothers and find out the truth. I just don't know when Sarah will be up to that.''

''Wait until tomorrow.''

''Yes.''

Suddenly she had to ask. ''Ethan?''

''Uh-huh?''

''Would you have shot Boyd?''

He gripped the chair with both hands. ''Probably. It's what I was trained to do. But in my experience I found that men like Boyd value their life more than anything else. He'd sell his soul to live. I was gambling he'd fold before I reached number five. If not…'' The words hung between them for a second, then he said, ''I wasn't letting him walk out of that room a free man.''

''What about Molly?''

''I was also trained never to trust a criminal. Any information he gave would probably be false. I knew I'd have to depend on the police department and my own instincts to find her.''

She could only imagine what that cost him, since he clearly loved his sister. It must've been tempting to let Boyd go, but everyone would've lost that way. What Ethan had done took enormous strength. She shuddered at the situations he'd been involved in—life-or-death situations. He was remarkably kindhearted for a man who had witnessed so much; he wasn't jaded or disillusioned, and she loved that about him. She loved *everything* about him—even his stubborn pride.

"Can I ask you something else?"

"Sure."

"Can I stay with you tonight?"

His breath melted in his throat at the entreaty in her voice. *Yes,* his heart said, but his mind was telling him something different. He needed her, but as soon as Molly was better, he'd be going back to Junction Flat and Serena would resume her life in Fort Worth. Their lives would go in opposite directions—away from each other. And that hurt more than he wanted to admit. Last night had been their special moment, a moment out of time, and it was over. When he'd left her this morning, he'd known that. Now she wanted to stay with him. Even though he loved her, he didn't know if it was a good idea. It would make their eventual parting even harder. Because he loved her but couldn't imagine a future for the two of them.

Why wasn't he answering? Serena wondered. Surely he wouldn't say no. She couldn't get through this night without him. His silence hurt; he was putting up walls again, trying to create barriers between them.

"Ethan." Daniel Garrett approached them. Neither had even noticed him. He was holding Serena's purse. "I need your truck keys."

Ethan stood and fished in his pocket.

"I was just down in emergency and they're bringing your sister up," Daniel said. "She looks much better."

"Yeah," Ethan answered. "She's going to be okay."

Daniel turned to Serena, who'd also stood. "I think this belongs to you, ma'am." He handed her the purse.

"Thank you," she replied. "I'd completely forgotten about it."

"No problem. The keys were in the ignition, so we brought your car to the hospital parking area."

"Thank you. I'm usually not that careless; but I was desperate to find Sarah." She held out her hand. "My name's Serena Farrell. I don't think we've been properly introduced."

"Daniel Garrett, and the pleasure's all mine, Serena." They shook hands. "How's your sister?"

"She's resting—and I'd better go check on her." She turned toward the hall.

"Serena." Daniel stopped her. "I know this is a difficult time, but I have to get a statement from everyone, and I'd like to do that first thing in the morning. I'll make it as easy as possible for everyone. The D.A.'s ready to go with this and I want everything in order."

"That's fine with me," Serena answered. "But I'm not sure about Sarah. We'll have to wait and see how she's doing."

"Of course."

"And thanks for my purse and for bringing back my car." She walked away.

Daniel stared after her.

Ethan frowned. "Daniel."

Daniel didn't answer. Ethan snapped his fingers in front of Daniel's face and he swung around.

"Are you coming on to her?" Ethan asked in a disapproving voice.

Daniel smiled. "I was being nice. That's what I do. I'm nice."

"Yeah, right." Ethan sighed in annoyance, not believing that for a moment.

Daniel slapped him on the shoulder. "We hit the mother lode on this one, Ethan. There's gonna be an investigation into the boys' club to weed out Boyd's accomplices. We got him six ways from Sunday."

"And you're feeling pretty damn good, huh?"

"You bet. Now give me your keys and I'll have your truck over here in no time."

"Thanks," Ethan said as he gave him the keys. "There's a toolbox upstairs at Teasers that belongs to Apex Plumbing, and I'll return this shirt to them as soon as I can." He paused, then asked, "Did your boys find the guy in the closet?"

Daniel smiled. "Oh, yeah, Ethan. A very good job." He bounced the keys in his hand. "I'll lock your gun in the glove compartment. That's where you keep it, right?"

"Yes, and thanks."

"No problem," Daniel said, and strolled toward the elevator.

Ethan hurried over to Molly's room, but before he reached it, he met Travis in the hall. "Why aren't you with Molly?" he asked with a scowl.

"Don't give me that look. Bruce is with her."

"What!"

"Yeah. She called him and he came."

"He did?"

"Said he was in town on business."

"That's right, I saw him this morning at your apartment—and Molly wasn't upset."

"She's not now, either. They're talking—rationally—so I thought I'd leave them alone."

Ethan ran a hand through his hair. "Who'd have thought this?"

"Not me," Travis said. "I'm going to talk to my boss at the construction company so I can get tomorrow off. I'll be back here in the morning."

"Okay," Ethan said distractedly, hardly aware that Travis had left.

Ethan continued down the hall. Why would Molly call Bruce? It didn't make sense, but he supposed, years of habit, years of loving, didn't change all that quickly.

He stopped outside the door, eased it open and looked in. Bruce sat on the bed with Molly in his arms. They were kissing. He slowly closed the door. He didn't know what was going on, but they definitely weren't arguing. Still, Bruce was getting married in four months, so what the hell was he doing kissing Molly? Deciding he needed to know, he knocked loudly on the door.

"Come in," Molly called weakly.

Ethan pushed open the door and walked in. Molly looked pale and disheveled and there was an IV in her arm. Bruce stood by the bed, hands shoved in his pockets. "I've got to go," he said abruptly. "I'll talk to you later." He glanced at Molly, then nodded at Ethan and left.

"What's he doing here?" Ethan asked calmly.

Molly played with the sheet. "I'm not sure. When I woke up in the ER, I wanted to see my son. I thought I was going to die and never see him again, but I couldn't tell him how stupid his mother had been. Bruce told me where he was staying, so I called him, instead. I guess he's my connection to Cole. I don't know why I did it, but I did, and he came and I..." She put her hands over her face. "Oh, Ethan, how could I have been so blind?"

Ethan sat on the bed, not sure if she was talking about Bruce or Boyd. But she soon made it clear.

"Rudy was nice to me. He showered me with attention and I needed that, needed to feel those feminine emotions again, but I knew something wasn't right. I just wouldn't admit it. You tried to warn me and I wouldn't listen. I'm not too good at listening, have you noticed?" She didn't give him time to answer. "In the last stages of our marriage, Bruce tried to tell me we needed to spend more time together, that we were growing apart. I didn't listen and he found someone else." She sniffled and impatiently dashed away tears. "You have a very stupid sister."

"And I love her," Ethan said lightly.

She hugged him. He wanted to tell her many things, but he knew that Molly understood she could always count on him. She leaned back. "Tell me everything that happened today. Travis said Rudy had a woman locked up."

Ethan did tell her everything and he didn't spare her feelings. The time for that was over.

"Oh, God, *I* picked up the drugs?"

"Yes. Some of the uniforms were soaked with opium."

"That's why Rudy was telling me how I should act today, what I should wear and how important the uniforms were. I'm the biggest fool who ever lived."

"He fooled a lot of people."

"And the stripper, how is she?"

"She's resting comfortably."

"This is too much to take in," she said weepily.

"I'll go so you can rest.

"Thanks, Ethan, for rescuing me."

"Anytime, sis," he replied. "If the doctor lets you out tomorrow, we can go home to Junction Flat."

"I'd like that. I have to see Cole. I have to see my son."

Ethan kissed her forehead. "G'night. I'll be here in the morning."

He wandered down the hall and sank into a chair. He was tired to the bone and his hip ached. The day was now taking its toll, reminding him of his age and infirmities. Right now, he craved sleep, a chance to recover, to…

He looked up and saw Serena standing there, her red hair shimmering like a halo. She was everything he needed, everything he wanted, and tonight he was too weak to resist. He didn't even want to.

He just wanted her.

CHAPTER THIRTEEN

"ARE YOU READY to go?" Ethan asked.

"Yes," Serena answered, surprised and pleased. Apparently he'd made up his mind.

He took her hand and they walked to the elevators. It felt so right to be with him. Now she could face the night.... But that frightened her, because she'd never needed anyone the way she needed him. Still, she wasn't questioning that right now. She was too exhausted.

In the elevator she said, "Sarah seems better."

"That's good. Each day she'll continue to improve."

"And I called Gran. I didn't tell her about Sarah. We decided we should do that together. I just told Gran I'd had some problems today and that I was fine. I asked her to meet me in the hospital lobby tomorrow."

"So tomorrow's the big day."

"I suppose," she sighed, too tired to give it much thought.

He squeezed her hand.

"How's Molly?" she asked.

"Better, too." He told her about Bruce. Normally he wouldn't have shared that with anyone, but he was breaking a lot of habits with Serena.

"Maybe they'll get back together," she said as they stepped out into the June-warm air.

"I don't know. I'm too drained to even think about it."

He looked at the rows of cars. "Now where the hell did Daniel park our vehicles?"

"There." She pointed to his white truck and her black car.

"We might as well go in my truck," he said. "You can pick up your car in the morning."

"Okay."

They got into his truck, left the parking area and headed for the motel. They didn't talk much; the day's events weighed heavily on both of them. As they drove up to the motel, he said, "I haven't eaten all day except for those doughnuts this morning." He parked the truck. "I'll go to the restaurant and get us some chicken-fried steak."

"Sounds good," she said as they climbed out. "And I'll take a shower. I desperately need one."

He handed her his room key. "Be back soon."

Serena opened the door and went inside, staring at the made-up bed, remembering last night and all the emotion and passion they'd shared. Most of all, she was remembering this morning and how sad she'd felt knowing she might not experience that again. Now she would, and she refused to think beyond that. She had one more night.

She threw off her clothes and went into the bathroom, then stopped dead. Her overnight bag was in her car. Damn, now what? She'd just improvise. She took a relaxing shower and wrapped a towel around her body. She hung her clothes neatly in the closet because she'd have to wear them tomorrow.

As Ethan came through the door with a large paper bag, he stared at her in the towel. Again he thought she was the most beautiful woman he'd ever seen. Sarah looked just like her, yet he didn't have these feelings for Sarah. There was something about Serena that touched his heart and his soul.

"My bag's in my car," she explained when he continued to stare at her.

He set the food on the coffee table in front of the sofa. "If you need it, I can go back for it."

"No, I'll make do," she replied. "Mmm, that smells good."

She sat on the sofa and he joined her there. They ate in silence. Ethan finished his dinner in record time, while she was still picking at hers.

"Aren't you hungry?" he asked.

She pushed her plastic fork through the mashed potatoes. "I guess I'm just so exhausted…."

"Then go to bed and I'll take a shower."

She cleared away the remains of their meal, then removed the bedspread and folded it. She pulled back the sheet and crawled in, leaving the towel on the floor. The bed felt like heaven and her body moved lazily against the cotton sheets. But there was one thing missing—Ethan.

Ethan showered quickly and toweled dry. There wasn't any doubt or indecision about tonight. He wasn't anxious; Serena had cured him of all that and he yearned to be with her. He left the bathroom naked and turned out the lights. He climbed into bed and took her in his arms. Her skin was so silky it felt good just to touch her.

She snuggled against him. "How's your hip?"

"I'm too tired to feel it," he replied. "But holding you, my body's recharging."

Out of the blue she started to cry. All day she hadn't shed a tear, but now they came unabated and she couldn't stop them.

His heart lurched painfully at the sound and he gently turned her onto her back, his hand smoothing the hair from her face. "Serena, sweetheart, what is it?"

''I have a sister—and she's hurting and...I feel so helpless.''

''Shh,'' he said, stroking her hair. ''I felt the same way when I learned that Boyd had given Molly heroin, but there's just so much we can do. Tomorrow will be better.'' He'd also felt that way when he couldn't find her. Knowing she was in that dreadful place was almost more than his heart could take.

''Tonight is better.'' She hiccuped and wrapped her arms around him. ''Thanks for letting me be with you.''

''I don't think you should thank me for that.'' He kissed the hollow of her neck. ''Because I need you just as much.''

''You seemed to hesitate when I asked you, and I could feel you raising a barrier between us. Why did you do that?''

He rested his forehead against hers. ''Serena.''

''Why, Ethan?'' she persisted. ''You believe in honesty, so be honest with me.''

She was right; he had to be honest. ''We've known each other only a few days and we got involved so deep, so fast, that it scares me. I feel most of our...closeness has to do with the situation we've found ourselves in. I told you before that I didn't want to take advantage of that, but I couldn't resist you. Truth is, I don't want to hurt you. Tomorrow I'll take Molly back to Junction Flat and you'll return to Fort Worth to sort out your life. We'll probably never see each other again.''

She swallowed the constriction in her throat. ''That makes me very sad,'' she said in a small voice.

Me, too, he wanted to say, but he had to be completely honest with her now. ''You see, my life is pretty well written for me. I had the marriage and the child, and all of that's behind me. I'll spend my days on the ranch and

I'll take occasional cases, but you have your whole life ahead of you. You're young and deserve a family, but I don't want any more children. I can't put myself through that again."

Now she understood. He had such an aura of strength, but he was afraid of life—afraid of all the emotions that had hurt him. She knew it was useless to argue with him. That stubborn streak of his wouldn't allow him the joy of feeling again. But he *was* feeling; last night proved that. He just wasn't aware of it yet. Would she ever get through that male pride? Well, she decided, there was only one way to do it. She would be patient and she would wait. She wouldn't pressure him, either. She'd just enjoy the time she had with him tonight.

"Your mind seems made up," she said.

"I'm sorry. I should have told you earlier."

"You mean before last night?"

"Yes."

"Oh, Ethan, you don't know a thing about how a woman's mind works."

"No, I was never very good at that part of the puzzle."

"I'll say. The point is, it wouldn't have mattered," she told him. "What we were feeling last night came from here." She laid her hand over his heart.

"And other places," he added with a grin.

"Mmm. Let's not think about anything except how we feel right this minute."

"But, Serena—"

"I'm not upset that you haven't pledged your undying love and asked me to marry you and bear your children—which you've just told me you don't want. But you've assumed I feel a certain way about that and you haven't even *asked* me for my views. But it doesn't really matter because that's much too intense for a two-day relationship.'' She was being blasé, but she had to be or she'd start crying again.

Ethan was stunned. She *wasn't* a one-night stand. She was so much more and he wanted to tell her that—but she was right. Things were too intense.

''Besides, Ethan, I don't know what tomorrow's going to bring, but I definitely don't plan on never seeing you again. You said you'd look me up from time to time to ask for a massage. I'm holding you to that.'' As she said it, her hand trailed across his stomach to his hip.

Tired as he was, his lower body jerked to life. She had that effect on him, and all he wanted to do was love her until… He ran his hands through her hair, holding her face as he kissed her deeply. She moaned and his hands slid from her hair to her breasts and lower. ''Ethan, Ethan.'' His name came out on sighs of pleasure and her hands found his hard flesh, kneading, stroking with soft, gentle movements.

Their hands and lips moved feverishly, as if they both felt an urge to savor as much as they could. His lips found hers again and he pulled her on top of him. Their bodies welded together, flesh against flesh, heart to heart. But it wasn't enough.

''Tonight,'' he murmured breathlessly, ''I'll give *you* a massage—with my lips.'' And he did—tantalizing her to the point of sheer torture. This was what she needed—Ethan's kiss, Ethan's touch—to block out everything but him.

Serena enjoyed the moment as long as she could before her hands touched his body with equal intensity. He groaned and entered her with one driving thrust. The room, the world, disappeared and it was just the two of them on a journey that took them to heights of unparalleled pleasure. Afterwards Ethan pulled the sheet over them and they drifted into peaceful, exhausted sleep.

WHEN ETHAN AWOKE dawn was struggling to creep through the blinds. He had the same feeling as he had yesterday morning—as if he'd experienced something rare. His arms tightened around Serena and she stirred.

"Is it morning?"

"Yes. I guess we'd better get up and get dressed so we can make it to the hospital early."

She stretched languorously. "You know what, Ethan?"

"No, what?"

"You don't limp when you make love."

Amusement flickered in his eyes, then he touched her cheek softly. "Your bruise is fading."

She smiled. "Because you kissed it and made it better."

He met her smile. "I'm glad."

"Kiss me so we can start this day together."

Together. That sounded so right, but he pushed his hopes and desires aside. He kissed her tenderly, with love, holding back his passion. Then he crawled out of bed. "I'll get dressed and buy coffee and doughnuts."

She pushed up against the headboard, watching him walk naked to his carryall. The jagged scar blemished his hip and he limped slightly, but he was handsome, stirring and beautiful to her. He moved with a sureness and a confidence that made his injury insignificant. But she knew that confidence to Ethan was very fragile—where his masculine pride was concerned. With her, though, it wasn't a problem anymore. It suddenly occurred to her that maybe it wouldn't be a problem with other women now, either. She didn't like that idea, not one bit.

The thought made her sound testy as she said, ''Is there a law that we have to have doughnuts?''

He slipped into his underwear. ''No, not that I'm aware of.''

''Then let's stop somewhere and have a good breakfast.''

''Sure,'' he replied. ''If that's what you want.''

She didn't. What she wanted was never to leave this room—or Ethan. But that was wishful thinking, like looking for rainbows. She forced herself to dress and within fifteen minutes they were sitting in a café. Ethan had bacon and eggs, and she ordered fruit and a bran muffin. The difference between men and women, she thought as she ate cantaloupe and strawberries.

Ethan finished his meal and glanced at her. ''You're very quiet.''

''I feel self-conscious in day-old clothes and no makeup.''

''You're beautiful, so don't worry about it.''

And she didn't. There were too many other things to worry about. Like her grandmother, her sister, Sarah, and never seeing Ethan again.

SARAH WAS STILL ASLEEP when they checked her room, so Serena accompanied Ethan to Molly's. Ethan wanted her to meet his sister. There were two men in the room with her when they arrived. Ethan introduced Travis, Bruce and Molly. Molly had short brown hair and brown eyes, like Ethan's. The side of her face was dark with bruises, but she smiled. Serena liked her instantly.

Travis walked up to her. ''I'm real sorry for the way I acted that day in Fort Worth.''

''I'm not sure why men do things like that.'' The words came out before she could stop them.

Travis held up his hands and stepped back. ‘‘I’m not answering that.’’

‘‘It’s all right,’’ Serena assured him. ‘‘I’m sorry. I’m a little on edge this morning.’’

‘‘After yesterday, you have a right to be,’’ Molly put in. ‘‘We should make a list of all the things men do that annoy the hell out of us.’’

‘‘On that note, I’ll leave,’’ Bruce said, looking at Molly. ‘‘I hope you feel better.’’

‘‘Thanks,’’ Molly replied feebly. As he left, Ethan knew that Molly still loved him. He sighed. What was it about love? Why did it have to hurt so badly?

‘‘The doctor was by earlier and he said I could go home today,’’ Molly added quickly.

‘‘That’s great, sis,’’ Ethan told her. ‘‘But you have to give Daniel a statement before we do that.’’

Ethan was leaving. *No, no, no.* It was too soon! As the clock ticked on the wall, Serena knew that her time had just run out.

‘‘I’d better see if Sarah’s awake,’’ she said abruptly.

‘‘I’ll go with you.’’ Ethan followed her down the hall and into Sarah’s room. Serena couldn’t speak. There was nothing left to say.

Sarah was up and sitting in a chair by the window. Serena ran to her and hugged her carefully. ‘‘You’re awake—and you look great!’’

‘‘I feel…human again. I’m free, Serena. I’m finally free.’’ Her voice was high and excited.

Serena held her hand. ‘‘Yes, it’s wonderful.’’ She nodded at Ethan. ‘‘You remember Ethan?’’

‘‘Yes. Thank you for rescuing us.’’

‘‘That seems to be my calling this week—rescuing beautiful women.’’

‘‘Boyd’s in jail?’’ Sarah asked tentatively.

"Yes, and he'll never terrorize a woman again."

Sarah shuddered.

"It's all right," Serena whispered.

"I know, but I guess it'll take a while to lose this fear inside me." She made what seemed to be a resolute effort to change the subject. "Would you do me a favor?"

"Sure, anything."

"Can you get me a hairbrush, toothpaste and a toothbrush?"

"Sure. There has to be a place in the hospital that carries those items."

"It's on the ground floor," Ethan said. "Want me to run down for you?"

"I'll go. It won't take but a minute." Serena wanted to do this for Sarah.

After Serena left, Ethan sat on the bed. "It's so…strange seeing the two of you together."

"I know. The first time I saw Serena, I thought I was hallucinating. I thought my mind had finally snapped." A pause. "I feel weird when I look at her, but she's so caring. I don't know what I would've done if she hadn't found me."

"You've been through a lot. Give yourself some time."

"I suppose," she said softly, and Ethan realized that the hardness he saw in Sarah was only a disguise, protection against the world. She'd probably been building it for years—during all the hard times.

He noticed the way she kept holding her robe together at the neck, as if she didn't want him to see any of her body. He was making her uncomfortable, so he decided it was time to leave.

As he stood, Serena breezed back into the room. "I was lucky," she said. "I didn't have to wait for an elevator and there was no one else in the shop. I'll put these in the bathroom for you."

"Thanks, Serena."

"I'll go call Daniel," Ethan announced.

"That's Greg's boss?" Sarah asked.

"Yes, and he wants to get a statement this morning. Do you think you're up to it?"

Sarah grimaced. "I'm not sure."

"The sooner you do it, the sooner they can build a case against Boyd."

Sarah twisted her hands.

"Just try your best," Ethan suggested.

"All right."

"Good." He turned toward the bathroom. "Serena, I—" He stopped as the door opened and an older woman walked in. Her white hair was neatly coiled at the base of her head and she had an ageless beauty. There were diamonds and pearls in her ears and around her neck; diamonds also sparkled on her fingers. She wore a beige suit with matching shoes and purse. She had to be Aurora Farrell.

Aurora hurried over to Sarah. "Serena, darling, what happened? Were you in an accident?"

Serena froze in the bathroom doorway. Her grandmother was here. Why had she come so early? How had she found this room? And why hadn't she waited in the lobby? Serena wasn't remotely ready for this. Oh, God. She should go to her grandmother, but her feet wouldn't move.

"How did you get undressed so fast?" Aurora said to Sarah, still talking to her as if she were Serena. "I saw you downstairs and followed you."

Sarah didn't say a word.

Aurora turned to Ethan. "And who are you?"

Ethan stepped forward. "Ethan Ramsey. We talked on the phone."

"Yes, yes," Aurora mumbled. She frowned at Sarah. "Serena, why don't you say something?"

"Because I'm not Serena," Sarah said quietly.

Serena emerged from the bathroom. "I'm here, Gran."

Aurora looked from Sarah to Serena. "Oh, oh, oh." She held a hand to her chest, stumbling backward. Ethan quickly shoved a chair behind her, and she collapsed into it. "I hoped this day would never come," she murmured.

"But it has," Serena said, and walked closer. "Meet your other granddaughter. Her name is Sarah Welch."

"I know," Aurora said, to Serena's surprise. "Jasmine named both of you before she died." Aurora raised a hand to her forehead. "I'm not feeling very well. Let's go home, Serena. We can talk later."

"No, Gran, we're gonna talk right here. Right now."

"Don't be difficult."

"I'm going to be a lot more than difficult," Serena said, trying not to lose her temper. "You knew who I was talking about when I mentioned the woman who looked like me. That's why you were so nervous and why you got angry."

"Yes, I knew," Aurora said in a low voice.

"Why, Gran? Why would you keep this a secret?"

"Oh, Serena, don't—"

Almost on cue the door opened, and Ethan saw who it was before anyone else did. Celia, in white Capri pants and a flowered blouse. Ethan moved aside, letting revelations unfold naturally.

"Sarah, are you..." Celia fell silent as she saw the people in the room. "Ohmigod. Ohmigod." She seemed to lose her balance and Ethan caught her by the arm.

There weren't any more chairs in the room so Sarah got up and gave Celia hers.

"What are you doing here, Celia?" Sarah asked.

"The hospital called and said you were… What's going on?" Her eyes were on Serena.

"That's what we want to know from the two of you," Serena said.

"I always wondered what you looked like," Celia said. "It's amazing. You're absolutely identical."

"Yes, we're twins—and no one bothered to tell us."

The silence became almost a tangible thing. It stretched awkwardly—thirty seconds, a minute—but no one said a word. Ethan felt he should leave, yet he also felt he should be there in case Serena needed him.

"Why did no one tell us?" Serena asked sharply, breaking the tense silence.

Celia crossed her legs. "I think I'll let you answer that, Aurora."

"I'm not talking about it," Aurora replied stubbornly.

"That's Aurora's answer to everything," Celia added. "When something becomes unpleasant, she just ignores it."

"You know Aurora?" Serena asked, surprised.

"Yes, we were best friends in high school."

"Oh." Nothing was making sense to Serena. Sarah sat on the bed, letting her do the talking; she seemed almost detached from the situation. Ethan stood a few feet away and that gave Serena strength.

She bit her lip. "Then why do you hate each other so much?"

"Honey, just let it go." Celia waved a hand. "You won't be happy hearing the truth." She glanced at Sarah. "Neither of you will be."

"I think we deserve the truth," Serena told her. "No, we demand it."

"Aurora, aren't you gonna say anything?" Celia asked.

"No." Aurora clamped her lips shut.

"God, you make me so mad. You always did." Celia brushed a speck from her pants. "You see, Aurora and I fell in love with the same boy in high school."

"John never loved anyone but himself, Celia. Haven't you learned that yet?" Aurora's voice fell. "Oh God, I can't talk about this."

Her grandmother's evident anguish touched Serena, but she hardened herself. "What can't you talk about?"

"Serena..."

"Tell me, Gran."

"John Welch is your father."

"Yes, I know that."

"No, you don't understand. John Welch, Jr., is not your father. John Welch, Sr., Celia's husband, is."

CHAPTER FOURTEEN

"WHAT!"

"You wanted the truth and that's it," Aurora said.

The room did a crazy spin, and Serena shook her head. She couldn't think clearly. "Gran, that doesn't make sense."

"It's true, honey," Celia said.

"He must have been much older...and married."

"Yes." Aurora nodded. "She was eighteen and he was forty. With a wife."

"Me," Celia whispered.

"But, but..."

Aurora studied the handle on her purse. "I know it's hard to believe, darling, but there it is."

"Then you're not really my grandmother?" Sarah asked, staring at Celia.

"No, I'm just your father's wife."

"And your son *wasn't* my father?"

"No, honey. John, Jr. died two years before you were born." Celia gave a quick shrug. "It just seemed the best story at the time."

Sarah grew quiet, and so did Serena. Ethan wanted to go to her, but this was out of his hands.

"How did it happen?" Serena demanded.

"This isn't easy to talk about," Aurora said in a hoarse whisper.

"Just tell me, Gran. I need to know and so does Sarah."

Aurora linked her hands together. "When I was in high school, I fell in love with John Welch. John was very active...sexually—I guess that's how you young people say it. I was raised to be a lady and he couldn't understand why I wouldn't sleep with him. I thought he loved me and would wait, but later I found out he was sleeping with other girls, including Celia, my best friend. I was devastated and broke up with him. He got angry, saying it was all my fault because I was frigid." She paused. "Celia was pregnant, and John and Celia got married. After high school our lives went in different directions. I met Henry and we had Jasmine, and life was almost perfect. Then Jasmine reached her teens and she became very rebellious. She even seemed to hate us at times. We gave her everything and she...she didn't appreciate anything. We bought her a Corvette, but she bought herself an old Chevy. That's how it all started."

Serena and Sarah glanced at each other in confusion.

Aurora closed her eyes for a second, then continued. "She took her car into *his* shop to get it repaired. He knew who she was when he saw her, because she looked a lot like me. He showed her lots of attention, worked on her car for nothing. When I found out, I went to see him and asked him to stay away from my daughter. He laughed at me and said Jasmine wasn't as frigid as I was—and I knew he was only trying to get back at me for what had happened in high school. I pleaded with Jasmine, trying to make her see sense, but she wouldn't listen. She said I was jealous. He'd poisoned her mind against us. Henry and I even talked to the police, but there was nothing we could do, since Jasmine was eighteen. They did talk to

John, though, and things cooled down for a while. Then…''

Aurora took a breath. ''Jasmine found out she was pregnant and moved in with him above that awful shop. Henry wanted to go after her, but I wouldn't let him. She'd made her decision. During the next few months she called Henry a couple of times. She wouldn't talk to me. The night she died she'd called and said the babies were due any day. Henry begged her to come home and she said she'd think about it. That was the first time she'd told him anything like that, and we waited and waited, but she never came and…''

Celia cleared her throat and took up the story. ''She and John had had a big argument and she wanted to go home. He tried to stop her from leaving. John didn't take rejection well. She broke away from him and got into the car. He got in, too, before she could drive away. They crashed a mile from their apartment.''

Serena's mind reeled with shock. But everything was becoming clearer. The shame of it all was too much for Gran; that was why there were no pictures, no reminders of Jasmine in the house. Why Gran had never wanted Serena to find out. But still, a few questions needed answering.

Serena looked at Celia. ''Why would you raise a child of your dead husband's lover?''

Celia glanced at Aurora nervously.

''Tell her, Celia. There're no more secrets.''

''I stuck with John through his women and his many affairs. Jasmine was younger than the rest, but I knew he'd eventually tire of her and come back to me. He dropped by the house several times and I told him how crazy he was for getting involved with Jasmine. He said it was his business and to stay out of it. He was thrilled about the babies, though. You see, our son was killed in a motorcycle accident and John, Sr. saw the babies as a second chance at family. And Jasmine had the polished sophistication of her mother. I'm sure that made him feel young again, especially since Jasmine was Aurora's daughter—that was too tempting for John to resist. I think he knew it wouldn't work, because he never asked me for a divorce.''

''Our parents weren't married?'' Serena already knew that, but she had to hear it.

Celia shook her head. ''No, and it didn't seem important to Jasmine. I believe John's main attraction was that he'd once been Aurora's boyfriend—and that he found Jasmine more attractive.''

''I still don't understand why you raised one of her children,'' Serena said.

''The night of the accident I went into the ER. John was still alive and able to talk. The only thing he said was that he was sorry and to look out for the babies, because he knew Aurora wouldn't want them—and he was right.''

''What!''

''Aurora didn't want either one of you.''

''Gran.'' Serena appealed to her grandmother.

''It's true,'' Aurora admitted painfully, twisting her hands. ''I didn't want anything to do with Jasmine and John's babies. I didn't even go to the nursery to see you. I couldn't. My daughter was dead, and that was all I could think about. I told Celia she could have the babies, and I left the hospital. I didn't sleep that night, and neither did Henry. That morning Henry disappeared and I didn't know where he was.'' She paused. ''He went to the hospital to talk to Celia and to see the babies. They made a deal. He would take one baby and she would take the other. When Henry brought you home and I saw your big blue eyes and red hair, my heart just melted. It was almost as if we were bringing Jasmine home again.''

''But what about Sarah? Why didn't you go back for Sarah?''

Aurora swallowed nervously. ''I had my daughter back. That was all I could think. Selfishly I believed it was my second chance—a second chance to raise my daughter. That was a little insane, but it came out of my grief, and after a while I could see that. You weren't Jasmine. You were Serena and you were everything I wanted you to be. By the time I realized that, Celia had already bonded with Sarah. Henry and I discussed it over and over. Should we try to get her back? We finally decided it was best to leave things the way they were. And...'' She looked at Sarah. ''I'm so sorry.''

Sarah couldn't speak and her face was blank.

''It wouldn't have done you any good,'' Celia said. ''I wouldn't have let you take her. She was all I had left of John, and no one was taking her away from me. It's been you and me against the world, hasn't it, honey?''

''Yeah, you and me,'' Sarah muttered, then added, ''but you lied to me. You said you were my grandmother and I had no family left and that's why you raised me.''

Celia grimaced. ''A little white lie to keep you from getting hurt. It seemed the best solution at the time. I was afraid Henry and Aurora would still try to take you, so I moved to Oklahoma, then Arizona. Everyone thought you were my grandchild and I didn't correct them.''

''I should've been with my family,'' Sarah said in a cold voice.

Celia's skin paled. ''Well, honey, it didn't work out that way and I—''

Sarah climbed off the bed and walked into the bathroom.

Serena wanted to go after her, but she couldn't. Her emotions were in upheaval and she felt physically ill. She had to get some air. She moved toward the door; Ethan followed.

She ran down the hall, jarring her hair clip loose. Her copper hair tumbled down her back. It was hard for Ethan to keep up, but he wasn't losing sight of her. A family-gathering area opened onto a patio and that was where he found her, gulping in fresh air.

He went to Serena and wrapped his arms around her. She clung to him. "I can't believe any of this!" she cried. "I've been lied to all my life and so has Sarah. I've had this fantasy in my head of my mother and father being star-crossed lovers, defying their parents to be together. I thought it was romantic, but it wasn't. It was sordid and dirty and..." She turned away and looked out over Dallas. "I wish I'd never asked for the truth. I'd rather live with the fantasy."

"No, you wouldn't. That's why you wanted me to find Sarah."

"I'm not sure anymore, Ethan," she said in a forlorn voice. "Where do we go from here? How do we put our lives back together?"

"Take a deep breath," he said, and tucked her hair behind her ears. "A whole new life is starting. You have your sister now. She needs your support and you'll forge a new relationship. I think Aurora will also forge a bond with her. She seems inclined to do that now."

"I don't understand Celia's part in all this," she muttered. "How could she love John Welch so much that she'd agree to raise his child by his teenage girlfriend?"

"I don't know," he admitted. "But love makes people do crazy things."

"I suppose." She leaned her head against his chest. "I'd better go back."

"Are you all right?"

"No. I feel like I'll never be all right again."

He cupped her face, gently lifting her chin. "Oh, I hate to hear that. I rather like that fighting spirit and determination of yours. It's helped *me* a great deal."

"Has it?"

"Enormously." He kissed her nose. "Your family needs you now."

"And your family needs you," she said tonelessly.

"Yes, I have to see about getting Molly out of this place."

"You won't leave without saying goodbye?" She couldn't keep that note of despair out of her voice.

"No, I would never do that."

"Good." She smiled slightly. "I'll see you later."

As she walked through the door, he thought his heart would never leave her.

WHEN SERENA GOT BACK to the room, Aurora, Celia and Sarah were talking. Aurora immediately came over to her. "Darling, are you still upset?"

"A little."

"I'm so sorry to disillusion you."

"Well, I came here searching for the truth and I found it."

"Oh, darling." Aurora held her for a moment and Serena couldn't help feeling puzzled. She'd never seen her grandmother this strong. As far back as Serena could remember, Aurora was always the one who needed taking care of. Maybe things were changing.

''Sarah was telling us about the ordeal she's been through,'' Aurora said. ''It's just terrible.''

Serena smiled at Sarah over Aurora's shoulder. ''I know, but because of it, we found each other.'' She went to stand beside Sarah. ''Are you okay?''

''Yes, I'm feeling better,'' Sarah replied. ''I've been talking to your grandmother—'' she paused ''—I mean *our* grandmother, and she's invited me to come and stay with you when I leave the hospital.''

Serena looked at Aurora. ''Has she?''

''Yes.'' Sarah frowned. ''That doesn't bother you, does it?''

''No, I think it's a wonderful idea,'' she said, and meant it. She was just surprised Aurora had thought of it.

Serena and Sarah sat on the bed, and Aurora and Celia took the chairs. ''I have to warn you, though,'' she told her sister, ''the bank is about to beat down our door.''

''Oh, my.'' Aurora covered her mouth. ''I was supposed to have a meeting with Mr. Wylie this morning and I forgot all about it. I need to call him.''

''That's all right, Gran,'' Serena assured her. ''I'll do it when we get home.'' Old habits were hard to break.

''No, Serena, you won't,'' Gran said decisively. ''I can't keep letting you take care of everything. I have to start taking responsibility. May I borrow your cell phone?''

This wasn't the Gran she knew, and for a moment she was dumbfounded.

''Serena?'' Gran prompted.

''Oh, yes, yes.'' She grabbed her phone and handed it to Aurora.

Aurora pulled a piece of paper out of her purse and punched in a number. Within moments, she was talking to Mr. Wylie and arranging to meet him the next morning. She returned the phone to Serena.

"Now," Aurora said, folding her hands in her lap. "That's done."

"Gran, tell us about the past," Serena suggested. "We need to hear more."

Aurora stared down at the floor. "I'm not sure what else to say, but I loved my daughter and I wanted her to have everything life had to offer. She, in turn, seemed to hate me and rebuffed all my efforts. We could never get back the relationship we had when she was a child. She was my little princess and I—"

"For heaven's sake, Aurora," Celia snapped. "Take off the blinders."

"What do you mean?" Aurora raised her head, sitting straight in her chair.

"Jasmine was not a doll for you to dress up and parade in front of your friends. She hated it."

Aurora blanched. "That's not true."

"It *is* true," Celia argued. "She never thought she was as beautiful as her mother. She felt inferior. And she hated the way you tried to make her look like you—the clothes, the makeup…"

"How do you know that?"

"She told me."

The words hung in the room for a moment, until finally Serena asked, "You had conversations with our mother?"

"Yes, many times. I wasn't letting John go without a fight. I wanted to know if she loved him or if their relationship was the standard thing John had with all his girlfriends."

"What did she say?" Serena asked with a catch in her voice.

"She said she loved him, but that no one understood

it, especially her parents. I told her she was attracted to John because he was her mother's boyfriend years ago. She admitted it had started that way, but according to her, John thought she was beautiful and special and she didn't have to wear expensive clothes or jewels or drive fancy cars for him. He loved her just the way she was. That was her fantasy—to be loved for herself—and she found it with John.''

A whimpering sound left Aurora's throat before she said, ''You didn't know my daughter, Celia.''

''Obviously neither did you,'' Celia shot back.

Aurora met Celia's eyes. ''I know John took her from me out of spite and you did nothing to stop it.''

''Me?'' Celia's mouth fell open. ''What could I do? John and I were already separated and he was living in the garage apartment.''

''You and John were separated?'' Serena repeated.

''Yes, but that was typical for us. After our son died, we could only stay together a few months at a time. John always came back, though. He and Jasmine fought like hellcats, and in the end all that held them together was the babies. He wanted to be a father again. That was one of John's good points. He loved kids. That's why he tried to make sure the two of you had a good home.''

Silence once again dominated the room.

''Then…he wanted us?'' Serena asked, softly.

''Yes,'' Celia answered. ''I don't know what kind of future they had in mind for you, but both Jasmine and John wanted you.''

''Shut up, Celia!'' Aurora said angrily.

Serena could see that Gran was having a hard time facing the truth—just as she had in years past. She stood up and then knelt by Aurora's chair. Sarah followed suit.

''Gran,'' she said, quietly, ''I don't think Jasmine meant to hurt you.''

''Yes, she did. Oh, yes, she did.'' The words were low and bitter.

Serena patted her clasped hands. ''Let it go, Gran. Let it go.''

''I can't,'' Aurora choked out. ''Jasmine did a terrible thing—but so did I. I forgot about Sarah. I pretended she didn't exist and I didn't want you to know about her. I kept holding on to my secret because...because I didn't want you to know you had a terrible grandmother.''

''You should've told me,'' Serena couldn't help saying, ''if not when I was a child, then when I mentioned the other woman who looked like me. I had a right to know and Sarah definitely had a right to know her family.''

Aurora's eyes filled with tears. ''Sarah, I hope someday you'll be able to forgive me and understand that I was overcome with grief and didn't realize what I was doing. And...''

''And what, Gran?''

''I guess I should tell you everything.'' Aurora reached into her purse for a handkerchief.

''I was wondering if you were ever gonna get around to it,'' Celia said.

Aurora shot her a dark look, but didn't say anything.

''What?'' Serena asked again. ''Please don't keep any more secrets.''

A nerve in Aurora's neck pulsed erratically, and Serena wondered what could cause her such distress. Her stomach felt queasy and she didn't know if she could take much more, but that was the coward's response. She *had* to know the whole truth.

''Gran?'' she prompted softly.

"Before...before Jasmine...died, she signed papers granting custody of the babies to Celia."

It took Serena a moment to assimilate this information. Then she had one question. "Why...why would she do that?"

Aurora couldn't answer, so Celia answered for her. "Because Jasmine didn't want Aurora to raise her babies."

Serena shook her head. "She was planning on coming home, so why wouldn't she want Gran to raise us?"

"Just because she was planning to return home didn't mean she'd let Aurora have her babies. She planned to raise you herself."

Serena still didn't understand. She looked at Celia. "But why would she want *you* to raise us?"

"When John asked me to take them, I was thrown for a loop, and I had to know how Jasmine felt. They let me see her and she said she wanted it, too, and asked the nurse to get the papers. She said her mother would make replicas of herself out of you. She wanted more for her children."

A sound of agony left Aurora's throat, and for the first time Serena truly grasped the bitterness in the relationship between mother and daughter. How did their lives get so out of control? She'd probably never understand it, because she had such a different relationship with Aurora. There'd been occasions when Aurora had tried to dress her up as a miniature version of herself, and Serena had said point-blank she wasn't wearing that and Aurora had accepted her decision. Maybe that willingness to accept Serena's refusal had come from her mistakes with Jasmine.

"Tension and emotions were running high that day." Celia's voice penetrated Serena's numb mind. "I'd agreed to take the babies, but I didn't know how I could afford to raise two kids. I was glad when Henry showed up the next morning. At first he offered to help me financially, but then when he saw the girls, he had a better plan. He said he and Aurora were Jasmine's parents and they should have one of the babies. He didn't know how Aurora would take the news, but he said she'd adjust. I wasn't sure what to do, but I knew I couldn't handle two babies. Afterward I felt good about that decision. With the money Henry gave me, I was able to move out of the trailer park and rent a nice place in Oklahoma City for Sarah and me. Having her gave me a new lease on life. It wasn't easy, but we got by. Separating the twins was the best solution then, but now...now I wish we'd worked out something else."

"What you and my grandparents forgot was that Sarah and I are connected by a single birth, a special bond, and no one had a right to take that away from us," Serena said sternly.

"Darling, don't be angry," Aurora pleaded, seeming to regain some of her strength.

"I'm confused, Gran," Serena admitted. "I don't understand why we weren't told we had a twin. Why did it have to be a secret?"

Aurora and Celia glanced at each other. Celia was the first to speak. "It wasn't initially a conscious decision, but later I didn't want any contact with Henry or Aurora because I was afraid they'd hire a lawyer and try to take Sarah. They were her grandparents. So I stayed away, hoping they wouldn't find us. We only came back to Dallas about five years ago because I had an aunt who died and left me her house."

"And we were afraid, too," Aurora added. "Celia had legal custody and we felt that as long as we had no contact, she couldn't try to get Serena. The secrecy just came about as a way to protect ourselves.''

Serena stood up. ''I don't know what I'm feeling right now. I'm so mixed up inside. But I'm glad Sarah and I have found each other. We won't lose touch again.''

Sarah stood, too, and they embraced.

Celia walked over to them with tears in her eyes. ''Well, I guess I always knew this day would come.''

Sarah turned to her. ''You shouldn't have lied to me, Celia.''

''I realize that now, honey, but back then things were different.''

''I'm trying to understand, but it's hard. All I know is that I need time to be with my family,'' Sarah said.

Celia stroked Sarah's hair. ''Honey, I did what I thought was best.''

''I'm trying to believe that.''

''Try not to think too badly of me, your grandparents or your parents,'' Celia murmured. ''It was a difficult time.'' She paused for a second. ''I hope you feel better soon, honey. If you need me, you know where to find me.''

As Celia hurried out of the room, Serena thought about the power of love. Could it bring forgiveness—and put a family back together?

AFTER TALKING to Serena and Sarah, Aurora left to return home. Serena would bring Sarah once the doctor released her. Daniel arrived soon after with a man from his department, and Serena held Sarah's hand as she told her story. She faltered at times, but eventually everything was down on paper. Daniel had already taken Molly's statement, and he told them the D.A. was building an unbeatable case against Boyd. Since Boyd had killed a police officer, the D.A. was seeking the death penalty. Serena tried not to think about that. She was just glad Sarah seemed so much stronger. The truth about her birth seemed to bolster her, not traumatize her further. Serena knew Sarah had a long way to go before she was herself again, but they'd face the future together—whatever that future held. At the moment it looked bleak. Coping with their financial crisis wouldn't be easy. They had to make some tough decisions and live by them. But the question uppermost in her mind was how she'd live without Ethan.

Her love would now be tested. It would either survive and grow stronger or be overshadowed by their respective family problems. Serena knew in her heart which it would be. She would love Ethan forever. But would he love her?

CHAPTER FIFTEEN

TRAVIS HAD PACKED Molly and Ethan's bags and brought them to the hospital. Ethan had the release papers in his hand. They were ready to go except for one thing: he had to say goodbye to Serena. For a moment his courage faltered, but he had to do it. It would be the last time he'd see her for a while. He gave the papers to Travis.

"I'll be back in a minute," he said.

"Where're you going?"

Ethan didn't answer. He walked out of the room and down the hall to Sarah's room. He stood outside the door for a few seconds, irresolute, then he knocked and went in. Serena and Sarah were sitting on the bed talking. They'd be doing a lot of that in the days ahead, he thought. They'd share their lives and their hopes and dreams. It was a new beginning for both of them and he was happy about that. Then why did he feel so discouraged?

"Ethan," Serena said, easing off the bed.

"Could I speak with you?"

He was leaving. Serena found it difficult to draw a breath. She reminded herself that she had to let him go with as much pride as she could muster.

"Yes, yes," she replied, meeting him at the door.

"I wish you the best," Ethan said to Sarah.

"Thank you," Sarah answered. "And thanks for everything."

Ethan nodded, and he and Serena walked down the hall to the family room without saying a word. Several people were sitting there already, so they went out to the patio.

"Is Molly ready to go?" she asked as she sat on one of the benches.

"Yeah. She gave her statement earlier and now she just wants to go home and see her son."

"I'm glad she's okay." Serena was talking, but she wasn't sure what she was saying. She kept thinking this was it...this was goodbye.

"And Sarah will be okay, too," he said.

"I know." She went on to tell him everything they'd learned. "I can hardly believe that Jasmine didn't want Aurora to raise her children. She chose Celia over her own parents."

"It *is* hard to understand, but their relationship had probably deteriorated so much that Jasmine didn't believe Aurora could love her babies—especially since John Welch was the father."

"I suppose, but to give custody to Celia, her lover's wife, is, well...bizarre."

"Maybe, but Jasmine knew how much Celia loved John and probably felt she'd love his children."

"By another woman?" Her words were sharper than she intended, and she got up and walked to the railing. The wind blew her hair across her face and she shoved it impatiently away. "These people are my parents and I find it difficult to relate to them. I always thought of Jasmine as someone who was spoiled and pampered and misunderstood, but it was more than that. How could she hate her mother so much?"

"Only Jasmine can answer that."

"And that's not going to happen, is it."

There wasn't much Ethan could say, and for several

minutes they were absorbed in their own thoughts. It would take a while for her to adjust to these revelations. He wished he could help her, but that wouldn't happen, either. Their time together was over and he had to let her go…let her live the new life she deserved.

"I'm trying to find something to like about my father, but he seems a selfish, self-centered man."

"He gave you life," Ethan said.

She turned. "Any man could've done that."

"No, if another man had, you wouldn't be the person you are."

"I don't know if that matters."

"Oh, it does, believe me. You wouldn't be such a strong-minded woman with such determination. You'd be different from the Serena I know and I wouldn't like that."

"You wouldn't?"

"No."

Her eyes caught his. "So you like me the way I am."

"Yes," he said without hesitation, and for a moment she was lost in the warmth of his gaze.

Serena knew then that she couldn't let him go without telling the truth about how she felt. It might not be what he wanted to hear, but she had to tell him.

"I lied to you last night." The words came out in a rush.

He raised his eyebrows. "About what?"

She walked back to the bench and sat down. "I said it didn't matter that you didn't pledge your undying love. I lied. It matters a lot."

"Serena," he groaned, an agonizing sound.

"I don't normally sleep with a man after knowing him for only a couple of days. It took months for me to sleep with Brad, and I had to think about it for a long time, wondering if I was doing the right thing. With you, I didn't even have to think. I knew in my heart that it was right. Somehow we connected in a way that's never happened for me before. I realize you think it was too fast and that we were just swept up in the emotions, but it's more than that...for me." She took a long breath. "I love you, Ethan."

He closed his eyes as if he was in pain, then sank down beside her.

She watched as the pain continued to grip his features. "This is exactly what you didn't want, isn't it?"

"Yes," he admitted. "The last thing I wanted was to hurt you, but my feelings for you overshadowed my reasoning."

Hope unfurled inside her. "Then you do care for me?"

"Yes, you're more than a one-night stand to me—much more—but I should have stopped what was happening between us. I'm a man, though, and I selfishly took what you offered."

"You didn't take anything. I gave freely with all my heart."

"I know." He sighed tiredly.

That hope grew stronger. "You don't want children. I understand that, but you haven't even asked me how *I* feel. If I had a choice of spending my life with you or having children, it wouldn't be much of a choice."

"I'm not giving you that choice." His words were quick and final.

She trembled at his tone and all hope died. "Ethan."

He rose to his feet. "You deserve a lot more than I can give you. Right now our emotions are tempered by what we've been through. But in the days to come things will change, and we'll feel differently."

Her eyes narrowed. "Do you really believe that?"

No, he didn't, but he couldn't say the words. He'd taken enough from her. He inhaled deeply. "I have to."

"I see," she murmured, knowing their time was over—for now.

She moved into his arms. He didn't resist—just held her tight. She savored this moment, letting his arms soothe and comfort because she knew there was nothing she could say to change his mind and she had to accept that—for now. She raised her head and stood on tiptoe to meet his kiss. His hands tangled in her hair as the kiss went on and on, both taking as if they needed the closeness as sustenance for the lonely times ahead.

Finally he rested his forehead against hers. "I'm not saying goodbye," she whispered.

"I know."

"I realize we both have family commitments and..." Emotion clogged her throat.

"Yes." He finished her thought. "You have to be there for Sarah. She has the trial to get through, and I have to be there for my family."

He stepped back and removed a piece of paper from his pocket. As he handed it to her, she realized it was a check. "Ethan?" She glanced at his face.

"Just some money to tide you over."

"I can't take money from you!"

"I'll sleep a lot better knowing you don't have to struggle to stay afloat."

And I'd sleep better if you were with me.

"No." She gave the check back to him. "I have to do this on my own without borrowing more money."

"Just keep it," he insisted. "Tear it up if you don't need it."

"*This* isn't what I need." There was a wealth of meaning in her words.

Ethan stared into the blue of her eyes, wanting everything she was offering, but knowing he wouldn't take it.

"Look after yourself," he said quietly, and this time his stubbornness cost him more than he'd ever dreamed.

Serena's heart must have stopped beating. She knew that by the pain in her chest. She drew in a deep breath. "You, too."

They looked at each other for endless seconds, then Ethan turned and left the patio. She wanted to run after him, to plead, to persuade, but she did nothing. She had to let him go. It was what he wanted.

ETHAN FELT as if someone had ripped his heart out, but he kept walking...walking toward the life that was waiting for him. The future didn't hold much hope or promise without Serena. That was the way it had to be, though. Life would go on, and in time her memory would fade—just as her feelings would fade. That was life. They had touched each other's lives in a profound way and now...now he had a hard time believing the drivel in his head. In time he would, though. He had to keep telling himself that.

ETHAN WAS IN A HURRY to leave Dallas. He had to put some distance between him and Serena. Molly was in the bathroom and Ethan waited impatiently. Travis watched him for several seconds.

"Can I ask you a question?" Travis asked.

"Sure," Ethan said absently.

"When I picked up your stuff at the motel, there was a fragrance in the room—like a woman's perfume or scented lotion or something." His eyes narrowed. "Did you have a woman at the motel with you?"

Lavender...Serena.

"Yes," Ethan answered without a second thought. He didn't care who knew. It wasn't a secret, but it also was nobody's business—just his and Serena's.

Travis's eyes almost bugged out of his head in shock.

"What's the matter?" Ethan asked. "You don't think I'm up to that any more? So to speak?"

"No...I mean...hell, it's *you,* Ethan. You don't do things like that." He obviously realized how that sounded and quickly backpedaled. "What I mean is, you're not the type of man who picks up women."

"I didn't pick her up."

"Well, then—"

"That's all I'm telling you," Ethan cut in, glancing at his watch.

Molly came out at that moment and the conversation ended, but Ethan knew Travis was bursting with questions. Questions he wasn't going to answer. At least not today. Travis was supposed to join them at the ranch tomorrow, and Ethan hoped he wasn't planning to start up with *that* line of inquiry again.

The six-hour drive to Junction Flat was long and tiring. Molly slept most of the way and Ethan was glad. He wasn't in the mood to talk. He stopped for gas in Austin and she stirred long enough to drink a Coke. The aftereffect of the drug was still with her, as the doctor had predicted. It was ten o'clock when they reached the low, rolling, sandy terrain of Junction Flat. Ethan gently woke her and she smiled.

"Are we home?"

"In a few minutes," he said. "Thought you might want to freshen up." He turned on the inside light.

"Oh, yes." She grabbed her purse, brushed her hair and put on lipstick. "How do I look?"

"Like Molly."

"Is the bruise noticeable?"

"Yes." No point lying to her.

"I'll have to think of something to tell Pop and Cole."

"How about the truth?"

"Ethan, please don't make me do that. I feel bad enough without telling my son what a fool his mother is."

He heard the pain in her voice and didn't want to cause her any more distress. "Okay, whatever," he relented.

"Thanks, Ethan."

As soon as the truck stopped in front of the house, Molly jumped out and ran for the front door. Ethan followed more slowly. The porch light was on and Cole opened the door, caught Molly and swung her around, then set her on her feet. Suddenly he noticed her face.

"Mom, are you all right?"

"Yes, I'm fine."

"But your face, it's—"

"There was a fight at the club and I got caught in it." She touched her cheek. "It'll heal in a few days."

"You're home awful early," Pop said as he came to the door. "Didn't expect you for a couple weeks or more."

She hugged Pop. "City life was too wild for me and I missed my son."

"Ah, Mom." Cole shuffled his feet.

Molly took his hand and they went inside.

Ethan gave his father a hug, too. "How are things going?"

"Fine," Pop replied. "But you look a little down."

No matter how old he got, his father could always read him. "I'm just tired."

"If you say so."

That was one of the things Ethan loved about Pop. He never pressured him or asked pointless questions. He respected his privacy. He wished Pop and Travis had the same kind of relationship, but at least things were improving. Travis was coming home for the weekend and they needed family time together—to put Dallas behind them.

LIFE WENT ON, as Serena soon discovered. No one knew her heart was broken and no one suspected anything was wrong, other than the usual worries. Sarah came home with her from the hospital, moving into the room Gran had chosen for her. Serena and Gran worked on it for days, trying to make a special homecoming for Sarah.

When Sarah saw the house, her eyes grew big. "You live *here?*"

Serena drove into the garage. "Yes, this is where I was raised."

"It's so...grand. I've never been in a place like this."

"You are now." Serena smiled at her. "And will be—as long as we can stay in the house. We're sisters, and we'll stay together until one of us gets married."

"I'm never getting married," Sarah said quietly. "Greg is dead. He was the love of my life. Now I'm off men completely."

"Me, too," Serena replied. If she couldn't have Ethan, she didn't want anyone.

Gran met them at the door, embracing them with hugs and kisses. They showed Sarah the house, and she seemed overwhelmed by everything. Serena knew she was still dealing with a lot of emotion, but she intended to help Sarah overcome what had happened to her. In the meantime they both had to adjust to their pasts and accept their lives the way they'd turned out. Placing blame wouldn't benefit anyone or accomplish anything. They had to move on and make the best of the situation.

Sarah settled into the house with relative ease, and Serena soon learned that even though they looked alike, they were very different in personality. Serena tried to run two miles every morning before breakfast; Sarah hated exercise and didn't like to get up too early. Sarah was a night person; Serena was not. Serena loved to draw and paint, while Sarah wrote poetry. Serena loved the outdoors; Sarah didn't. But different though they were, they were forming a strong bond. They spent most nights staying up talking, or at least until Serena fell asleep.

Aurora was also forming a bond with Sarah, and Serena soon realized that her twin sister was a lot like Gran. She loved clothes, jewelry and expensive things, and Gran indulged her with Serena's wardrobe and her own. Sarah enjoyed dressing up, which pleased Gran. Gran introduced Sarah to her friends. But Serena sensed a latent hostility simmering in Sarah, and she wondered how long Sarah would restrain it.

Sarah talked to Celia regularly, and Serena knew that helped her twin. Celia was Sarah's past, and although there were still some confused feelings, they cared deeply for each other.

Gran had met with Mr. Wylie and he'd given her an extension on the loan. Serena didn't know what good that did because the money still had to be paid back and the interest was building. They couldn't ignore it. Gran was now focused on Sarah, and Serena was once again left with the worry. It had to be resolved soon, but like Gran, she wanted Sarah to have time in the house—at least until their fool's paradise came to an end.

Serena tried not to think about Ethan. But he was in her every waking thought and all her dreams. Time and distance had not diminished what she felt for him. So often she wanted to call him just to hear his voice, but she resisted, knowing it would only increase the hurt.

She kept Ethan's check in her purse, although she knew she'd never use it. His mere thoughtfulness gave her the added boost she needed to get through each day. The only solution was to sell the house. She had to talk to Gran about that, and soon.

The district attorney was pushing the trial date forward. Both Daniel and an assistant D.A. had been out to the house several times, briefing Sarah, getting her ready to testify. One day Sarah would be fine with the questions; the next she'd break down and say she couldn't do it. Sarah's emotions were teetering on the brink of eruption.

And as close as they were becoming, Serena still wasn't sure how to help her.

DAYS TURNED into weeks, and life was almost back to normal—except for the big hole in Ethan's heart. He kept waiting for Serena's memory to fade, but each day it grew stronger. So he tried to ease his frustration with hard work. That wasn't the solution, either. His body wanted her that much more. Emotions he'd thought he could control were getting the best of him, and he was turning into an unbearable grouch.

Molly was improving, though. She was cooking and cleaning again, even singing around the house. They didn't talk about Rudy Boyd. That subject was forever closed. Daniel had called and said Molly wouldn't have to testify. The D.A. was trying to get a conviction on the murder charge, and if that happened, it would all be over.

Ethan had been wanting to remodel the house. They needed another bedroom and definitely another bath. He hired a contractor and they considered ways to enlarge the place. Molly became interested in the project and spent many hours going over details with the contractor.

The relationship between Molly and Bruce had improved greatly, and Cole was now talking easily with his father. He'd even visited him a couple of times. Ethan was relieved that Molly's experience with Boyd hadn't left her depressed. To the contrary, it seemed to give her a new perspective on life.

Travis was coming home every weekend, making the long trip to spend time with the family. He was even riding a horse again, and he and Pop weren't snapping at each other with every other breath. They were getting along, adjusting, pulling together as a family. Ethan should be happy, but he wasn't. Without Serena life didn't hold much meaning, and that rattled him. He and Beth had been young and in love, but he'd had no problem leaving her for weeks at a time when his job demanded it. So what kind of hold did Serena have on him? Even as he asked himself the question, he knew the answer. He loved her beyond anything he'd ever felt. He'd only known her a short time, but the feeling was real and intense. He realized he couldn't keep lying to himself; he had to make a decision. Could he ask her to live a life without children—or could *he* change? He wrestled with that thought for days and he still didn't know.

SERENA AND SARAH decided to go through their mother's things in the attic. Serena had been unaware that the stored boxes belonged to Jasmine; she'd always thought they were old things of Gran's so she'd never investigated. Now she would—with her twin sister, Sarah. Together they sorted through the photos, toys, clothes and memorabilia that had been part of Jasmine's life. There were baby clothes, kept in plastic, that were almost new, and frilly dresses and Mary Jane shoes. Then there was a box of worn black shirts and pants. Photos also told a story, from a beautiful little girl with pigtails and a big smile to a young teenager with a sullen expression. Rebellion showed on her face, showed that Jasmine was trying to break free from a mother who wanted her to be something she wasn't—perfect.

They sat on the floor with all Jasmine's things around them. Sarah picked up a photo and stared at it. "I want to feel some connection to her," she said in a somber voice, "but it's hard when you've never known someone."

Serena nodded. "John Welch is a stranger to me, yet he's my father and I want to like him, feel something for him."

"Celia talked about him constantly. Of course, I thought he was my grandfather, but he seemed to be a loving person who enjoyed life. He was charming, affable—and had a way with the ladies."

"I think we're well aware of *that* quality," Serena remarked with a smile.

Still staring at the photo, Sarah answered, "I guess we'll never know how they really felt."

"No."

Sarah fingered the photo with a thoughtful expression. "Were you rebellious as a teenager?"

"No."

"I wasn't, either. Celia worked as a waitress and as soon as I could, I started working, too, so I could save money for college. Celia never understood my desire for college, but I had to be more than a waitress. I just thought Celia and I were different, but it was a lot more than that."

Serena was reluctant to say she'd never worked a day

in her life until she'd started teaching school, because she didn't want Sarah to feel any worse than she already did. They both knew that the difference in the way they were raised was an issue. Serena was hoping it would be minor.

"I wish we could've grown up together," Serena said honestly. "I wish we could've had girl talks, pillow fights, discussions about boys and shared our dreams."

"Me, too," Sarah replied sadly.

"But we have each other now, and that's what counts."

"Yes, it does."

Serena picked up several framed photos of Jasmine. "Let's go hang our mother's pictures in the house where they belong."

They made their way downstairs. When Aurora saw the photos, tears rolled down her cheeks.

Serena put both arms around her.

"I don't know how I could've done such a thing," Aurora said miserably. "How could I alienate my own daughter?"

"It's in the past, Gran," Serena said. "So try not to dwell on it."

"How can I not?" Gran choked out. "I let my pain overshadow everything, and I made such bad decisions. I let my granddaughter go when I should've fought for her. I should've done more."

Sarah patted her shoulder. "It's all right, Gran. As Serena said, it's in the past and we can't change it."

There was something in Sarah's eyes that bothered Serena, but she didn't know what it was. She just had a feeling that Sarah wasn't being sincere....

That night the three of them sat on Gran's bed, going through family albums. There were pictures of Jasmine and Serena from the day they were born to schooldays and beyond. Every year was depicted with holidays and family vacations. Aurora and Serena explained each picture as they went through the albums.

"I should be in these pictures," Sarah said in a hard voice.

Serena was taken aback by the tone, and before she could say anything, Sarah grabbed the album and threw it on the floor. Pictures scattered everywhere.

Sarah jumped to feet. "I should have been in those pictures," she repeated, her eyes on Aurora. "But you just forgot about me and went on with your life. You had Serena. You didn't need me. Why didn't you pick *me?* Why did you pick Serena?" Sarah fell to her knees and began to cry, her sobs loud and heartbreaking.

Serena immediately knelt beside her, as did Gran. Serena tried to hug her, but Sarah pushed her away. "Don't…touch me," came out on a sob. "Just leave me alone."

"Listen to me, Sarah." Gran spoke up strongly. "I didn't pick Serena, and neither did Henry. When he got to the hospital, Celia had the babies ready to go. They talked, and after they'd made a decision, she handed him one. We didn't know which baby we had until we looked at the bracelet on her wrist."

"You…didn't?" Sarah asked brokenly.

Serena felt like crying herself; she couldn't stand to see her sister like this. The emotions Sarah had been holding in had finally broken free.

"No, darling." Gran pushed Sarah's hair back. "We were grateful just to have one. It didn't matter if it was you or Serena. Over the years I had to force myself not to think about you, but Celia had legal rights, as we told you, and Henry and I didn't want to rock the boat. We were afraid Celia would take Serena from us. We just couldn't lose another child." Gran wiped tears from

Sarah's face. "I have you now, darling, and you will be in every picture from here on—just like you're in my heart."

"Oh, Gran." Sarah hugged her tightly. "I'm sorry. I'm just—"

"I know, darling. I know."

Serena put her arms around both of them. "I wish I could've changed places with you."

Sarah drew away and looked at her with tear-filled eyes. "You mean that, don't you."

"Absolutely. You're more like Gran than I am. She hates it when I wear jeans and sneakers. She prefers me in heels and tailored suits."

"Yes," Sarah hiccupped. She smiled, then hugged Serena. "I just lost it there for a minute. I don't know what came over me, but I don't blame you for what happened. I don't blame anyone. It's just..."

"Hard to accept," Serena finished for her.

They laughed and stood up, hand in hand.

"I think someone's going to have to help me," Gran said from the floor. Serena and Sarah quickly lifted her to her feet.

Gran put an arm around each of their waists. "No matter what happens in the future, we'll be together," she vowed.

"Together," they chorused.

After that, Sarah bounced back with vigor. The depressed look was gone from her eyes and she smiled a lot. Serena was relieved and knew that Sarah was well on her way to recovery. Life was promising and full of delight, except for the problems that hung over them—their financial situation and the trial.

During the day, Serena was busy drawing cards and

painting and trying to raise everyone's spirits. At night she held her pillow, wishing for Ethan and his strength and love. She needed him, but he didn't need her.

How long could she go on without him?

CHAPTER SIXTEEN

THE TRIAL WAS SCHEDULED for the first week in September, and the D.A.'s office had Sarah ready to testify. As the day drew near, Sarah was nervous, but Serena was certain she'd be fine.

Serena had returned to her teaching job and was gone most of the day. Sarah was adjusting to life with them; she planned to resume her college classes the following term.

One Sunday morning Serena opened the door to find Daniel on the doorstep.

"Can I speak to you alone, please?" he asked. Sarah would be testifying on Monday, and Serena wondered if plans had changed.

She led him into the living room. Sarah and Gran were still sleeping. "What is it?"

He glanced around. "Where's Sarah?"

"She's upstairs. Why? Do you need to talk to her?"

"No, I need to talk to you."

"Oh." She sat on the sofa and he took a seat in a straight-back chair.

"You're making me nervous," she murmured when he said nothing else.

He clasped his hands. "I'm sorry. I'm trying to think of a way to say this without having you go ballistic on me."

Oh, God. Something's happened to Ethan. Her skin grew clammy and her stomach churned.

"Is this about Ethan?" she asked.

"Ethan?" Surprise showed on his face. "No, why would you think that?"

"Then Ethan's okay?"

"As far as I'm aware." He shot her a knowing glance. "You and Ethan have... I'm not sure how to word this."

"Me, neither," she replied frankly. "But Ethan and I became very close and I..."

"You love him," he said.

"Yes," she answered without hesitation, meeting his eyes.

"Well, I'll be damned." He smiled. "That Ethan's a lucky man."

If only Ethan felt that way.

"Thank you," she said, not sure what else to say. "What did you want to talk about?"

"The trial."

"Has something happened?"

"Yes, we heard something from a snitch who brings us information from time to time. Sometimes what he says pans out, sometimes it doesn't, but this isn't one we can ignore."

"What did he tell you?"

"Boyd's hired someone to make sure Sarah doesn't testify."

"What?" She could feel the blood draining from her face.

"We have to take it seriously, so we'll be moving you and Sarah to a safe place until she testifies. You'll be guarded twenty-four hours a day."

"Me, too?" she asked in a puzzled voice.

He waved a hand. "You're identical. The hit man could

mistake you for her, and we don't want to take any chances.''

''Oh.'' She thought about that for a second, and her mind was in a short-circuit state. How much more could they handle? She couldn't think about that; they had things to do. She turned to Daniel. ''Do you want us to go now?''

''Yes, I have a police escort outside that will take us to the station. From there you'll go in an unmarked car to an undisclosed hotel.''

''And you want me to tell Sarah?'' she guessed.

''Yes, ma'am, but be assured I'm gonna make damn sure nothing happens to either of you. We have an expert team that'll guard you. They do this all the time, so they know what they're doing.''

She stood. ''Thank you. I've already made arrangements at the school to take off two days to help Sarah through this.''

''That's good. She'll need you.'' He paused, then asked, ''Is there somewhere your grandmother can spend the night? I'd rather she didn't stay here, either.''

''Yes, she can visit with one of her bridge friends.''

''That would be best.''

''Okay,'' she replied. ''I'll tell Sarah and Gran and we'll pack.'' She was afraid to even speculate what Boyd might do. She just had to be there for Sarah.

Daniel glanced at his watch. ''I'll give you an hour. Is that enough time?''

''Yes,'' she said briskly.

''I'll be waiting outside. Try not to worry.''

Serena climbed the stairs on feet that felt numb. Just when she thought life couldn't get any worse, it did. *Oh, Ethan. Please come back. I need you.*

ETHAN WAS HAVING a bad night. He'd spent too many hours in a saddle today and his hip was bothering him. He turned onto his left side; that didn't help. He lay on his back; that didn't help. What he needed was Serena. One touch, and all his aches and pains would leave him. He closed his eyes and imagined her hands on his body, soothing, lulling him… With a deep sigh, he crawled out of bed and reached for his robe. He didn't want to wake anyone so he didn't turn on any lights as he walked into the den.

As he settled into his easy chair, so many thoughts clamored in his head. Had Serena moved on with her life? Had she forgotten him? He had regular conversations with Daniel, who said the family was adjusting. He wanted to ask more but never did. God, why couldn't he…

He raised his eyes and saw Ryan's picture on the wall. It was clearly illuminated by the moonlight streaming through the window. A smiling three-year-old with his hair neatly combed. His hair was never neat because he was too active—too alive. But he *wasn't* alive. Ethan felt the pain as it ripped through his chest the way it always did when he thought of Ryan—but this time it was different. He was thinking about more than his death. He was thinking about his life, about the years he'd had with Ryan. Ethan wouldn't change those for anything. He remembered how it felt to be a father, that wonderful all-consuming emotion. He'd loved it. He'd loved everything about being a father. So why—

He heard a noise from Molly's room and his thoughts stopped. Was she crying? He hadn't heard her cry lately, but something was going on with her and he didn't know what. It could just be that she missed Cole since he'd gone off to college. But he wasn't far—in San Antonio—so she could see him anytime she wanted. No, that wasn't it. He frowned. She'd missed another meeting with the contractor and couldn't explain why. She said she'd just forgotten, but he didn't buy that. Another thing—Bruce's wedding was three weeks away and she hadn't said a word. He knew this was hard for her even though she and Bruce were now able to talk. She seemed fine during the day, but at night she was probably crying herself to sleep.

He got up and knocked on her door. "Molly, are you okay?"

There was a muffled sound. He opened the door slightly and stared in complete shock. Molly was tying the belt on her robe, her hair in disarray. Bruce sat on the bed hurriedly trying to pull on his slacks. Ethan turned and walked back to the den, flipping on lights as he went.

Molly and Bruce followed. "Let me explain," Bruce said.

Ethan sat in his chair. "I don't think I want to hear it." He looked at Molly. "He's getting married in three weeks. Did you forget that?"

"I called off the wedding," Bruce explained quickly.

"What?" Ethan was dumbfounded.

"He told me this morning," Molly said. "That's why I missed the meeting with the contractor. We—" she glanced shyly at Bruce "—had lunch and—"

"I don't need to know." Ethan raised a hand to stop her.

"I couldn't stay away from her so I came out here tonight," Bruce mumbled.

"He tapped on my window—just like he did when I was teenager—and I let him in." Molly grinned like the girl she used to be.

Ethan stood. "Well, I'll let you two handle your own lives."

"Ethan, we made some stupid mistakes," Bruce said.

"But we found our way back to each other. Please be happy for us."

"I am, but what about your fiancée?"

"Things have been rocky between us since I came back from Dallas and I finally had to be honest with her and with myself. I still love Molly."

Molly linked her arm in Bruce's, and Ethan could see how happy they were. "Have you told Cole?"

"No," Molly said. "We're going to the university tomorrow to tell him."

"He'll be thrilled."

"We think so, too." Molly leaned into Bruce and he wrapped his arm around her.

"And Pop?"

Pop came through the front door at that moment. "What about Pop?"

Ethan stared at him, puzzled. Pop had gone to bed hours ago. Now he was waltzing through the front door in his dress shirt and hat. Where had he been so late?

"What are *you* doing here?" Pop asked when he saw Bruce.

"Now don't get upset," Molly begged as she went over to him. "Bruce called off the wedding and we're getting back together."

Ethan waited for an eruption, but none came. Pop glanced from Molly to Bruce. "It's about time. I'm not pleased that you hurt my daughter so badly, but I was wondering if you two were going to be foolish enough to throw away everything you had together."

Ethan felt the urge to check Pop's driver's license to make sure this man was Walt Ramsey. He was acting calm and...happy. That wasn't like him.

"Thanks, Pop." Molly kissed his cheek.

"From your attire, I take it Bruce is spending the night," Pop mused.

"Well, no." Molly hesitated. "We plan to tell Cole in the morning, but Bruce came tonight to—"

"Sneaking through the window again, Bruce?" Pop asked with a grin.

"Yes, sir," Bruce admitted. "But I'll put the screen back on."

"You'd better."

Molly took Bruce's hand, and they went back into the bedroom and closed the door.

"That's great," Pop said.

"Yeah, it is." Ethan rubbed his chin. "Where've you been tonight?"

"That's my business," he snapped as he walked past Ethan.

Ethan sniffed. "Aftershave. This is getting mighty interesting."

"All right!" Pop turned back quickly. "If you have to know, Alma Ferguson invited me over for apple pie and a movie."

Ethan eyes widened. "Really?"

"Yes, really. I'm not too old to enjoy a woman's company."

"I didn't say you were. I just don't understand why you had to sneak out."

Pop shoved his hands in his pockets. "I feel kind of silly."

Ethan threw an arm around him. "But it's wonderful to be silly sometimes, don't you think?"

"Yeah, son, I do."

Ethan said good-night and went to his room, a smile on his face. His family could take care of itself. Now he had to think about his own future, and that meant... Serena.

ETHAN GOT UP EARLY, had a bag packed and was ready to go in minutes. He thought he should call her first, but he'd rather see her in person. He couldn't still the excitement inside him, nor did he want to. He heard the phone ringing, but he knew Molly or Pop would get it. It was probably Bruce, anyway.

"Ethan, it's for you," Molly called.

"Who is it?" he shouted back. He didn't want to talk to anyone; he was in a hurry to leave.

"Daniel somebody."

Daniel. Ethan immediately yanked up the phone, knowing in his gut that something was wrong. "Daniel, what is it?"

"Calm down, Ethan," Daniel said. "We have everything under control."

"What do you mean?"

"We got news through a snitch that Boyd was gonna have Sarah taken out so she couldn't testify, but like I said, we have everything under control. Serena and Sarah are heavily guarded in a safe place until Sarah gives her testimony. I thought I should let you know, since you have a personal interest in this."

"Why didn't you call me sooner?" Ethan demanded.

"Hell, Ethan, I'm not supposed to be calling you now. This is police business, and if anyone finds out I could be in a lot of trouble. But I owe you, and I know Serena wants you here."

"Has she asked for me?"

"No, but I think she needs you."

Ethan closed his eyes for a brief second. "What time does Sarah testify?"

"This morning. Probably around eleven."

"Dammit, I don't know if I can make it. I'll catch the first plane out."

"Okay, but don't worry. There's no way anyone can get to them."

He'd heard that story before. All too often, criminals found a way. "Daniel, don't you let *anything* happen to them."

"I won't."

Ethan hung up and called the airport. His luck was in. A plane was departing for Dallas in forty-five minutes. He took Pop with him so Pop could bring his truck back; he didn't have time to bother with parking if he was going to make the flight.

As they drove into the airport terminal, Pop said, "I don't guess you're gonna tell me where you're going in such a hurry."

Ethan grabbed his bag. "To do one of those silly things we talked about last night." He got out. "Wish me luck."

"Always, son. Always."

ETHAN MADE THE PLANE. His heart was in his throat the whole flight and time seemed to stand still. He knew Boyd would do anything to save his own life; once Sarah was no longer a factor, it would be hard to get a conviction. He, too, had heard Boyd confess to the murder, but his word wouldn't carry as much weight as Sarah's. And if Sarah's life was in danger, so was Serena's.

By the time the plane landed, his stomach was one hard knot. He had only the bag he'd carried on, so he didn't have to wait for luggage. He rented a car and headed straight for the police station, where he met Daniel coming out.

"Wow, you made it here fast," Daniel said in surprise.

Ethan glanced at his watch. Ten o'clock. "Yeah. Have you moved them yet?"

"No, that's what we're fixing to do," Daniel replied. "And Ethan, you have to stay out of our way."

"I won't interfere, Daniel, but I'm coming with you." The tone of Ethan's voice was unyielding.

"Fine." Daniel sighed. "I guess an extra pair of eyes and ears won't hurt."

"What's the plan?" Ethan asked as Daniel drove away.

"We have them at an older hotel that's being renovated. Several floors are empty so there aren't a lot of people around. We'll move them from the hotel to the criminal-courts building. The car will stop at a sally port to the courthouse and Sarah will be escorted to the Criminal Investigations Department and booked in as a witness. It's heavily secured and everything should go off without a hitch. We're gonna get them in as quickly and safely as we can."

It didn't take long to reach the hotel, which had underground parking. Daniel waved to two men at the entrance. "There's one way in and one way out," Daniel said. "No one gets in here unless we know about it." Daniel parked some distance from the glass doors that led to a foyer and a set of elevators to the upper floors.

They left the car and surveyed the parking area. There were several cars and three men were walking through the garage. Ethan recognized them as police officers. Lights burned dimly from concrete beams, and the water pipes of a fire-prevention sprinkler system were visible. The massive garage was eerily quiet.

"The cars have been checked and the place is secure," Daniel said.

Ethan nodded. "I figured that."

Daniel was on the radio. "Bring 'em down."

A car drove up and Daniel motioned for it to stop. He talked to the driver, another police officer. ''They're coming down. As soon as you see them, drive to the glass doors. I don't want them out in the open.''

''Yes, sir,'' the man replied, and they waited.

Suddenly a piercing sound tore through the silence.

''What the hell's going on?'' Daniel barked into his mike, but Ethan knew it was a fire alarm. So did Daniel.

''Goddammit,'' Daniel muttered. ''This isn't a coincidence.''

''No, it's a diversion,'' Ethan answered, knowing Boyd was pulling out all the stops. ''We'd better do something and fast.''

Daniel shouted into his radio. ''Abort and go back. It's too dangerous.''

''Sorry, sir,'' the officer said. ''We're in the elevator coming down.''

''Is everyone okay?''

''Yes, sir.''

''Tighten your guard on the women. Don't let anyone near them.''

''Yes, sir. We're proceeding with caution.''

''Goddammit,'' Daniel said again. ''Those elevators will come directly to the bottom floor and shut down.''

Ethan looked quickly around. Sirens mingled with the wail of the alarm. Uniformed and plainclothes police were waiting for Daniel's order. The quiet now felt tense, and every officer was poised and ready.

Daniel was on the phone talking to his superiors. ''We have to abort,'' he was saying. ''It's much too dangerous now.'' Pause. ''Yes, I understand. Yes, sir.''

Daniel scowled. ''We have to continue with the plan.''

''This isn't safe,'' Ethan said. ''Anyone can see that.''

Daniel shook his head. ''The D.A. wants Sarah to testify. He's not gonna let Boyd win this thing.''

''Daniel...'' But Daniel wasn't listening. He was on the radio shouting orders. This was going to happen one way or the other. Ethan had to get to Serena. He had to be there when she got off the elevator. That was his only thought.

He knew Daniel was trying to keep everything under control, but he sensed things were spiraling in the wrong direction.

''Everyone in position?'' Daniel bellowed into the mike. ''Okay, let's do it.''

Ethan removed his revolver, checked his clip, then released the safety. He kept his eyes on the glass doors, waiting and staying alert for anything unusual. Through the glass, he could see the elevator doors opening. Two armed officers stepped out, looked around, then motioned to the others in the elevator. Ethan started toward them, as did Daniel and several more officers.

''Okay,'' Daniel said into the receiver. ''Bring the car up. Now.''

Ethan got a glimpse of Serena and Sarah, two beauties, one in navy and the other in deep purple. The woman in purple was Serena. He knew it immediately and his heart beat a little faster at the sight of her. She was safe.

As Ethan moved aside to let the car ease by, the sound of screeching tires vied with the clanging alarm. He glanced toward the entrance and saw the speeding car a split second before everyone else did. He also saw the automatic weapons sticking out of the windows.

All his years of training kicked in and he leaped into action. ''Serena,'' he screamed as he made a dive for Serena and Sarah. They went down under a barrage of gunfire. Ethan felt something burn his arm, but he kept Serena and Sarah pinned to the concrete as the gunfire exploded around them.

The impact of the car crashing into a concrete pillar echoed through the gunfire, then everything became quiet. Deadly quiet—even the alarm had stopped. Ethan's left arm was on fire and he knew he'd been hit. Had Serena been hit, too? He wanted to ask. But he couldn't move.

He heard Daniel's voice. "Everyone okay?" Then it all went black.

Serena's chest was locked tight with fear, but she realized Ethan was with her and the fear eased. She raised her head and stared at him. He lay so still—and then she saw his arm, the ripped flesh and the blood oozing from it. "Ohmigod!" she cried as fear renewed its grip. "Ethan's been hit! Ethan. Ethan." She scrambled to her knees, hands trembling against his pale face. *Oh, God. No, no, no.*

Ethan lay on his stomach and Daniel checked his body. "It's just his arm, thank God. Get Serena in the car. Now!" Sarah had already been whisked away.

"No," Serena said. "I'm not leaving Ethan."

The people and the voices floated around Ethan in a hazy mist, but one thing was clear—Serena's touch, her voice. *She was okay.*

"You have to go with Sarah," Daniel insisted. "She needs you. I'll give you a police escort to the hospital when this is over."

"I'm not leaving Ethan," Serena repeated stubbornly.

Ethan knew she had to go to court. They'd been through too much to let Boyd win now. "Serena, go...please." He thought he said the words; he wasn't sure. All he could see were blinking red lights and he knew he was losing consciousness. He recognized this feeling. He'd had it before.

"Ethan, I—"

"Go" was all he could manage.

"Ethan! Ethan!" Serena cried as two officers literally dragged her into the waiting car.

An ambulance pulled up, and Daniel knelt beside him. "Hang on, buddy," he whispered, then he turned to an officer. "How many are down?"

"Five, sir, but everyone's alive."

Daniel closed his eyes briefly. "Make sure things are taken care of, and I'll be at the hospital as soon as I can."

"Yes, sir."

Daniel hurried to the passenger side of the waiting car.

"We can't leave Ethan here," Serena told him angrily.

"They're taking him to the hospital," Daniel replied. "That's where he needs to be right now."

"I should be with him. I'll never forgive you for this, Daniel."

"I'm not sure I'll forgive myself," Daniel answered quietly.

Serena glanced back at the scene around them. A bloody massacre. Along with Ethan, several officers were down and the shooters lay dead, sprawled half in and half out of the crashed car, which was riddled with bullet holes. Blood was everywhere and Ethan lay in a pool of it. Tears ran down her face. *Please be okay,* she prayed as she watched paramedics load his body onto a stretcher.

They had a police escort, sirens blaring, all the way to the courthouse. The car pulled into a sally port, and Serena and Sarah were escorted down a corridor to the Criminal Investigations Department, where Sarah was booked in as a witness. Armed officers were everywhere—on the alert.

As they waited, Daniel called the hospital. He turned

to Serena. ''They're taking Ethan to surgery. The bullet did some damage to his arm.''

Serena swallowed the painful lump in her throat. ''But he's alive.''

''Yes. I'll drive you over there as soon as Sarah testifies.''

Serena breathed in deeply, drawing fresh air into her starved lungs. ''I didn't mean what I said earlier, Daniel. I'm just...''

''It's okay—'' He stopped speaking as Sarah was escorted to the corridor. Daniel and Serena followed. From there, they went to the appropriate elevator, which would take them to the designated courtroom. The court officials weren't ready for Sarah, so they had to wait in a small room.

When they entered it, Sarah grabbed her and they hugged tightly. ''How's Ethan?'' Sarah asked shakily.

''He's in surgery.''

''You should be with him.''

''I know, but Ethan wanted me to go with you,'' Serena replied, wiping away a tear and noticing that her hand was covered with blood and there were dark stains on her suit. Agonizing pain tore through her and she fought for control. She knew what her sister had to do, and she had to make sure Sarah did it. ''You have to nail Boyd today,'' she said urgently. ''He's hurt too many people.''

Sarah trembled. ''I'm so scared.''

''I'll be sitting in the courtroom sending you all my strength. Just keep thinking about what he did to Greg, to you...and Ethan and those other poor officers. You have to do this, Sarah, and you have to do it with courage!''

''I...ah...''

''You've been through this a hundred times with the D.A. Just do what they've asked you to do.''

Sarah remained silent, staring at the floor, and Serena added, "Don't fail on us now. Their case depends on you."

Sarah raised her head, eyes bright. "Oh, I won't fail," she said in a resolute voice. "I'm putting Boyd away just like he put Greg away."

Daniel opened the door just then. "You ready?" he asked, looking at Sarah.

"I'm ready," she replied, and Serena knew that she was. Rudy Boyd's day of reckoning had come.

CHAPTER SEVENTEEN

ETHAN WOKE UP in a hospital room. His left arm was bandaged and there was an IV in his right. His body burned with a familiar pain; he'd been here before. He wondered how badly hurt he was this time.

A doctor stood by the bed writing on a chart. "Mr. Ramsey, good, you're awake."

"How's my arm?" he asked, and his voice sounded hoarse.

"The bullet ripped through the left medial upper arm, but missed the bone. A surgeon was able to repair the damage."

Damage. "How bad is it?" His voice was even hoarser.

"You've had some vascular injuries, but the surgeon will explain all that."

Vascular. "My arm will be weaker?" *No. No.*

"For now, but time will be the telling factor. All in all, you were lucky. You'll be sore and stiff for a few days, but exercise will help that. Tonight we want to get enough antibiotics in you to stave off infection, and the surgeon wants to evaluate you again tomorrow."

"When can I go home?"

"That's up to the surgeon."

"Thanks," Ethan mumbled. He was feeling so many things, experiencing so many reactions—and he didn't like any of them. He remembered another time and the long road back to recovery. *Not again,* was all he could think.

"There's a young lady in the hall dying to visit you," the doctor said. "Are you up to it?"

He didn't have to ask who it was; he knew. Serena. He'd waited forever, it seemed, for her to come, but now he was having second thoughts. He didn't want her to see him like this.

No, no, no, not now. I need time, went through his head, but what he said was yes.

When the doctor opened the door, Serena walked in and stopped abruptly. Ethan was so white that for a moment her heart stilled, then she ran to him. "Are you okay?"

"Yes," he nodded, trying to avoid that look in her eyes—that look of sympathy.

She smoothed his forehead with her hand. "I was so worried. I..." She couldn't go on. The trauma of the day had caught up with her and she needed to be close to him. She dropped her purse, resting her face against his.

"Oh, Ethan," she whispered in an aching voice.

Ethan breathed in her sweet scent, but something in him was shutting down. He could feel it. He needed to be alone. He didn't know how badly his arm was injured and he had to have time to adjust before he could be himself again. And before he could be with her....

"I'll leave you two now," the doctor said, sauntering out of the room and quietly closing the door.

"Are you in pain?" Serena asked.

"A little," he admitted.

"Oh, Ethan," she said again, and kissed his chin, his cheek, then his mouth, where she lingered.

"Serena," he groaned, and unable to resist, he kissed her softly in return.

"It was awful," she murmured. "I saw you, and in that split second all hell broke loose. The gunfire was terrifying, and when I saw you'd been hit, I thought I'd die. Then Daniel wouldn't let me stay with you." She shook her head. "I don't want to live through that again."

"Don't think about," he said. "Did Sarah hold up okay?"

"She did beautifully. Boyd didn't rattle her at all. She told her story and how Boyd shot Greg in cold blood. Boyd's attorney tried to shake her, but she never faltered. I was so proud of her."

"It's over, then."

"Yes, and not soon enough." She looked at the bandage on his left arm. "The doctor said the surgeon plans to evaluate you in the morning and they want to monitor you during the night."

"A casualty of taking a bullet, I suppose," he answered in a monotone.

"I can stay here with you," she offered, but he was already shaking his head.

God, no. He couldn't deal with that.

"I'll sleep most of the night," he said. "Medication does that to me."

She tucked her head beneath his chin. "Did you hurt your hip when you hit the concrete?"

"Stop worrying about me," he said, and there was tension in his voice she didn't like. He was pushing her away.

"I don't think I can," she told him honestly.

"Then don't make me feel worse than I already do."

She immediately straightened. "I'm sorry." She blinked back tears. "I didn't mean to do that."

"Serena..." He hated the way he was acting, but he couldn't stop himself.

"It all right, Ethan." She bit her lip to still the trembling. "It's been an emotional day. I'll come and see you in the morning."

"They notified Travis, and I'm hoping to go home in the morning."

Home. He was leaving again. And without her. She reached down to pick up her purse and took a moment to collect herself. "Well, then, I'll leave you to get your rest." She slid the strap of her purse over her shoulder. "Have a safe journey." She forced herself to walk out of the room.

"Serena," she heard him call, but she didn't go back. She couldn't. She couldn't take any more of this today. What had she been thinking? He'd made perfectly clear how he felt, but she was just so ecstatic that he was alive, that he was going to be okay. And he *was* glad to see her; she knew he was.

She pushed the elevator button much harder than necessary. As she waited, she suddenly understood. *His pride.* That stubborn pride of his. He didn't want her to see him when he was hurt, when he was vulnerable and wounded. That was why he'd sent her away—and even though she understood his motive now, a motive rooted deep in who and what he was, she felt angry. Furious. Didn't he know what love meant—needing to be with that special person during good times and bad? Leaning on the one you loved when you were weak and knowing that love would always see you through—no matter what.

She wasn't sure what to do now. Give up or fight for what she wanted?

The elevator doors opened and Travis stepped out. "Oh." He seemed startled to see her. "Serena, isn't it?"

"Yes."

"Have you been to see Ethan?"

The doors started to glide shut and she caught them. "Yes, he's down the hall and to the left. Second door, I believe. I forget the room number."

"How is he?"

"He's fine," she answered, and walked into the elevator. She couldn't talk; she had to escape and sort through her feelings—and the rest of her life.

The doors closed on Travis's puzzled face.

ETHAN SHUT his eyes in excruciating pain. It wasn't his arm or his hip. It was his heart, and he'd just shattered it into so many pieces that it seemed impossible to mend. Impossible to heal. He wanted her and needed her. He'd come here to be with her, but he couldn't stand letting her see him like this—like a…like a helpless cripple. But now he'd hurt her; he could see it in her eyes when he snapped at her. That look would be with him for a long time.

He was used to being strong, not needing anyone. He took care of himself and everyone else. He didn't need anyone to take care of *him,* except… Her blue eyes swam before him and he felt a crack in that wall of pride. He remembered the night she'd touched him and made him whole again. The crack spread, encompassing every part of him, and he knew beyond anything he'd ever known that he was always going to need Serena. *Oh, Serena, please forgive me. Please.*

Travis entered the room, a horrified look on his face. "My God, Ethan, what happened?"

"I'm sure you heard it on the news."

"You were in *that* shooting?"

"Yeah."

"When are you gonna learn to stay out of the line of fire?"

''When criminals stop trying to outsmart the cops,'' he replied. ''Did you see Serena in the hall?''

''Yeah, and she seemed upset.''

Ethan winced. He wished he could go after her and apologize, beg her to come back, but for now he was stuck here.

''I talked to the surgeon and he said you might be able to leave tomorrow, but he has to check you in the morning and you have to have therapy for your arm.''

''That's good,'' Ethan murmured, relieved. He wanted to get out of this hospital. ''The doctor I saw earlier said I had vascular injuries, but a surgeon did some repairs. With time it should heal. I don't know how long that'll take, though.''

Travis shoved both hands through his hair. ''You have to stop all this P.I. work. I can't handle much more of this. If anything happened to you...'' His voice gave out.

''I'll be fine,'' Ethan assured him. ''I just need a place to crash for the next few days.''

''You know you can stay at my place.''

''Thanks.''

Travis sank into a chair and was thoughtful for a second. ''Ethan?''

''Uh-huh?''

''Was Serena the woman at your motel?''

''Yes.'' He didn't see any reason to lie. But he was glad when Daniel walked in, interrupting the conversation.

Travis stood up quickly. ''I know you two want to talk, so I'll go get your clothes and stuff from the nurses and clean up the apartment.''

''My bag's in the rental car at the police station. The keys should be with my things.''

''Okay,'' Travis answered, then squeezed Ethan's right

hand. ‘‘I’ll see you tomorrow.’’ At the door he turned. ‘‘Do you want me to tell anyone at home?’’

‘‘No,’’ Ethan said. ‘‘I’ll do that myself.’’ He didn’t want Molly and Pop fussing over him. He didn’t want *anyone* fussing over him. He didn’t…couldn’t… God, would he ever get past his pride?

‘‘Okay,’’ Travis said.

Daniel dropped into a chair and buried his face in his hands. ‘‘I screwed up, Ethan. Bad.’’

‘‘You just underestimated Boyd’s desire to beat a death sentence. You had all your bases covered. There was nothing more you could’ve done. Some criminals find a way to slip through. You know that.’’

‘‘I keep thinking that those two beautiful women could be dead if you hadn’t acted so quickly.’’

‘‘A reflex action I learned a long time ago. I just happened to see the car before you did.’’

‘‘They figured they could race through, right in our faces, get the job done and disappear before the cops could gather their wits. They timed it perfectly. Another one of their guys was in the hotel and set off the fire alarm.’’

‘‘How did they know where Sarah was being kept?’’

‘‘A leak,’’ Daniel answered angrily. ‘‘We have a God-damn leak in our department. That’s how Boyd always knows when we’re coming and why every raid turns up nothing. Boyd got to someone, and I won’t rest until I know who it is.’’

Ethan shook his head. ‘‘A bad cop is a disgrace to all of us.’’

‘‘Yeah,’’ Daniel agreed. ‘‘The mission should’ve been aborted, but my superiors and the D.A. wanted Sarah there today—no matter what. I don’t think they even cared that her life was in danger. They just wanted to get Boyd.’’

"You did, too," Ethan reminded him.

"But not at the cost of human life."

The silence stretched for a moment, then Daniel got to his feet. "I'm getting too soft for this job. I should've gone into the family business like my father begged me to."

"You'd be bored out of your mind."

"Probably, but I'd be able to sleep at night."

"Did you lose anyone today?"

"No, thank God," Daniel said. "Their car plowed into the officers at the entrance, and they have some broken bones. The officers walking behind the women were hit by gunfire, but it was minor, thanks to their protective vests. Another was hit in the shoulder. Everyone's gonna be fine."

"Your men were able to take out the shooters in a hurry. That's what made the difference."

"Yes, once we knew… God, Ethan they were just kids. One nineteen, one twenty. Some of Boyd's faithful soldiers—willing to lose their lives for him. The other one's only eighteen. The officers subdued him without incident and he's talking his head off. He was sneaking around in the hotel, waiting to set off the alarm to divert our attention. Those boys had orders from Boyd to kill both women to make sure they got Sarah."

"It didn't work, though. Sarah testified, anyway, and now there's nothing Boyd can do."

"But at what cost?" Daniel stared at Ethan's arm.

"A small price to pay," he said, trying to make light of it. "I'll be fine, Daniel, so get that look off your face."

"I'm just glad you're alive, man."

"Me, too," Ethan replied, and realized that he was. So he had to work at getting his arm stronger. That was no reason to act the way he was acting. *Serena. Serena.*

"I wish you could've seen Boyd's face when Sarah walked into that courtroom. The judge ordered a recess because of the shooting, and when court convened, Boyd had this smug expression on his face—like he knew he was home free. Then Sarah walked in and he knew it was over."

"Sorry I missed that."

Daniel glanced around. "Where's Serena? I told her I'd give her a ride home."

Ethan swallowed the bitter taste in his mouth. "She left already."

"Really?" Daniel raised his eyebrows. "Thought she'd be here until they let you out."

Ethan clenched his teeth, pretending he hadn't heard.

Daniel watched him for a moment. "Ethan," he finally said, "try not to mess something up that could be wonderful for you."

Ethan didn't say anything. He couldn't.

"I'd better check on my guys," Daniel said. "I'll be back tomorrow."

Ethan let out a long sigh, knowing he'd already messed up. Now he had to figure out how to make it right.

THAT NIGHT Serena and Sarah sat in the den eating popcorn and watching an old movie. Gran had already gone to bed. Neither twin was really watching the movie, though. The day had been so traumatic they couldn't concentrate. They just wanted to relax, to talk a little. Serena told Sarah about Ethan and how he'd hurt her.

"Men are so predictable," Sarah said.

"What do you mean?"

"They have to be the stronger ones, never letting their pain show. Greg was just like that. When we first started dating, he fell and bruised his knee while he was apprehending a drug suspect. He was hurting like hell, but I could see he didn't want me to fuss over him, so I pretended nothing was wrong and that seemed to make him happy.''

Serena curled her feet beneath her. ''Ethan's like that, too, but it's much more extreme because of his hip injury. He's very sensitive about that, but I thought we'd finally gotten around it. I just want to be with him—to help him through this.''

Sarah pushed popcorn around in the bowl. ''What was Ethan doing in Dallas today? I'm glad he was here, but I was just wondering.''

Serena sat perfectly still. She hadn't even thought of that. What *was* Ethan doing in Dallas? ''I don't know,'' she said slowly. ''We never had a chance to talk about it.''

''I'll bet he came to make sure you were okay.''

''If he did, he didn't act like it when I saw him.'' Serena gazed at the TV, but all she saw was Ethan's face. ''I love him, Sarah, but when he shuts me out it hurts, and I can't figure out how to deal with him.''

Sarah placed the bowl on the coffee table. ''Oh, I think you'll find a way. Now let's go to bed. This nightmare's over and maybe tonight I can sleep.''

As they walked upstairs, Serena couldn't help thinking that *her* nightmare was just starting—a life without Ethan.

THE NEXT MORNING Serena called the hospital to see how Ethan was doing. The nurse said he was much improved, which meant he'd be leaving for Junction Flat today. She ignored the urge to call his room; Ethan didn't want her there and she had to respect his wishes, no matter how hard that was. The next move was Ethan's. She'd decided that last night. She had to wait for him to want her—but oh, God, she wasn't good at waiting!

The doorbell rang and she went to answer it, since Sarah was still sleeping and Gran had left for an early bridge tournament. She opened the door to find a man and woman, somewhere in their late fifties, standing there. Serena had seen them in the courtroom yesterday, and she wondered nervously what they wanted. Were they reporters?

"Can I help you?" she asked in a guarded voice.

"We're sorry to disturb you, Sarah," the woman said. "We're Marion and Fred Larson, Greg's parents."

"Oh." Serena was shocked for a second, then quickly composed herself. "I'm Serena, not Sarah, but please come in. I'll get Sarah."

"Thank you," they said, and followed her into the living room. "My, you look so much alike," Marion added. "Did Greg ever see you together?"

"No, but that's a long story and I'm sure Sarah will tell you about it. Have a seat and I'll go get her."

Serena rushed upstairs and found Sarah curled up in a chair with Greg's picture in her hand. "You're awake," Serena said, not entirely sure how to tell her.

"Yes, I just got through talking to Celia. She seemed upset when I called her last night and I wanted to reassure her that I'm okay."

Serena sat on the bed facing her. "I'm sure she's relieved that your testimony is over."

"Yeah." Sarah touched the photo. "I did it for Greg. As scared as I was, I had to do it."

"You did great." Serena smiled. "And speaking of Greg, there's—"

Sarah raised her head. "What?"

"His parents are downstairs."

"They are?"

"They want to see you."

Sarah jumped up and ran to the mirror. "Oh, I look awful." Frantically, she began to brush her long hair. "Maybe I should put my hair up."

"You look fine. Come on."

"Are these slacks okay?"

"They don't care what you're wearing. They just want to talk to you."

Sarah bit her lip, frowning. "I've never met them. You have to come with me."

"Okay, let's go." Serena got up from the bed. "They're waiting."

They walked downstairs and into the living room. Sarah stepped forward to shake their hands, but Marion hugged her and Sarah hugged the older woman back.

"It's so good to meet you in person," Marion said. "Greg talked about you a lot."

"He talked about you, too."

"Thank you for what you did yesterday," Fred said. "I know it was hard for you."

"Yes, and I'm sorry you had to listen to it."

"I had to know the truth about his death," Marion said in a quavering voice.

"I loved him very much." Sarah brushed away a tear.

"He loved you, too. He told us many times, and that's why we're here."

"Please have a seat," Sarah invited. As everyone sat, she asked, "How did you find me?"

"That nice Mr. Garrett told us. At first he was reluctant, but when we explained what we wanted, he agreed."

"I'm glad, because I've always wanted to meet you. Greg said when this case was closed we would. But..."

"I know. It wasn't easy for us, either, but when our

son became a policeman, we knew we might have to face this one day.'' Mrs. Larson reached in her purse for a tissue and dabbed at her eyes. ''I'm sorry,'' she said. ''It's still painful, but that's not why we're here. Greg was very proud of the way you were working so diligently to get your degree. He didn't make much on a cop's salary, but he wanted to help you.''

''He did that by just being there.''

Mrs. Larson dabbed at her eyes again. ''I'm not saying this right. You see, Greg had a life-insurance policy and we promised that if anything happened to him, *we'd* carry out his wishes and offer you financial aid.''

''Oh, no.'' Sarah shook her head. ''That's not necessary.''

Mr. Larson stood and handed Sarah a check. ''The policy was for five hundred thousand. We're giving you half, like he stipulated. We're using part of ours to start a scholarship fund in his name at SMU.''

Sarah stared at the check. ''No, I can't. Use this for the scholarship fund, too.''

''Sorry, Sarah,'' Mr. Larson said. ''It was my son's last request, and I couldn't live with myself if I ignored that. Take the money and try to find some happiness in this world. That's what Greg wanted.''

Sarah still wouldn't take the check, and Serena could see she was having a difficult time accepting their generosity.

Mr. Larson laid it on the coffee table and Mrs. Larson rose to her feet. ''It was nice meeting both of you.'' They turned and walked from the room, and Serena hurried to let them out.

When she returned, she stared at Sarah, who seemed to be locked in her own misery. Touching her arm, she asked, ''Sarah, are you okay?''

Sarah raised her head. ''How can I do this? It's money from Greg's death. How can I accept it?''

''Because Greg wanted you to have a better life. He knew how much getting your degree meant to you. It's a gift from him.''

''It is, isn't it?'' Sarah's eyes took on a vibrant glow and she picked up the check. ''I know exactly what I'm going to do with this.''

Serena smiled. ''Pay for your education?''

''Yes, that, too, but I have something else in mind.''

''Like what?''

''Pay off the note on this house.''

''Oh, no, Sarah.'' Serena was horrified. ''I've been meaning to talk to Gran, but with everything that's been happening, I haven't had an opportunity. We need to sell the house. That's the only way to get out of this financial mess.''

''No, Serena, you don't get to make that decision,'' Sarah insisted. ''I'm not saying that to be mean, but I never got to grow up here, to live with Gran and with you. Now I can make that happen—and I will.''

''Sarah, think about it,'' Serena begged. ''This money could open up a whole new world for you.''

''The world I want is right here.''

''Give yourself some time—that's all I'm asking.''

''I don't need time,'' Sarah said. ''I know exactly what I want, and the first thing we're going to do is get our great-grandmother's earrings back.''

''What!''

''You heard me,'' Sarah said. ''I'm going upstairs to finish dressing, then I'm heading over to the bank while you go to the jeweler to see where we stand on the earrings.''

''I'm sure he's sold them by now.''

Sarah raised her eyebrows. ''Are you with me or not?''

''Sarah.'' She sighed her frustration.

They looked at each other. Finally Sarah said, ''Greg wanted me to be happy, and getting this family out of debt will make me extremely happy. Please, Serena.''

''Okay.'' Serena gave in reluctantly.

Sarah ran up the stairs. Serena sank onto the sofa with a groan. This had to be the real Sarah. The one willing to take risks with a vivaciousness that was hard to resist. Serena just hoped they were doing what was right for everyone—especially Sarah.

CHAPTER EIGHTEEN

ETHAN SPENT the morning with the surgeon and a therapist, who evaluated his arm. He could move his hand, and the doctor said he had good circulation to his fingers. His strength had diminished considerably, but the therapist was confident that in time he would get it back. Afterward he felt better about the whole situation. He made arrangements to see the therapist again, then called home and told them what had happened. Molly was horrified; at Ethan's request, Travis hadn't told the family and they hadn't been listening to the news. Pop asked when he was coming home and he said he wasn't sure. And he wasn't. He was so restless that he couldn't think straight. He had to call Serena or he wasn't going to have any peace at all. He picked up the phone before he could change his mind.

He took a swift breath when she answered. "Serena, it's Ethan."

Serena heard his voice loud and clear, and she almost dropped the phone. "Ethan." His name came out in a whisper. *How are you? Are you in pain? Do you need me?* The questions hovered on her lips and she wanted so desperately to know, but she clamped her lips together.

"I called to apologize for last night," he said.

"You did?" Her chest felt tight.

"I lose my manners when I've been shot. I didn't mean to snap at you."

"Serena!" Sarah called from upstairs.

Serena put her hand over the receiver and called back, "I'll be there in a minute."

"Is someone with you?" Ethan asked when he heard the muffled sounds.

"It's Sarah," she explained, and before she could stop herself, she told him about the money. She wanted to share everything with him.

"That *is* good news."

"Yes, for her it is, but she's insisting on paying off the note on the house. And remember I told you about my great-grandmother's earrings, which I had to sell so the bank wouldn't foreclose?"

"Yes."

"She's planning on buying them back. I just wish she'd take the time to think this through. This is *her* money and I want her to do what's best for her."

"Maybe she is."

"What do you mean?"

"What she probably needs now is to feel a part of your life and your grandmother's. By helping you, she'll gain confidence and a sense of security. A sense that she belongs."

"I suppose," Serena said, still not sure.

"I'd better let you go. I…just wanted to apologize and let you know that my arm will be fine."

Suddenly Serena became angry. She'd held in all her emotions, all her questions, trying not to mention his arm because it would distress him. But now that he was on the mend, it was okay to talk about his injury. The words spilled out unheeded. "Since you know you're going to be a whole man again, you can talk to me. Is that it? Well, things don't work that way, Ethan. You hurt me last night and an apology doesn't make it better. I just wanted to be with you, offer you some comfort and thank you for saving our lives, but you didn't want me near you. You didn't want me to see you in that condition. What you don't understand is that it wouldn't have mattered to me if you could never use your arm again. All that mattered was that you were alive. And—'' she swallowed ''—all I needed was *you,* but you let your pride take over and you pushed me away. I'm having a hard time with that, because to me, love means accepting people as they are. But you didn't even think about *my* feelings, and that's what hurts the most.''

''Serena—''

''I've got to go,'' she said abruptly, ending the call. She wrapped her arms around her waist to stop the trembling. What had she done? She immediately picked up the phone again, then slowly put it down. She had to stand by what she'd said. If Ethan felt anything for her, he'd find his way back to her. Then they could talk more rationally. *But what if he didn't?* No, she—

''Serena, are you ready?'' Sarah's voice broke into her thoughts.

''Yes.'' She met her sister at the bottom of the stairs.

''I thought maybe you should go to the bank with me, since this Mr. Wylie knows you.''

''Okay,'' Serena agreed unenthusiastically.

Sarah caught her arm. ''What's wrong?''

''Ethan just phoned.''

''That's good, isn't it?''

''Yes, but I lost my temper and told him how hurt I was about his behavior last night.''

''And from the expression on your face, I'd say you regret doing that.''

''Yes. No. Oh, I just want to go to the hospital and see him, but I can't do that, either.''

"Why not?"

"Because Ethan has to make the next move."

Sarah lifted an eyebrow. "Is this a chess game?"

Serena smiled and it felt good. "No, it's a puzzle, and Ethan hasn't got a clue about how all the pieces fit."

Sarah swung her purse over her shoulder. "Does any man ever know?"

"No," Serena answered, "even when we keep giving them hints."

"Don't despair," was Sarah's advice. "I have a feeling that someday Ethan will find the piece that'll make it all fall into place for him—and you."

Serena hoped so, but she didn't know how long she could wait for that to happen.

ETHAN STARED at the phone but resisted the urge to call her back. She had a temper to match that red hair, and he deserved every word she'd said. His pride had gotten in the way once again. He had to do something about that, and he had to do it now. There was no other option.

Travis came through the door with Ethan's release papers. "Let's go," Ethan said as he got off the bed.

"Hey, what's the hurry? We have to wait for the nurse to bring a wheelchair."

"I don't need a damn wheelchair. I can walk." Before he'd finished speaking, a weak feeling overcame him, and he realized he had to accept that he was hurt and needed help. He couldn't keep pushing people away. Well, his new attitude would begin with getting into that wheelchair, which he did as uncomplainingly as he could manage.

In the truck Travis said, "The apartment's all clean and ready for you."

"Thanks, but I need to do something first."

"What? You've just gotten out of the hospital. The doctor said you should go home and rest. And you have to be careful the wound doesn't start bleeding."

Ethan closed his eyes briefly as Travis pulled into traffic. "Don't argue with me. I have to do this."

The urgency in Ethan's voice reached Travis. "It must be important," he muttered.

"It's the most important thing I'll do in my life."

SERENA AND SARAH spent the morning at the bank. Mr. Wylie was shocked but very pleased that Sarah wanted to pay off the note. Since the check was so large, they had to wait until it cleared, but Sarah set up an account and made arrangements to return and finalize the deal. From there they went to the jeweler's—and discovered that the earrings had been sold. Disappointment overwhelmed Serena; she hadn't realized how much she wanted the earrings back. Subconsciously, she supposed, she'd dreamed of wearing them on her wedding day—to Ethan.

They went home and told Gran what they'd done. Gran was happy about the money, but refused to let Sarah do such a thing. However, Sarah said it was a fait accompli and Gran might as well accept it. Gran began to cry then, and they all sat on the sofa crying together. In a strange way, those moments drew them closer than anything that had happened before. They were a family now.

LATER THAT AFTERNOON Mr. Hudson, the jeweler, called. He said that the man who'd bought the earrings was interested in selling them. He'd purchased them as an investment. He gave Serena the address where the buyer was staying, which was a hotel.

Sarah insisted she go and see what the man would take

for them. Serena was reluctant, but in the end she went. It couldn't hurt to ask, she kept telling herself.

The hotel was one of the most elegant in the city, and on the ride up in the elevator, she felt like forgetting the whole thing. For some reason, though, she didn't turn back. She walked down the carpeted hall to the room number Mr. Hudson had given her. On the door was a plaque that read Honeymoon Suite. Mr. Hudson must have given her the wrong number. The man couldn't possibly be on his honeymoon and wanting to sell jewelry. Could he? Unless he'd bought them for his new bride and then changed his mind. No, that seemed too odd.

Since she was here, she might as well find out. When she knocked on the door, it opened slightly. It was unlocked. She poked her head into the room and said, "Hello. Anyone here?"

No answer.

She pushed the door wider and walked in. The room was a sitting area, very plush, done in reds, browns and dark green. A huge vase of roses sat on the coffee table. She could see there was something else on the table, but couldn't tell what it was. Serena moved to back out of the room; she didn't want to intrude on such a private affair.

Suddenly the bedroom door opened and Ethan stood there, his left arm bandaged and in a sling. She blinked; she had to be seeing things. It *couldn't* be Ethan. He was on his way to Junction Flat by now. But he was still standing there and he was smiling.

"Ethan?" she said tentatively.

He walked farther into the room. "Yes, it's me."

He looked much better. His color was back and... Her eyes narrowed. "What are you doing here?"

"I wanted to apologize in person." His voice was low

and filled with so much emotion that her heart wobbled crazily inside her.

"You said that loving means accepting people the way they are, so I'm assuming you're willing to accept me and all my faults, even my pigheaded pride."

Serena was sure she was dreaming, because nothing he said was making sense. But she enjoyed every word coming out of his mouth.

"You were right that I didn't want you to see me in that condition," he went on. "I felt weak, incapacitated, and I want to be strong for you. But I've finally realized that's not always possible. From time to time I have to bend and let someone I love care for me, fuss over me." He took a deep breath. "That's not easy for me to admit."

Her heart was beating so fast she had trouble thinking, but she had to be clear on one thing. "Someone you love," she repeated in a trembling voice. "Is that anyone I know?"

"Oh, yeah." He walked close to her and gazed into her eyes. "She's standing in front of me."

The breath she'd been holding solidified in her throat. She moved into his right side and he slipped his arm around her. "Ethan, I love you so much it's making me crazy." She kissed the warmth of his neck. "I'm sorry I got angry this morning, but I felt so hurt."

Everything in him suddenly relaxed, and he held her close. "You had a right to be angry. I was a jerk yesterday."

She raised her head and he kissed her gently, softly, but soon a driving need took over and the kiss deepened. She threw both arms around his waist as his hand cradled the nape of her neck. "Serena," he groaned, "I love you and I'm sorry for hurting you. Yesterday I couldn't face another injury, a long recovery. It made me feel less of a man.'' He shook his head. ''You'll have to help me when my pride gets in the way.''

They stood holding each other, savoring the moment. Ethan swayed slightly and Serena drew back to look at his face. She saw happiness and joy, but also strain. ''Ethan, you shouldn't even be out of the hospital.'' She led him to the sofa.

He sat and rested his head against the cushion, while Serena sat on his right side. ''Better?'' she asked.

He caught her hand and held it. ''Much better. Because you're here.''

She watched the strong lines of his face soften, and all she wanted was to be with him—but there were questions clamoring in her head. ''Ethan?''

''Uh-huh?''

''What are you doing in this room? Mr. Hudson from the Diamond Store gave me this room number. Someone who bought my great-grandmother's earrings is supposed to be here.''

''I know,'' he replied, and let go of her hand. He reached for the bag on the coffee table and pulled out a small box.

She recognized the box immediately; she'd never expected to see it again. With his thumb he popped open the lid and the diamonds sparkled at her. ''Oh, Ethan! You bought the diamonds!''

''Yes.''

''How did you know where they were?''

''You told me that first night we spent together in Dallas.''

''Oh, and you asked Mr. Hudson to send me here.''

''Yes.''

''Why, Ethan? Why would you do that?''

His eyes melted into hers. ‘‘Because I want you to wear them on our wedding day.’’

‘‘Oh…’’ Tears trickled down her cheeks.

‘‘Sweetheart, please don’t cry.’’ He brushed away her tears with his thumb.

‘‘I can’t help it,’’ she sniffed. ‘‘This is the sweetest thing anyone’s ever done for me.’’ She hugged him carefully, trying not to jostle his injured arm. ‘‘Can you afford this? I mean I don’t want you to—’’

He placed a finger over her lips. ‘‘You never cashed that check I gave you, so I decided to spend it on something that would make us both happy. Besides, I get a good pension from the government. So, yes, I can afford it.’’

‘‘Are you…asking me to marry you?’’

‘‘Yes,’’ he answered without taking a breath.

‘‘Oh, Ethan.’’ She curled her arms around his neck again and kissed him until they were both breathless.

‘‘I’ll take that as a yes,’’ he said, grinning.

‘‘Yes, yes, yes.’’ She punctuated each word with a kiss, then snuggled against his side, her heart about to burst with happiness.

She picked up the diamonds and they glistened with every color of the rainbow. Finally she’d found her rainbow and it was Ethan—just as she’d known. She removed the earrings and put them on. ‘‘How do they look?’’

Her hair was up, so Ethan could see them clearly. ‘‘Beautiful,’’ he murmured, gazing raptly into her eyes. ‘‘I thought our daughter might wear them one day, too.’’

She sat perfectly still. ‘‘You don’t have to say that. I know how you feel about children and I’m fine with it.’’

‘‘But I’m not.’’

She didn’t know what to say.

‘‘I’ve been doing a lot of thinking since I left here,’’

he explained. "It's all I've been doing. For so long, I was focused on Ryan's death, but I began to remember his life—what joy he brought me and how much I enjoyed being a father. I wouldn't have missed that for the world." He paused. "I'd like to experience it again...with you."

"Ethan." Her voice was hesitant. She didn't want him doing this because he thought it was what *she* needed. All she needed was him.

He took her hand again and answered her unasked question. "I'm not saying that because I feel it's what you want to hear." He rubbed his thumb over her palm. "Did you wonder why I was here yesterday?"

"Sarah and I talked about that last night."

"I'd already made up my mind that I wanted a life with you. I was packed and ready to go when Daniel called and told me about the situation. I had to get to Dallas as fast as I could, so I flew, instead of driving. I got here just in time."

She leaned her head on his chest. "I'm glad you did."

He caressed her neck. "I love you so much that it almost killed me when I hurt you last night. That pain was worse than my arm."

"Then don't do it again."

"I promise."

He became quiet and she raised her head to look at him. His eyes were glassy, and she sensed that he was in pain.

"Ethan, what is it?"

"The surgeon gave me a prescription for pain medication. I took the pills a little while ago, and now I feel like I'm fading out."

She stood and clasped his hand. "Then we should get you to bed."

He smiled. "Ah, I like that."

When he'd clambered to his feet, she placed an arm around his waist and together they walked into the bedroom.

Serena paused at the big round bed, but only for a second. "In your condition, all you're going to do tonight is sleep."

"Oh, I don't like that."

She helped him off with his shirt, then removed his boots and socks. As she worked on his jeans, he said, "I like *this.*"

"See, it's not so bad to let someone help you, is it?" she asked as she pulled the bedspread back.

"No," he agreed as he crawled into bed, feeling woozy. "Damn, I shouldn't have taken that medicine."

Serena quickly shed her clothes and slid in beside him. He reached for her with his right arm and took the clip out of her hair. "I prefer it down."

"I noticed." She ran her hand over his bare chest. "You've finally found the piece that completes the puzzle."

He grinned. "You'll have to tell me what it is because I'll be damned if I know."

She sighed. "It's unconditional love. Every woman wants that."

"And every man wants unconditional sex."

"Ethan." She nipped his chest with her teeth.

"Oops. Must be the medication."

"Go to sleep, Ethan. We'll talk in the morning."

His lips curved into a peaceful smile and in a few moments she knew he was asleep. She kissed his forehead and let the events of the night wash over her. She'd been feeling so low, and now she was so high she didn't think she'd ever come down. Nor did she want to. She just wanted to spend the rest of her life with this man. It didn't matter that they were different in so many ways; the differences between them only enhanced the love they shared.

She snuggled against him—and suddenly her eyes flew open. She'd forgotten about Sarah. She had to call and let her know what had happened. Easing out of bed, she reached for the phone.

Sarah picked it up before the first ring stopped. "Serena, is that you?"

"Yes, it's me," she whispered, not wanting to wake Ethan, although she didn't think there was much danger of that.

"Why are you whispering? Are you in trouble? What happened? Gran and I are worried sick."

"Calm down. I'm fine. Ethan was the one who bought the earrings and he was here waiting for me and..."

"You made up," Sarah guessed.

"Yes, and it was wonderful. I called to let you know, so you wouldn't worry. I'll phone again tomorrow. Good night."

Serena went into the living room to get the roses. She set them on the nightstand and breathed in their fragrance, thinking that her life was exactly as she'd always hoped it could be. She had a sister and they were forming a bond as strong as if they'd known each other all their lives. The financial crisis was resolved. And she had Ethan. That was the best of all. She slipped back into bed, snuggled against him again and drifted into the rainbow of her dreams.

SERENA AWOKE feeling blissful, and she stirred to see Ethan coming out of the bathroom. Naked. Her stomach fluttered with excitement.

He sat on the bed and stared down at her. "Morning," he murmured.

She sat up. ''Morning. You look better.''

''I *am* better. Much better.'' His eyes lingered on her face and disheveled appearance, then traveled to her breasts.

''What are you doing up so early?'' she asked.

''I have to be at the hospital at ten to get my arm checked,'' he told her. ''I've already shaved and I was going to shower, but I need help.''

''Why do they need to check your arm?'' she asked anxiously.

''They're just making sure I have good blood flow to my fingers and that there isn't any excess bleeding—minor stuff. I'll begin my therapy in two weeks.''

''Oh.'' She pushed the hair away from her face. ''What can I do?''

The diamonds sparkled on her ears, but they didn't match the glow in her eyes. ''Kiss me,'' he said.

''That can be arranged.'' Smiling, she leaned over and met his lips eagerly.

''Mmm, that's nice.''

''What else?'' she asked.

He pointed to a piece of plastic lying on the bedside table. ''I have to wrap that around my arm so I won't get it wet in the shower. It's difficult to do with one hand.''

''So that's why you don't have your sling on.''

''Yes.''

Her smile broadened. ''There's a big tub, so why don't I fill it and we can take a bath together.'' She made to crawl over him, but he caught her around the waist. ''Tempting as that sounds, I want to talk first.''

''About what?'' she asked. Then he began to kiss her back, and her senses hummed with delight. ''Ah, oh...'' Each kiss was an erotic tease.

''How do you feel about living in Junction Flat?''

"I, ah, I can't think when you do that." His lips continued to the base of her spine.

"Do you know you have freckles on your lower back?" His tongue gently touched each one, and her brain went haywire.

"Yes, I know," she answered in a small voice.

He stopped and brought his mouth to her shoulder. "How do you feel about living in Junction Flat?" he repeated.

"Will you be there?"

"Of course."

"Is there a school?"

"Yes."

"Then I don't have a problem with it."

"Are you sure?" he asked as he pushed her hair away and kissed her neck. "You're just getting to know your sister, and I thought you might not want to leave Fort Worth."

As his lips traveled to her ear, she had trouble speaking, but she managed. "Sarah and I are old enough to understand that our lives will go in different directions. We'll never lose touch, but my life is now with you."

"Oh, Serena." He kissed her lips briefly. "How do you feel about renovating an old ranch house?"

"Sounds like fun."

"The house has needed renovating for a long time, and I decided to let Molly work on it, hoping it would cheer her up, but she has other interests now. She and Bruce are getting back together."

"That's great!"

"Yeah, they both realized they still love each other."

"True love never dies."

"I believe that now," he replied. "But before I get completely sidetracked, I have to tell you that my father lives with me. Pop gave the ranch to his kids and I bought out Travis and Molly because they weren't interested in ranching.''

''I have no problem with that, either, but I have to tell you that my grandmother and Sarah will be visiting from time to time.''

''I wouldn't have it any other way.'' He ran his hand through her hair. ''I want you to be sure about this. I've lived all over the world and I can adjust to living in Fort Worth if that's what you want.''

She touched his face. ''Thanks for offering, but let's try Junction Flat. You love it there and I love the outdoors—and you.''

''Oh, Serena, I love you,'' he whispered, and they kissed deeply, passionately, until primal needs emerged.

She felt his arousal against her hip. ''Ethan, we shouldn't do anything strenuous,'' she breathed in an uneven voice.

''They said exercise was good for me.''

She laughed softly. ''I don't think this is what they meant.''

''I want you.'' He kissed her breasts. ''So bad.''

She tried to still the need inside her, but she couldn't. ''Me, too,'' she murmured. ''But we have to be careful.''

''I don't want to be careful. I want to make mad, passionate love to you.'' His lips found hers again and for a moment silence mingled with pleasure.

''Okay,'' she moaned raggedly. ''*I'll* make love to *you.*'' She'd never done this before, but with Ethan she was sure it would come naturally, like everything else she'd experienced with him.

''Serena...''

She put a finger over his lips. ''Your pride is getting in the way.''

He grinned, accepting everything she was offering.

''Just let me love you,'' she said as her lips slid down his chest and lower.

And he would...for the rest of their lives.

EPILOGUE

One year later

SARAH WELCH scribbled notes and attached them to her date book. She'd just returned home from counselling people on the Crisis Hotline, where she did volunteer work three times a week. She wanted to check with this person again tomorrow. The woman was in an abusive relationship, and Sarah needed to make sure she had all the facts and understood all the options open to her. It was so hard not to just say, "Get out and don't look back," but she'd been trained to let people make that decision on their own, with a little guidance if necessary. Sarah wondered if she was equipped to give such guidance. She'd studied for years and had finally received the masters degree she'd been working on, but at times she felt inadequate to deal with such problems. That stemmed from her own life, of course. She'd endured so much and still…

She stood up and walked over to the window, which faced the landscaped backyard—a yard that needed regular maintenance, as did the pool. It cost so much to live in this house, but she couldn't bring herself to sell it. Maybe she would eventually, but for now she needed to be here—where she should've been as a child with Serena and Gran. She was still sorting through a lot of emotion from the past, and she knew that soon she'd have to make some decisions about the future. But today she wasn't analyzing her life anymore. Today Serena and Ethan were coming home for a visit, and Sarah was excited. She hadn't seen them in a month.

"Sarah," she heard Serena calling a moment before she burst into the study with a big smile.

Sarah ran across the room and they embraced. "I'm so glad you're home," Sarah murmured.

"Me, too," Serena said as she stepped back.

"Where's Ethan?"

"In the den with Gran. I wanted a few minutes alone with you."

Sarah stared at her sister's smiling face. "Okay, what gives?"

"I couldn't tell you on the phone," Serena said in a rush. "I had to tell you in person."

"You're pregnant," Sarah guessed, smiling, too.

"Yes."

"Oh, Serena." Sarah hugged her again. "I'm so happy for you and Ethan."

"Thanks." Serena's smile broadened as they sat down. "I can hardly believe it. I'm going to be a mother."

"So Ethan finally talked you into it."

"I had to be sure he really wanted another child, and I also wanted this year alone with Ethan. I've even adjusted to living in Junction Flat, because the people are so nice and the kids don't have that hardness they do in the city. They're fresh and eager to learn and I have some great art students."

"You're so happy that it's—"

"Infectious," Serena finished for her.

"Yeah, infectious," Sarah said with a wry grin.

"You'll find that kind of love, too," Serena told her.

Sarah looked down at her hands. "I don't think so. That part of my life ended when Greg died."

"I know you've been through a lot, but you have to start living again. It's time to start dating."

Sarah got up and walked to her desk. "A man is the last thing I need."

"You're a licensed therapist. You know it's not healthy to suppress your emotions. There are plenty of nice guys out there. Give them a chance. Give *yourself* a chance."

When Sarah didn't respond, Serena added, "Boyd's appeal is coming up soon and I know you're worried about that."

"It's crossed my mind a few times," Sarah admitted.

"But you can handle it. I know you can."

"Yeah, I've learned how to apply some of the knowledge I've acquired to my own life."

"That's the spirit," Serena said. "And I know there's a perfect guy out there waiting for you."

"Serena, stop pushing. Love, marriage and all that stuff—that's you, not me. I'm happy just living here with Gran."

Serena stood. "I have to say you've done a wonderful job getting her to stay on a budget. She actually listens to you. I'm impressed."

"Thanks. It just took patience."

"And a lot of other things," Serena insisted. "But you're not happy, Sarah. I know it. And so do you."

Sarah rolled her eyes. "Your life revolves around one man. Not everyone's made that way. Please, let me be me."

Serena shook her head. "Oh, Sarah, you haven't even found the real you. You've built all these defenses around you for protection. I know about that—I had to break through Ethan's. One day you'll meet a man who'll do the same for you, I'm sure of it.''

''Speaking of Ethan,'' Sarah said. ''Let's go find him before I strangle you.''

Serena threw both arms around her and held on tight. ''I'm glad you're home,'' Sarah whispered again, and they walked out into the hall.

But Sarah couldn't help thinking that her defenses would never be breached by anyone and her life would never be as happy as her sister's. Still, Serena seemed convinced that love would find Sarah, too—and her twin sister *had* been right about lots of other things....

* * * * *

Look for Sarah's story in 2004